The Silent Guest

Ian Erikson

Chapter One

Kate

Highway 83 twisted through miles of dense Montana forest alongside a chain of lakes connected by the Clearwater River. It was spectacular scenery. I could recognize that objectively, but I couldn't focus on the road, let alone appreciate the scenery. I couldn't process it, let alone appreciate it.

The evening sky outside was heavy and gray, closing in more and more the further north we drove. Mile by mile, the rusty old Ford truck was leaving everything I knew behind.

Stan, the grey-haired man who picked me up at the airport in Missoula, didn't seem to mind. He hadn't stopped talking since I stepped into the cab of his truck. Like an old-fashioned tour guide, he rambled on about the Native Americans who live nearby, the geology of the area, and all the wildlife we were passing. I didn't reply because I didn't care. It had been ten days since I had been released from the rehab hospital in Seattle, and I swear I could still feel the effects of the medicine they had forced me to take. I might have been here by choice, but I was angry at the world and beginning to question my choices.

In the hospital, I had studied maps of the area and tried to memorize the key roads and landmarks. Experience has shaped me into a person who likes to know how to get away from wherever I am.

We passed the little town of Seeley Lake and drove another half-hour to the north, then turned east on a gravel road that pointed straight at the Swan Mountain Range, a series of sharp peaks covered with snow.

"The lodge is quite a relic," Stan said, glancing at me from under the brim of his cap. "Lots of history. Used to be full of folks all summer long. Bustling during the high season. Haven't opened back up since the pandemic." His voice trailed off as he tapped the steering wheel in time with the rumbling engine. "Used to be quite a place."

I nodded, unsure how to respond. His friendliness was genuine, but foreign to me after years in Seattle's noise, energy and cool anonymity.

The old man was the type of talker who asked and answered his own questions. "Me? I worked at the sawmill in town," he added. "Thirty years. Then it shut down last year. That's why I'm driving."

The rutted road jolted through the suspension. "Ever been up this way before?" he asked.

"No," I said, pulling my coat tighter. "First time."

"Miss Hedden will take good care of you," he said with a reassuring smile. "She's been out here a long while."

Rachel Hedden. The lodge manager and the woman who had hired me from an online ad and a phone interview conducted while I was still wearing slipper-socks at the hospital. Needless to say, it wasn't a video chat. She had introduced herself as the only other resident at this isolated spot.

Four miles on the rough road and there it was—Holland Lake—stretched out like a black mirror in the dim light; and beyond it, the lodge. It was enormous. More of a huge log hotel, like something from Yellowstone National Park. Far bigger than I'd expected. Dark wood framed it against the mountains, its wide windows reflecting the dark sky. It was beautiful in a way, but heavy and still.

The Ford creaked to a stop. Stan glanced at me. "Good luck out here," he said. "Not everyone takes to the quiet."

I tried to smile, getting out of the cab. "Thanks for the ride," I said, grabbing my bags and slamming the door.

He nodded and rumbled off, the taillights blinking as they disappeared down the road and into the trees.

I turned to face the lodge. A woman was waiting on the steps. This must be Rachel. She was smaller than I'd imagined when I spoke with her on the phone, but her posture was rigid, just as I'd pictured. Her movements, when she raised a hand in greeting, were sharp and birdlike. She had shoulder-length salt and pepper hair and a smile that looked about as forced as mine. Perhaps I wasn't quite what she'd pictured either. "Kate, right?" she said, extending a hand as I walked up to the steps. When we shook, her grip was firm and her hand was as dry as 150 grit sandpaper.

"That's me," I said. "You must be Rachel."

She nodded. "Come on in. Let's get you settled."

We walked through the massive front door, and my eyes took a moment to adjust. The lobby was vast, with dark plank floors under a high, vaulted ceiling. A massive stone fireplace dominated one wall. I thought of Stan's description of this place years ago and shivered. The space around me felt as empty as a tomb and just as cold. My footsteps echoed as we moved through the cavernous room.

Rachel led me down a wide hallway lined with guest rooms and then down a narrow hallway to the employee wing. "As we discussed on the phone, the lodge is closed to the public, so it'll just be you and me," she said. "I'm in the caretaker's cabin, a couple hundred yards up the lake."

Her words sounded rehearsed. I nodded, looking at the old photographs lining the hallway. Smiling guests, families by the lake, couples near the fireplace. Ghosts of a time when the lodge had been pulsing with life and energy.

We reached a door, and Rachel pushed it open. "This'll be your room," she said. "It's not fancy, but it's comfortable."

The room was small and simple—a bed with a worn quilt, a stone fireplace, a window overlooking the woods. A rack of firewood was stacked near the hearth..

I set my bag down and looked out the window. From here, the forest and lake outside looked endless and frozen. Not a single ripple was visible on the lake's inky surface. Not a single branch or creature moved in the woods beyond it.

Rachel lingered in the doorway, watching me with that same tight smile. "I'll show you the rest tomorrow," she said. "Your job isn't too complicated—just basic maintenance. Keeping the old place running."

She paused, looking to the window, then back to me. "It's pretty isolated out here," she said, her voice dropping. "Let me know if it starts getting to you."

There was something in her tone that made me uneasy. I tried to smile. "Thanks, I think I can handle it."

"Good. Help yourself to whatever you find in the kitchen. We're well stocked. If you need anything else, I'm just a short walk away." She left, the door closing softly behind her.

I moved to the old-fashioned sash window, pressing my hands to the cold panes of glass. My view from the hospital had also looked out over a lake. In that two months, I got to know the landmarks there like the back of my hand. I wondered if I would also come to despise this view. Getting out of Seattle and leaving everything behind had seemed like such a great idea after all that had happened during the past year. I'd fantasized about winter in Montana, but now I was here and was hoping I hadn't made a mistake.

I turned back to the room, the sudden silence making my stomach churn. Rachel's words looped in my mind. The stillness. The isolation. Her offer—if you need anything—felt more like a warning than a comfort.

I sat on the bed, feeling the place settling over me. I was alone in this massive lodge. Rachel had warned me that there was no cell service, no Wi-Fi, and no way to call out other than an emergency satellite phone. She was my only connection to the world beyond. And as the snowflakes began to fall outside, winter seemed to be coming faster than I was ready for.

Chapter Two

Rachel

The new girl arrived today. Another in a long line of young women who've passed through these halls. Kate, her name was. Pretty and quiet, with that hesitant look they so often have when they first cross the threshold into my world. I've seen it all before—the way their eyes widen as they take in the grandness of the lodge, the nervous energy that makes their hands twitch when I ask them simple questions. It's always the same. But Kate had something different in her eyes, a shadow that lingered when she thought I wasn't watching. We've always hired girls who need a fresh start; girls with pasts they'd rather not talk about. They come here to escape something or someone. Maybe Kate's shadow will lighten, maybe it won't.

Time will tell.

I slide the sash on the kitchen window to the side and gaze out into the night. It's dark out there. So dark that all I can see in the glass in my reflection staring back at me. My expression is, as usual, completely neutral as I consider the lodge's newest employee and her background.

She was up front about a stay in a drug rehabilitation facility near Seattle. Her voice was flat like she was daring me to judge. I didn't. Why would I? This place was built for second chances, for wiping the slate clean. Out here, there's no past and no future, just the slow rhythm of the present. Work, nature, and the silence that seeps into your bones. It's not for everyone. Some crack under the stillness. Others flourish. I wonder which direction Kate will take.

After settling her in the winter caretaker's room, I made my way back to the kitchen; the hallway creaking faintly beneath my feet. These floors, these walls—they're my life's work, my family's legacy. My great-great-grandfather built this place with his own hands, and those of a few hundred workers in 1913. Every log cut from the surrounding forest. The lodge has stood through wars, fires, the Great Depression, even COVID. But it's more than just a building. The logs, the stones, the beams, they hold stories, secrets. You can feel it if you stand still long enough. I wonder if Kate will feel it, too, when she's alone tonight. They usually do.

The lodge hasn't hosted guests since the pandemic shuttered its doors, but it's still a sanctuary—for me, for the girls who come here, for the memories that linger in every corner. One hundred and twelve rooms stand empty now, waiting for life to return. Until then, it's up to me to keep it ready. The fire in the grand hearth will roar tonight as I feed it freshly cut cordwood. The fire will bring warmth and light to the shadows stretching across the room.

Kate will have plenty to keep her busy. Cleaning, maintenance, and hauling wood. I'll teach her the rhythm of it all. Some pick it up quickly; others balk at the work. The ones who stay learn the beauty in the hard work and routine. The way dusting a mantle or refinishing a floor can quiet the mind.

Kate's a quiet one. Maybe she'll take to it. Or maybe she'll break.

I squint out into the night but, predictably, am unable to sense any movement. I rarely can. Finally, I release the curtain and focus my attention on making myself a cup of hot chamomile tea and retrieving a couple of cookies from the pantry. The door groaned shut behind me; the sound echoing through the stillness. Above me, the Milky Way stretched across the sky, dazzling and infinite. Nights like these remind me why I've never left.

The path to my cabin winds through the woods just in from the lakeshore, the soft step of my boots on the frozen ground was the only sound. Inside, the embers in the woodstove still smoldered from the morning. I coaxed them back to life, settled into my chair, and watched as the wood caught and began to burn. The lodge may be silent, but it's never truly empty. It has a way of speaking to you, whispering its secrets when the world outside forgets you exist.

Chapter Three

Kate

I slept little that first night. Exhaustion from the long trip from Seattle to Holland Lake should have knocked me out, but I laid awake, staring into the darkness. The lodge was quiet. Too quiet. Every small sound—branches tapping, floorboards shifting—echoed in the silence, magnified until I couldn't tell if the noise was real or in my head.

By morning, the dim light and the sound of an approaching vehicle on the road were a relief. I dragged myself out of bed, combed my tangled curls into a topknot, and made my way to the kitchen, which smelled divine. Rachel was already there, talking to an older woman I hadn't met.

"Kate, this is Marta," Rachel said, her tone brisk. "She comes by to cook and stock the freezer. Keeps us from living off mac and cheese all winter."

Marta looked up, her eyes kind but distant. "Hola," she said softly, gesturing toward a pot on the stove. "Sopa de Pollo."

The smell had hit me down the hallway—garlic, herbs, chicken broth. "Nice to meet you. Smells great." I said, my stomach grumbling.

Rachel leaned in, whispering, "She doesn't speak much English, but she's the best cook you'll meet."

I sat at the table, grateful for the warmth of the stove. The kitchen pulled me back to Sunday dinners in Seattle. Marta moved with practiced efficiency, humming as she worked.

Rachel poured me a cup of coffee, slid it across the table, and sat down across from me. "How did you sleep?"

I shook my head. "Not great."

"It takes getting used to," she said, almost sympathetic. "Some people love it. Others... not so much."

Her eyes focused on the window. "There's a stillness here in winter. You'll feel it. You just need to stay strong."

Stillness. It was more than that. It was total isolation. But I said nothing, just nodded and looked down at my coffee cup, which was filled with coffee so black it reminded me of the lake at night.

After breakfast, I wandered the lodge, trying to wrap my head around its size. The halls seemed to stretch on forever, the kind of place where you could disappear. Every step echoed, as if the building itself was amplifying my movements. The air felt colder here, with strange drafts and patches of especially frigid air, and had a different feeling than anywhere I'd ever been.

The dining hall was also vast, with tall windows casting a pale light over rows of heavy plank tables. Drop cloths covered the chairs, lined up as if waiting for guests who would never return. I ran my fingers along a table, disturbing the dust in four parallel lines. The lodge felt abandoned, like no one had been here in decades, as opposed to just a handful of years. If I'd been a fanciful person, I would say the atmosphere inside the lodge felt bereft, empty and mournful.

Upstairs, the air was colder still. The first rooms I entered felt grand, with dark wood furniture and antique rugs. At the end of the hall, a door stood ajar. I pushed it open and stepped inside. The room was like the others, except for one thing—a deep red scarf was draped over a chair.

I moved closer, touched the fabric. It was soft, but cold and damp, as if it had been outside in the rain. There were no visitors. Why was this here? My nervous stomach returned.

I made my way back downstairs. Marta was folding her apron in the kitchen. She gave me a nod. "Hasta la próxima semana," she whispered. "Tenga cuidado."

"Gracias, Marta," I replied, though my voice felt small in the large space. She gave me a piercing look, then walked out the kitchen door to her car without looking back. I understood very little Spanish, but I cast my mind back to sophomore Spanish class and didn't cuidado mean hot? No, that was caliente. Wait, was it... 'be careful'?

I was mulling this over when Rachel appeared in the doorway of her office across the hall, her eyes sharp. "How's the exploring?"

"It's... interesting," I said. "Bigger than I thought."

She smiled, a strange, knowing smile. "It grows on you. There's always something new to find."

Her words lingered as she turned and disappeared back into her office. I stood by the tall windows in the lobby, watching the wind pick up outside. I couldn't shake the feeling I didn't belong here, like I was stepping into someone else's reality, but I couldn't tell if it was the space itself or my own mindset that had me feeling so unsettled. I thought of what the staff had taught me at the facility in Seattle and how they had encouraged me to focus on my breath to work through my anxiety. I took a series of deep breaths and tried to release the tension that I could feel building between my shoulder blades, but to no avail. The lodge was too still. It felt like it was holding its breath, even as I released my own.

Chapter Four

Rachel

I sat down at my desk and arranged my paperwork into three neat piles. It was Monday and everything needed to be in order to get the week started off just right. Marta had arrived early, driving up from Seeley Lake like she has for twenty years. How anyone can live in this country that long and not pick up a word of English, I'll never understand. She's affordable and she can cook, but the woman drives me mad. She knows about my allergies. I've had descriptions of them translated into Spanish, printed, highlighted—despite that, she forgets. Good help is hard to find, especially here in what most people would call the middle of nowhere. But I swear that if I need to use my EpiPen again, Marta is fired.

At least Kate was up early, already busying herself in the lodge. That's a relief; I've had girls who wanted to sleep till noon, dragging their feet through the day. These old floors—plank wood polished to a shine since they were cut at the sawmill before World War I—take work to keep up. Wax is the secret, layered on twice a season to protect the wood, and every five or six years we strip it down and start fresh. It's a back-breaking job, and now that I'm in my late fifties, I'd rather not spend weeks on my knees with a scraper and rag. Seniority has its perks, you know. Kate seems willing enough to do it, and I intend to check on her often, keep her busy, making sure she's learning the ropes. New girls need a close eye at first. They get distracted otherwise.

There was a sudden crunching of gravel outside as Dale Petrie pulled up, his dump truck full of cordwood for the season. We order fifteen cords every fall; enough to keep the fireplaces roaring if we lose power. And we will lose power. We've got a generator, but during a cold snap, it's those fires that keep this place cozy. Or at least as cozy as possible.

I walked out onto the front porch and over to the woodshed.

"Thanks, Dale," I said, watching as he lowered the bed to unload. He grinned down at me and nodded once. That man's been trying to get me to go on a date for most of two decades, a fact that's never failed to amuse me. He's got a spare tire that could wrap around him twice, and a nose like a lumpy potato.

"Happy to help, Rachel, my dear," he said with that too-familiar twinkle in his eye. "Anything for you. You know that."

We banter about this and that, the way we always do. About the winter coming on, about his plans to head down to Mexico soon. "You'd love it there, Rachel. White sand, warm ocean, cheap living. And loads of golden sunshine," he said, giving the lodge a pointed look. "This old place needs its pipes drained and to be left alone in the winter. No reason to do all this work if there aren't even any guests."

"That'll be the day. You know as well as I do, Dale, the only reason you're going to Mexico is for the cheap whores." The words snapped out of me before I had the chance to soften them. Dale's face fell, his eyes hurt. He shook his head, mumbled a goodbye, and left. I watched him drive off without waving..

I had hurt him, but no one tells me what to do with my lodge.

Chapter Five

Kate

R achel dropped by frequently. At first, it was cool. She helped me learn the ropes and get my list of daily tasks organized. It broke up the monotony and gave me something to focus on other than the silence pressing in after I'd finished work for the day. Even a quick chat felt like a lifeline, reminding me I wasn't alone in the lodge. She stopped by while I cleaned or when I made coffee on a break. Small talk at first. But soon, her visits stretched longer and her questions dug deeper than I felt comfortable with.

One evening, while I folded laundry in my room, I heard a soft knock. Rachel stood in the doorway, arms crossed, that faint smile on her lips.

"Hey," she said. "Thought I would see how you're doing."

"I'm fine. Trying to stay busy."

She stepped inside without waiting for an invitation, her eyes wandering over the room—the bed, my stack of books, the drawn curtains. "Not much to do around here, is there?" Her voice was casual, but the way she said it made my skin prickle.

"No distractions."

I nodded. "I'm managing."

Rachel lingered, watching me, her expression thoughtful. "So," she said, "why'd you take this job? I know you were upfront about your time in the hospital, but why not go back to your family? Your parents, maybe?"

"Needed a change of scenery," I said, keeping it vague.

"A change of scenery," she repeated. "Well, you picked a good place for that."

I reminded myself she was my boss, and she had the right to check in. I reached for another shirt, but something made me stop. Rachel's sleeves were rolled up, and there, on the inside of her forearms, were patches of burn scars. Twisted and rough and unmistakable. I looked away, but not fast enough.

Rachel caught me staring. Her expression shifted—embarrassment or anger, I couldn't tell. She pulled her sleeves down, as if suddenly realizing the scars were visible.

"Sorry," I muttered, softer than I intended.

"It's fine," she said. She waved it off, but her smile disappeared, replaced with something sharper. "That was a long time ago."

There was no room for questions, so I didn't ask. I folded the last of the clothes in silence as she watched me work.

Outside, snow was falling again, drifting down against the fading light in total silence. I hadn't noticed before now, but now it blanketed the world outside. A shiver ran through me. Winter had arrived.

Rachel followed my eyes to the window. "The snow's started," she said, her voice low. "Won't be long before the roads get bad. It's fairly often that we can't get to town."

I knew winter here would be rough, but I hadn't considered being cut off completely. The idea of being trapped settled uncomfortably in my mind.

"You're saying we could get snowed in?" I asked.

"It happens," Rachel said, "But it's peaceful once you embrace it." She smiled, but it didn't reassure me. If anything, it made me wonder if she didn't welcome the isolation.

"You know," she added, her voice softening, "it's nice to have some company again."

"Yeah," I said, though the words felt hollow. "I'm glad you're around."

"I'll let you get back to it," she said, turning to the door. "But if you need anything... you know where to find me."

"I'll keep that in mind," I said.

She left, her footsteps fading down the hall. I couldn't quite place what it was about Rachel that unsettled me. Maybe it was that odd smile, the way she lingered, or that strange familiarity in her voice when she talked about being alone. I realized I knew almost nothing about her. She was always around, asking questions, but she never revealed much about herself. Those scars told a story, one I couldn't begin to understand. But there was something about her, about this place, that made me feel like I didn't belong. Did Rachel ever feel like that? Or did she feel embraced by the lodge, rather than repelled? I looked around the room, suddenly aware of how small it felt. For all her friendliness, there was tension in the air when Rachel was nearby, an almost static charge.

Outside, the snow fell harder, becoming a white curtain. The roads would be buried soon. The idea of heading to town tempted me, but it was getting dark and I didn't like the idea of driving in this weather. I finished putting away the laundry, sitting on the edge of the bed as the wind rattled the windows. Rachel's words made me wonder just how long it had been since she'd had someone to talk to out here. And what happened the last time she did? The lodge shifted softly, the sound of it settling into the earth. As I sat alone on my bed watching the gathering storm, I couldn't shake the bone-deep chill that was creeping in.

Chapter Six

Rachel

The snow was finally falling. Winter is the season I wait for with more anticipation than any other. I could tell right away that Kate was going to need a little hand-holding. A city girl like her was rattled at the idea of a Montana winter with snow that piles up and seals us off. Personally, I love it. The lodge snowed in, stocked up with firewood, food, water, and thick blankets. If you're prepared, there's nothing to fear. It's part of who I am.

This lodge was built to take anything winter throws its way. Back in the 1920s, my great-great-grandfather—always thinking ahead—had his workers dig a tunnel connecting the lodge to the caretaker's cabin. His silver mine in eastern Montana gave him the idea. Mining towns often had underground tunnels for moving around when snowdrifts piled up and the temperature dropped below zero. Some towns even ran a tunnel under Main Street, with side passages leading to the barber, the bank, the saloon—some even led straight to homes. Great-great-grandpa was a genius and knew how to make a place not just survive, but thrive.

On nights like this, I make my way down to the end of one of the long hallways, step into a storage room filled with unused furniture and banquet tables, and descend the twenty-eight steps into the tunnel. The air down there holds a steady 56 degrees year-round, winter or summer—a comfortable refuge in any blizzard. I need to replace the light bulbs in the tunnel, but the flashlight does well enough for now. The walls are rough stone, the ceiling low, but at my height, it suits me just fine. Someone over six feet might find it a squeeze.

Over the years, I've decorated the tunnel to make the short walk more cheery. Over the rough stone, chiseled by hand all those decades ago, I'd painted bright, feminine colors. I'd added plastic flowers and bright streamers of crepe paper. As long as I have a secret place of my own, why shouldn't it be pleasant and uplifting? In past years, I've thrown parties or held high tea in the tunnel, with guests and costumes and music. To some it, would seem odd, but it is joyful and helps bring life into the lodge.

At the other end, another staircase leads up into the back porch of my cabin. I walked in, took a big breath and stoke the wood stove, add a few pieces of wood to the embers. I loved to watch the flames catch. The warmth spread through the cabin, driving out the chill. I sat in my chair, thinking over what still needs doing around the lodge. Quiet tasks, things I like to get done while Kate is sleeping. Chores she doesn't need to know about.

On the table beside me was a letter I'd read more than a dozen times, crinkled at the edges. A New York investment bank, offered $25 million for the lodge and the land. It's was a fortune, more than I'd ever dreamed. But I looked out the window at the lodge—my family's legacy, built by hand. That meant something. A place that stood as a counterpoint against the world's noise.

Still, $25 million is a substantial offer. What would Mother do?

Chapter Seven

Kate

By the fourth night of the storm, five feet of snow had piled up around the lodge, effectively sealing us inside. The silence was different now, somehow deeper; deadened, like the snow had smothered the world beyond. It was the kind of oppressive silence that made me feel trapped.

Rachel stayed in her cabin, a five-minute walk through the woods when there wasn't snow. It's impassable now. She'd warned me early on that the generator only ran during the day to save fuel. That left the lodge in total darkness as soon as the sun set. I kept a fire going in my fireplace near the window, its flames lighting up the walls. But the cold still found its way in, slipping in through every tiny crack.

I laid in bed, staring at the ceiling, waiting for sleep. It didn't come. At first, the lodge seemed silent, but as my breath and hearing adjusted, I began to make out faint noises. A rustle here, a faint thud there. At first, I told myself it was just the building settling, the way old wood shifts in the cold. But tonight, the rhythm was different. Irregular. Off.

It sounded like footsteps.

I squeezed my eyes shut, trying to block it out. No one could be out there. Snow buried the roads and covered the paths, leaving only Rachel and me. It had to be the lodge.

But then I heard it again. A soft, deliberate shift. The faint press of weight on the floorboards, like someone—or something —was moving just outside my door.

My heart raced. I sat up, straining to hear. I fumbled for the flashlight on the nightstand. My hands were cold and clumsy as I switched it on. The beam of light cut through the darkness, and for a moment, I felt relief.

I tiptoed to the door and eased it open. The hinges squeaked softly. The hallway beyond was dark, the shadows stretching long and still. This lodge felt different at night, larger, like the walls had expanded in the dark. My flashlight barely pierced the gloom, its beam passing across the wood paneling. My breath sounded loud in my ears as I crept toward the stairs.

When I reached the lobby, I swept the light across the open space. The tall windows reflected the faint glow of snow outside, but everything else was still. Silent. Then I turned the light toward the front door.

It wasn't shut.

It hung open just a crack, swaying in the icy wind. My pulse quickened. I knew I'd locked it earlier. I could still picture the latch clicking into place and I would have noticed if it hadn't closed all the way. I stepped closer, the cold air biting at my skin. The smell of snow and pine hit me as I pushed the door closed, the latch clicking back into place. But a sense of deep unease stayed with me. I scanned the lobby one more time, and there was nothing; just shadows and silence. I took a deep breath and headed back to my room, telling myself I was overreacting. It was the cold, the darkness, the isolation. Nothing more.

But as I walked down the hallway, I couldn't shake the feeling that someone—or something—had been here. As if their energy had left an imprint on the surrounding space. The open door, the shifting sounds, the oppressive quiet—it didn't feel like coincidence. I told myself it was my nerves, but a small voice in the back of my mind whispered otherwise.

I climbed back into bed, pulling the blankets up to my chin. The flashlight stayed on, its beam resting on the wall. Shadows flickered and shifted in the soft glow of the fire. The flames crackled, but its warmth felt distant, as if it couldn't quite push back the cold creeping into the room. I lay there, wide awake, listening.

The lodge sent a deep, slow sound traveling through the walls. It didn't feel like the building settling. It felt alive. Like it was trying to tell me something.

When the first light of dawn crept through the window, it was a relief, though the gray morning was nearly as dark as the night that came before. I knew I must have slept, but it couldn't have been for long. I got up, stiff from lying still for hours.

I walked to the window and looked out at the blanket of snow that stretched to the edge of the lake and over the ice. The old lodge seemed smaller in the daylight, less threatening, but the feeling from the night before lingered. There was something here—something buried in the shifting walls. I didn't know what it was yet, but I was feeling like I was alone in some ways and yet, at times, not alone at all.

Chapter Eight

Kate

The day started with breakfast and a few hours of work on the floors. By mid-morning, the sound of an engine broke the quiet. I glanced out the window and saw a big four-wheel-drive truck pull up to the lodge. The man behind the wheel looked young, my age maybe, late twenties, with dark hair and a clean shave. He stepped out, his breath visible in the freezing air, and grabbed a toolbox from the back of the truck.

Rachel was at the front door, waving him inside with a smile that felt a little too bright. "Dominic, you made it," she said.

"I wouldn't miss it," he replied with a grin, stepping in the door. "Generator trouble's no fun this time of year." He turned and gave me a quick nod. "You must be Kate."

"That's me," I said, smiling back. Up close, I noticed his eyes—a striking blue, the kind that stands out in any light, even the dull half-light of a grey winter's day.

He was handsome, this man with the beat-up toolbox, and I stood a little straighter.

"I'm Dominic," he said, offering his hand. "I'll be fixing your generator problems today."

"Nice to meet you. Thanks for making the drive." I replied, shaking his hand. His grip was firm and I couldn't help the little flutter of interest. Best of all, it was warm. It had been a while since I'd met someone new, and his effortless charm was a pleasant change.

Rachel stepped in closer, her expression tightening. "The generator engine's been acting up," she said. "We need it running reliably, especially with more snow coming in." She shot me a glance, something sharp in her eyes. I didn't know her well enough to be sure, but it felt like irritation.

"I'll take a look," Dominic said, his eyes lingering on me. "Shouldn't take too long."

As he headed out back outside, I noticed Rachel watching him go, her face tense. For a moment, she looked almost angry.

Later, on my break, I walked to the side of the building and found Dominic working on the huge, old generator. He was happy to have company and was in a good mood, cracking jokes, talking about life in Seeley Lake. It felt easy, and after a half-hour, I realized I'd been laughing for the first time in weeks.

Rachel drifted in and out of the lodge, hovering as Dominic and I talked. Every time she appeared, I caught a tightness in her jaw. It didn't take long to figure out she wasn't happy with the attention Dominic was giving me. When he hit me with a snowball, her face hardened.

"Well," she said sharply, "let's make sure you're focused on that generator." She smiled, but it didn't reach her eyes. "We need those problems fixed."

Dominic chuckled. "No worries. Almost done here."

Rachel walked away, her posture stiff, her boots almost stomping as she went back around to the front of the building.

Dominic finished up, wiping his hands on a rag before packing his tools. "That should do it," he said, flashing me a smile. "If you need anything, just gimme a call. Good to meet you." He winked before walking back to his truck.

As he drove away, I glanced at Rachel, standing near the window, staring after him. When she caught my eye, her expression was unmistakably cold, almost hateful. It was just a flash, a moment of something raw, but it left a knot in my stomach. I tried to shake it off as I went about my day cleaning rooms, making sure everything was in order. The generator hummed steadily, and I let myself feel a little relief. But that ease didn't last long.

Later, during my rounds, I noticed something strange—a small, folded piece of paper tucked under my door. I picked it up, my pulse quickening as I unfolded it. My name was written on the front in delicate, looping letters.

I hesitated, then opened it. The message was brief, just three words: Don't walk on the lake.

I looked up and down the empty hallway, but there was no one, just the quiet stretch of closed doors and dim light filtering in from the windows. My first instinct was to find Rachel.

When I showed her the note, she barely glanced at it before shrugging. "Just something left behind by the summer staff before we closed," she said, her tone dismissive. "Kids were always playing pranks on each other."

She crumpled the note, calm and almost bored, as if this was nothing unusual. "It means nothing."

Her explanation felt too easy, like she hadn't given it much thought. I searched her face for any sign that she might be hiding something, but Rachel's expression stayed neutral, unfazed.

"Are you sure?" I asked, "It just seems strange to find it now, with no one else around. With my name on it."

"You're letting your imagination get the better of you," she said firmly. "It's an old lodge. Things get left behind. You're not the only Kate who has worked here."

I headed back to my room. The delicate handwriting felt too personal, too deliberate. Whoever wrote the note wasn't playing a prank. I sat on the edge of the bed, thinking of the words: Don't walk on the lake.

The temperature was dropping again, the shadows in the corners lengthening as the light outside faded.

Chapter Nine

Rachel

At long last, I settled into my chair, the cabin quiet but for the soft hum of the radio. I twisted the dial until I found the classical station from Missoula—a string quartet, delicate and drifting. I pick up my basket of yarn, running my fingers over the different textures, sorting through the colors. Humming with the music, I choose the thickest wool, some pinks and purples, and begin my evening's work: a nice, warm pair of socks for Mother. Her feet have always been cold, ever since I can remember. I smile, picturing her surprise. She taught me to knit when I was just a girl, sitting right by her side in the lodge's parlor, her hands moving swiftly over each stitch. Those days feel close on nights like this.

I knit on, the rhythm of the needles almost meditative. I let my thoughts drift, turning, as they often do, to the lodge and its workings. Sometimes, a bit of uncertainty can do wonders for people, and push them to grow. Mother knew that well. When she taught me to run the lodge, she'd let me stumble through my own mistakes, never stepping in too soon. It hurt her, I could tell, but she was wise enough to let me find my way. That taught me more than anything, and it made me the woman I am today.

I take a slow breath, steadying my hands as I turn the heel. Kate is doing well enough, but maybe she's gotten a bit too sure of herself. I'll keep an eye on her, make sure she feels that gentle nudge—enough to remind her that loyalty to the lodge is our guiding principle. The lodge, this place, comes first. It has been a priority, *the* priority, for everyone who's worked here, generation after generation. That's why it still stands, over a hundred years since my great-grandfather built it. We all learned to put it before our own desires. Those who didn't paid a terrible price. She'll learn that, too.

I glance out the window; a few stars have started to appear in the clear sky. The first storm has passed and another is on the way. There's always another storm. But there's a tranquility to this isolation, to the quiet duty of maintaining something so solid, so enduring. I'll admit, I've always been a night owl. During high season, when the lodge was filled with vacationers, nighttime was my only chance to see the place as it really is. With everyone sleeping, I'd walk the halls and check the floors, the walls, the railings—searching for smudges, dust, a footprint out of place. Staff knew perfection was our standard because I'd see to it. We've been closed to the public for years but I still feel most connected to the lodge at night, like its heart is beating with mine.

In the early days, there was no generator, no electricity at all. We had kerosene lanterns, fireplaces, and clear water straight from Holland Lake, pure as any you could find. But now, our heat depends on the boiler, and that boiler needs power. The generator's been giving me trouble lately, but a replacement would cost $100,000 we don't have. Finding a reliable mechanic isn't easy out here. We've got Dominic, who knows his way around it, but he flirts with every girl who comes to work here, and this year's apparently no exception. I sigh heavily. He's a disrespectful fool, really, but he keeps the machine going. The day I find a better option, he'll be fired.

I shift the yarn in my lap, working the needles as the lovely music flows through the room. A thought crosses my mind, one I've turned over more than once. Some people say loyalty to the lodge, to the family's legacy, is old-fashioned. But I know better. This place is worth every bit of devotion I give it.

My fingers keep a steady rhythm as I finish the heel, the soft wool taking shape, stitch by stitch, the colors blending just right. A simple thing, these socks. But I think of Mother, her feet wrapped in that warmth, and it makes me smile.

Chapter Ten

Kate

The plow had come in the night, clearing the road to the highway. I needed to get away from the lodge, even just for a few hours, so when Rachel offered me her old pickup to head into town for a few supplies, I didn't hesitate. The keys were cold in my hand as I climbed into the cab. The truck creaked, old and spotted with rust, but it started on the second try, and that was good enough.

I hadn't driven a stick shift in years, but muscle memory kicked in and the truck lurched forward, the wheels spinning on the frozen ground. Even after the big county plow, the forest-lined road to Highway 83 was a mess—rutted ice, patches of frozen mud, gravel crunching beneath the tires. Every bump sent a jolt through me, and I gripped the steering wheel so tightly that my knuckles turned white.

The trees thinned as I drove, but the feeling of isolation didn't lift until I was on the blacktop, over Summit Pass and descending into the valley. The road from the lodge was terrible, but the asphalt wasn't much better; slick, with patches of black ice. I kept the truck in the lane, eyes glued to the road ahead.

With the roads so treacherous, Seeley Lake was almost an hour's drive away. The town was quaint, but mostly shut down for the season. The local lumber mill had gone out of business, laying off a hundred workers, and the lot sat vacant. A few trucks were parked outside a diner, and small shops lined the quiet highway. In the summer, I imagined it would be lively, full of tourists spending their weekends by the lake. But now it felt empty, waiting for life to return.

I scoffed, sensing some common themes with the place I'd been living for the past few weeks. All this stagnant energy felt oppressive. The idea of working hard and being alone with my thoughts, all while being surrounded by the peace and tranquility of winter, had appealed to me when I'd been in rehab. Now, after less than a month, I wondered if I should have pursued something entirely different. Perhaps hosting BINGO on a tropical cruise ship?

As I drove through the little town, I spotted a snow-covered tennis court in a small neighborhood park, its net sagging drunkenly on one side. My heart ached as I thought of the two decades I had spent on courts, learning tennis in grade school, competing in high school and college and joining the pros six years ago. My entire world came to revolve around tennis and competition, and I was good, possibly world class. My parents had never pushed me; I had loved it from the start and that love, that bone-deep passion, had propelled me to train harder, faster and push myself relentlessly. Perhaps it was this intensity, this drive towards perfection, that led to my downfall because a knee injury had sidelined me two years ago. With three surgeries and no hope of ever returning to the game on a serious, professional level, I had felt completely unmoored emotionally.

That injury had brought all my dreams and plans to a crashing halt, but it had also brought opioids into my life. It was a fateful and ironic prescription provided by the doctors. My low self-esteem and diminished sense of self-worth didn't help matters any. Those pills had cost me my relationship with Decker and nearly ruined my life.

I parked outside the general store and gas station. The engine rattled to a stop as I switched off the key. it. A few people at the gas pumps glanced my way, all bundled against the cold. They knew I wasn't from here. They could spot an outsider a mile away.

The bell above the door chimed as I stepped inside. The smell of fresh coffee hit me immediately. Aisles were packed with hardware, fishing tackle, and random necessities. I grabbed a basket and picked up the list of items we needed back at the lodge.

The old man behind the counter gave me a nod as I approached. "How're you finding life at Holland Lake?" he asked.

The question seemed casual enough, but there was something in his tone. I forced a smile. "It's quiet," I said, setting my items on the counter. "But I like it."

He rang me up, nodding like he'd heard that before. "Quiet's good. But most folks don't like it once the snow piles up." He glanced out the window, his brow furrowed. "Storm's coming."

I followed his eyes to the grey sky out the window. "How do you know?"

He chuckled, shaking his head. "Weather service is wrong half the time out here. No radar in this valley. But locals know when it's gonna snow."

I had nothing to say to that. I'd already learned that this part of Montana didn't follow the same rules as anywhere else.

As the clerk bagged my items, he gave me another look, more intent this time. "Miss Hedden taking good care of you?"

It was a simple question, but something about the way he said her name made my stomach lurch. Too familiar, like there was something I wasn't in on; some inside knowledge.

"Yeah," I replied, "She's been helpful."

He nodded, like that was what he expected to hear. "Good. She knows the place well."

I paid for my things, thanked him, and headed for the door. Above the door, the bell chimed again as I stepped back into the cold. The sky was darker now, heavy with the weight of snow. The clerk was right—a storm was coming. Even I could sense that.

The drive back felt longer than the drive down. The icy road kept me on edge and the closer I got to the lodge, the more I seemed to dread returning.

I have no reason to dread the lodge, or Rachel. It's a winter job that pays well, gets me out of Seattle for a while, and delays the task of finding housing by six months. This way, I don't have to live in with my parents or my ex-boyfriend. It is a good move. I can't let my mind run away with me.

The truck's headlights cut through the gathering dark. By the time I turned off onto Holland Lake Road, the snow had already started and while the tiny flakes fell so heavily that I was reminded of the confectioner's sugar my grandmother used to sprinkle over her beignets.

Just as I pulled up to the lodge, the wind picked up, blowing the trees and sending swirls of snow up the face of the building. I killed the engine but didn't get out right away. I sat there for a minute, staring at the structure looming ahead, a hulking, symmetrical beast made of logs and stone, standing sentry beside the lake. Its windows were dark and soulless, the edges blurred by the falling snow.

I grabbed my bags and stepped into the cold. As I walked toward the door, I couldn't shake the feeling that I was even more alone than I'd been in the hospital.

Chapter Eleven

Kate

R achel's visits had become routine—one I never welcomed nor asked for and her appearances, often so sudden they startled me, unsettled me more with each passing day. It wasn't just the frequency or the suddenness that unnerved me; it was the curious way she seemed to brush aside any respect for my privacy.

Tonight wasn't any different. She knocked softly, but didn't wait for an answer before coming in. I hadn't even finished putting my book down before she was sitting in the armchair by my bed, crossing her legs like she was settling in for an interrogation.

Her eyes swept over my room. "Looks like you're right at home," she said.

"More or less," I said, forcing a smile. "Still getting used to things."

Her smile widened, but it was sharp, not comforting. "You'll learn to appreciate it. It's peaceful once you let go."

I didn't know what to say to that, so I stayed quiet, folding my legs under me on the bed. Rachel wasn't done, though. She never was. The silence seemed to make her uneasy, and she filled it with questions that felt too close, too personal.

"Seattle. That's become a big city," she said, her tone light but probing.

I nodded. "Yeah."

"You must miss it," she said, her eyes locked on me. "All the energy, the people. And you're so young, it must've been fun, living in the city."

Her words weren't compliments. They were reminders of my youth, of the life she thought I left behind. "I guess," I said, trying to keep my voice neutral. "I grew up there but was ready for something quieter."

"Hmm. And you left because of... Decker, wasn't it?"

I froze. She'd said his name like she had a right to; like she knew something. My pulse quickened. I hadn't mentioned Decker more than once, and even then, it wasn't an invitation to dig into my past.

"Yep," I said, my voice tight. "It didn't work out."

Rachel tilted her head, not satisfied with my vague answer. "That must've been hard. A breakup like that never comes out of nowhere."

My hands were clenched in my lap. "It wasn't out of nowhere. We were together for a long time. Things just didn't work out."

"That's tough," she said softly, her tone sympathetic but her expression curious. "But when you're so young, you've got your whole life ahead of you. Must be nice."

There it was again—that subtle dig wrapped in a compliment.

I forced a laugh, brushing it off. "Yeah, I guess. Still got time."

"You're lucky. When I was your age, I didn't have that luxury. Must be nice, knowing you've got so many options."

Her tone had something unspoken—jealousy, resentment. I had the sense that she was picking at me, trying to see how I'd react, trying to get under my skin.

"I try not to think about it too much," I said, keeping my tone calm, but my patience was thinning.

"Well, you should. From what I've seen, if you can keep your mental health on solid ground, the future is bright."

Mental health. I didn't respond. I just sat there, feeling her eyes on me, dissecting me piece by piece. She didn't say it, but I could feel the question behind her words—why would someone like me, with my whole life ahead of me, end up here? Alone. In the middle of nowhere.

The flames in the fireplace crackled, the only sound between us. As usual, the fire seemed to give off light with little actual heat. I glanced at the window, the darkness setting in, the snow blowing again outside. The room felt claustrophobic.

Rachel leaned back, crossing her legs again, getting even more comfortable. "It's hard, being alone out here," she said, her voice dropping. "It makes you think about things you'd rather not."

"I'm used to being alone," I said. Her words sent adrenaline into my limbs, but I didn't let it show.

Rachel's expression showed that she didn't believe me. "Good. You'll need to be."

The words felt like a warning, wrapped in false warmth.

After what felt like forever, Rachel stood, smoothing down her sweater. "Well, I'll let you get back to it."

"Thanks," I said, my throat tight.

She paused at the door, turning back with that sharp smile. "And remember, if you ever need anything, I'm here for you. We're a team."

"Thanks," I said, balling my fist up under the duvet, wishing she would leave.

Rachel lingered for a moment longer, her eyes still on me, before slipping out the door and closing it behind her. Her words echoed in my mind—*you've got your whole life ahead of you.* But it didn't feel like encouragement. It felt like something I didn't want to examine too closely.

I glanced out the window at the snow, still falling in thick sheets. And for the first time, I wondered if Rachel wasn't just checking in on me.

Maybe she was making sure I stayed exactly where I was.

Chapter Twelve

Kate

The days stretched on, a blur of scrubbing and stripping wax from the lodge's worn floors. My hands grew raw and cracked while my kneecaps turned purple. After the third day, they were a kaleidoscope of fresh and half-healed bruises; lavender, navy blue, yellow and finally, towards the very edges, a sickly brown. At night I would sit in a bathtub filled with barely warm water and study them closely, fascinated by the visible sequence of healing and wondering about other kinds of healing—the invisible kind. Did we progressively heal like the bruising on my knees? Or did we heal in fits and starts, sudden staccato bursts?

Each layer I peeled back revealed strata of dirt and grime, but the wood beneath, though scarred from generations of use and abuse, was luminous. I couldn't help but wonder how many winter caretakers like me had knelt on these planks.

When we had spoken on the phone, Rachel had mentioned that there used to be a permanent caretaker, back when the lodge was a thriving holiday destination, but that in recent years, there had been a new caretaker every year.

The work was slow; the old wax was stubborn, refusing to give way. But I kept at it, inch by inch, scraping it from the cracks, making slow but steady progress. It was satisfying in its own way, but after lunch on the second day, a draft of cold air, whether real or imaginary, I couldn't say, caused all the hairs on the back of my neck to rise at once. It was a feeling never abated. In fact, it grew more pronounced as the days wore on. A nagging feeling followed me up every creaking staircase and through every abandoned room, landing, and hallway.

It started small. A book I left on the nightstand would end up back on the shelf. I thought maybe I'd moved it without realizing it, distracted by the work, long days and my headspace, which I could admit still felt a little off after my time spent in the hospital and everything that had led up to that.

If nothing else had happened, I could have convinced myself that the book moving from one room to another was in my head, and I would have given enough time and distraction, but small strange occurrences kept happening over the coming days. My hairbrush, left on the bathroom counter, would reappear neatly placed on my dresser, its wooden handle placed perpendicular to the edge.

By the end of the week, I found myself second-guessing everything. Was it me? Was I losing track of my routine? Or was something else going on? I had tapered my medications under a doctor's care and now only took a mild antidepressant. I felt like I was losing it, though. Maybe the anti-psychotics had been more necessary than the doctors thought. I started chewing my cuticles again, a nervous habit I'd outgrown years ago, and between my new-old habit and the manual labor, my cuticles grew torn and ragged.

The breaking point came when my gray cashmere scarf went missing. I had draped it over the footboard of the bed that morning. I tore my room apart, searching every corner, every drawer, even my bags. It was nowhere to be found.

Frustrated, I left the room, pacing down the hall. And then I saw it—neatly folded, sitting just outside my door. Someone had placed it there. Deliberately.

A cold jolt shot through me. My pulse quickened, and I knelt to pick up the scarf. Someone, Rachel, had been in my room. She had moved it. I hadn't misplaced it; I was certain of that now—the scarf didn't just move itself into the hallway.

I exhaled deep and nibbled anxiously at the broken skin near my thumb. As disturbed as I was by Rachel's actions, there was a relief in finally having certainty about at least one of the recent events that had left me feeling so off-kilter.

I carried the scarf into my room and put it in a drawer. It had been a gift from my mom last Christmas. I couldn't shake the feeling that Rachel was playing some kind of game I didn't agree to. My boss had once again invaded my little island of privacy. That I hadn't been there when she did so made it feel all the more violating.

That afternoon, Rachel stopped by the lobby where I was working, as she always did. She was in one of her moods—bossier than usual, pointing out every flaw. "You missed a spot," she said, her voice clipped as she gestured to the floor I'd been working on for hours. "And the dust is piling up in the corners."

I bit back my irritation. "I've been stripping wax all day. It's a process," I said, trying to keep my tone even.

Rachel crossed her arms, her gaze sweeping the room. "You need to stay on top of it," she said sharply. "There's still plenty to do."

The constant criticism grated on me. It wasn't just about the cleaning anymore—she was asserting control, reminding me who was in charge. I took a deep breath, forcing myself to stay calm. "I'm on it," I muttered, focusing on the floor.

After a long silence, I brought it up. "By the way," I said, not looking at her, "my scarf went missing earlier. I found it in the hallway, folded."

Rachel raised an eyebrow, her expression unreadable. "Folded?"

I nodded, watching her. "I left it in my room, but somehow it ended up outside my door. Do you know anything about that?"

She waved a hand, dismissive. "You just forgot where you put it. Happens to the best of us."

Her cavalier response irritated me. The tone of her voice, the wave of her hand, communicated that I was overreacting. My chest tightened as she brushed off my concern, like she was trying to make me doubt myself.

"No," I said, my voice firm with conviction. "I didn't forget."

Rachel smiled, but like so many of her smiles, it was thin, forced. "It's easy to lose track of things out here," she said, her voice soft but her tone condescending.

I clenched my jaw, swallowing back the frustration. Something about the way she was looking at me made my skin crawl, like she knew more than she was letting on. Like she was playing with me, twisting the situation around so I would doubt myself, doubt what I had seen.

I forced my molars to unclench but didn't argue. After all, what was the point? As we stood there, staring at each other in the fraught silence, the tension between us felt palpable. I looked away first, breaking eye contact to focus my attention on the window beyond her. Rachel lingered a moment longer to look around the room before she turned on her heel and left.

As the door to her office clicked shut behind her, I let out a breath I hadn't realized I'd been holding. Rachel's energy seemed to squeeze my chest. I'd never thought of it as oppressive but I could barely breathe. I looked down at the cleaning sponge in my hand. I was squeezing it so tightly that a tiny drop of blood was forming at the corner of my thumbnail, where the cuticle had shredded. I watched it bead up near the broken skin before it began a slow descent down the tip of my finger and onto the newly stripped floor below.

I huffed out a sigh and knelt down with the sponge to wipe it up and get back to work.

Chapter Thirteen

Rachel

I hate to say it, but lately I've had some doubts about Kate. Over the past couple of weeks she's seemed distracted, almost evasive, with little lies here and there. They're harmless enough on their own—forgotten details, strange little stories about things that make no sense. But they're adding up, and I can't ignore it anymore.

She arrived here straight from a drug rehab facility, or maybe an asylum, whatever they're calling it these days. I knew she was on medication before coming here, though she assured me she was stable. But I've begun to wonder if they released her before she was ready.

In a place as remote as this, with only us and the lodge stretching across the empty winter landscape, I can't afford any risks. Already, a month into her stay here, there are the stories about missing and moved items. What next? It is possible that these mild delusions, or lies as the case may be, could escalate over time? I've always felt it was my duty to help those in need, especially young women. Life's hard enough for them without support. I know that better than anyone. But there's a fine line between being helpful and being reckless, and if Kate's not well enough to be here, I might have made a mistake.

Just yesterday, I caught her rummaging around in the back office, supposedly "looking for extra cleaning supplies." The shelf she was looking through didn't hold a single bottle of soap or a dust cloth. I've decided to lock up my valuables tonight, tucking away anything small enough to go missing. Her behavior seems to be getting less and less predictable.

Better to be safe than sorry, as Mother always says.

Maybe I'm being too cautious, but something about her has me wary. And while I'd hate to let her go, I have my responsibilities to think of.

If things don't improve, I'll call her parents. I'll let them know what I've noticed, ask if there's any medication she's supposed to be on, or any methods they've found to keep her steady. It's a delicate thing, bringing up someone's troubles, but hopefully they'll understand and perhaps they will all be grateful for my interference.

I sip my tea and look out the window at the frozen forest beyond. The wind has died down, for the moment at least, and the branches of Alpine Fir trees are so stiff and angular against the grey backdrop of the sky that I'm reminded of rigor mortis.

Enough of that, I think as I take another sip of tea. Tomorrow, when I make my supply run to town, I'll swing by the library to post a new job listing online. I've never had trouble finding applicants; in fact, sometimes there are too many to sift through. If it comes to that, a replacement won't be hard to find. Kate had seemed like the right fit at the time—she had a story that tugged at me and was from the Northwest, close enough that she could easily come and go. I've learned to avoid hiring anyone from the East Coast or the South; it's more complicated for them to go home if things don't work out.

I picture the faces of past winter caretakers, each one who

passed through these halls over the years. Many of them came from troubled backgrounds, and I welcomed them. For some, the work and solitude were a balm, and they grew into the place. For others, the isolation drew out their demons. I don't want that for Kate, but I won't let her bring her problems into the lodge, either. She's still young, unsettled, and while I'd like to help her, I need her loyalty and focus. That's all I ask for here—a commitment to the lodge and the discipline to put personal struggles aside.

I pause, listening to the quiet creak of the walls around me. This old lodge still stands because we've all put it first, each of us who passed through. Kate will either do the same, or she'll be moving on soon.

Tomorrow, I'll talk with her, watch her reactions, and look for any sign she can steady herself here. This lodge isn't just a place to get back on your feet. It's a test.

Chapter Fourteen

Kate

I t was early, maybe three or four in the morning. Something had woken me. The cold hit me like a slap in the face the second I stepped into the hallway. My stomach tightened. The front door was open again, just like last time. I stood in the lobby and stared at it, my pulse quickening. The heavy door swayed in the breeze, creaking, the frigid air rushing inside like an unwanted guest.

I knew I had locked it.

My legs felt heavy as I crossed the great room, eyes fixed on the door. Each step echoed in the quiet building. When I reached the threshold, I saw it—another note, pushed into a crack in the floor just inside the doorway.

I closed the door and knelt to pick it up. The paper felt cold, the ink sharp and clear. *"Keep steady, Kate. Your efforts don't go unnoticed."*

A cold sweat prickled the back of my neck. I stood there, staring at the words, heart pounding. Someone was playing with me, watching me. I glanced around, suddenly feeling exposed. The shadows in the corners of the wide-open lobby of the lodge felt like they were moving toward me. The door rattled on its hinges; the wind pushing its way inside.

I didn't know what to think anymore. *Was this a prank, like Rachel kept insisting, or something worse? Something deliberate.* Who else was here? My hands clenched around the note, crumpling the paper.

I pulled on a pair of snowshoes from the rack beside the entrance. I flung the door open and marched straight for Rachel's cabin, the icy air nipping at my face as I strode through the woods. The deep snow compressed underfoot, the lodge fading behind me. My thoughts churned with a mix of anger, fear, and, finally, doubt. I didn't want to believe Rachel was behind it, but her indifference, her constant dismissals—it was gnawing at me. Something wasn't right.

At her cabin, I trudged up on the porch and knocked harder than I meant to. Rachel opened the door after a moment, her face calm, like she was expecting me.

"I found another note and the front door was open," I said.

She glanced at the words and handed it back without hesitation. "Like I said before," she replied, casual. "Its just left over from the summer guests years ago. You're letting this get to you, Kate."

Her nonchalance grated on me. I stared at her, waiting for more, but she just stood there in a long, flannel robe, her expression mild, almost bored.

"This isn't a prank," I said. "Someone's messing with me, Rachel. I know I locked that door."

Rachel raised an eyebrow, her smile tight. "It's easy to let one day run into the next out here. It's such a big place. I know what it's like to lose track."

I kept my voice even. "I didn't lose track of anything. And this note... it's not funny anymore."

Rachel's eyes flickered, something shifting behind them.

She sighed heavily, almost sadly. "You're getting worked up over nothing. Whoever left those notes is long gone. If they wanted to do more than scare you, don't you think they would have by now?"

"I don't believe you," I said.

Rachel's smile faded. For a moment, her calm expression slipped. "You don't have to," she said. "But there's nothing out here but us and the snow."

It wasn't Rachel's unnatural calm that bothered me. It was the way her expressions, words and tone of voice all seemed to be implying that *I* was the one losing my grip on reality.

Gas-lighting, right? Wasn't that the term for behavior like that?

I nodded once and turned without another word, snow-shoeing back into the cold, the wind stinging my face as I made my way back to the lodge. This place felt less like a refuge and more like a trap with each passing day. The adrenaline that had propelled my angry march to Rachel's cabin was wearing off quickly, and I suddenly realized that I was out in the dead of night without a jacket. I shivered as the air seemed to seep down into the very marrow of my bones. In the forest that lay between Rachel's secluded cabin and the lodge itself, I felt vulnerable, exposed, and impossibly cold.

But my boss's inexplicable manipulation? That was far colder still.

Chapter Fifteen

Rachel

My cabin has always been my sanctuary, the one place where the endless tasks and duties of the lodge don't confront me. It's small, private, and utterly mine. Unlike the lodge, which is too large and too alive, this modest cabin feels like an extension of me. The lodge is shared—always has been. Caretakers and still contractors pass through its halls regularly, and guests once came and went like waves on the shore. My cabin, though, is sacred. No one intrudes here.

So when Kate came hammering on my door at four in the morning, rambling about some note she'd found, it felt like a violation.

Her voice was frantic, her words tumbling over each other in a rush. Something about how the notes seemed to be encouraging her, praising her efforts. I tried to listen calmly, nodding in all the right places, but inside, my patience was unraveling.

Kate was unraveling.

The nervous glances, the endless questions, the unsteady energy—it's all building up to something, a crescendo of sorts, and I'm tired of holding it together for her. She's off her medication or simply unfit for this kind of work. That's not my fault. As I've told her from the beginning of her tenure here, this place isn't for everyone.

I'd stood there in Mother's old robe and given her the same detached reassurances I've given before; I told her the lodge was old, full of quirks, and that she was just reading too much into things. But it's getting harder to stay stoic in the face of her skittering nonsense and obvious delusions..

Her babbling about resilience and dedication, though—that hit a nerve.

Those words used to belong to me.

When she left, I stood in the doorway for a moment, breathing in the frosty night air. It had a way of settling my thoughts, grounding me when the weight of the lodge threatened to tip me over. I exhaled deeply, attempting to expel the last lingering effects of Kate's chaos, before I closed the door and turned back to the warmth of my cabin. *My space.*

The fire crackled in the stove as I sank into my chair, letting the silence wrap around me. My fingers tightened on the note I'd found earlier, tucked into the kitchen windowsill. I didn't have to read it to know what it said, but I did anyway, the paper cool against my skin.

"Keep steady, Kate. Your efforts don't go unnoticed."

The handwriting was unmistakable—strong but trembling, aged but precise. My mother's hand.

The words churned in my chest like an old ache, familiar and unwelcome. Mother always had her ways of making her thoughts known, even now. She never needed grand gestures. A simple note, left in the right place at the right time, was enough to remind me of her presence. Of her judgment.

This wasn't just encouragement; it was evaluation. A silent measuring up.

Of all people, Kate.

It stung more than I wanted to admit. I'd spent years earning Mother's approval, working harder than anyone, holding this place together with my bare hands. And now? Now she was leaving her little praises for Kate, this outsider who didn't belong here.

I crumpled the note in my fist, the paper crinkling like dry leaves. A deep resentment pooled in my chest, hot and heavy. Kate was resilient, sure. She cleaned well enough, followed instructions. But she didn't understand this place. She didn't know its history, its demands. She couldn't possibly meet Mother's standards.

And yet...

The thought gnawed at me. Mother was watching, assessing. Could she see something in Kate that I'd missed? Could she be... considering her?

The word left a sour taste in my mouth. *Replacement. Successor.*

No.

This lodge is mine.

The firelight flickered as I uncrumpled the note and smoothed it out on the table. My mind sharpened, narrowing in on a plan. If Mother wanted to test Kate, then Kate would fail.

It wouldn't take much. A few carefully placed obstacles, subtle but effective. I'd give her tasks that looked simple on the surface but were impossible to complete perfectly. Washing windows, stacking firewood and stripping floors? We were done with all of that now. Going forward, Kate would wax the uneven and age-pocked floors, scrub miles of baseboards, clean the ornate paneling in the old lounges—small, detailed work that would exhaust her, frustrate her, trip her up.

And nothing but perfection would do.

I'd inspect her work afterward, pointing out every flaw. If Mother saw the imperfections, her approval would fade.

Kate would falter. And then she'd fail, just like all the others.

Of course, here was another matter to address: boundaries. I'd given Kate too much freedom, let her wander too far. She was curious, I'd noticed, always poking around where she didn't belong. It was only a matter of time before she found the tunnel—the hidden passage linking my cabin to the lodge.

The tunnel was a necessity in the winter, a safeguard against the worst storms. But it was a secret. If Kate discovered it, she'd have access to both spaces, slipping between them at will.

The thought chilled me. No one should have that kind of freedom here.

Tomorrow, after I assigned her tasks, I'd secure the storage room door where the tunnel began. Lock it tight. She didn't need to know it existed, much less use it. Her place was in the lodge, under my eye and under my thumb, her movements confined to the work I gave her.

I leaned back in my chair, staring again at the note on the table, tapping the edge of the table with an index finger. *Tap, tap, tap.* The fire cast long shadows across the walls, its warmth unable to melt the knot of resentment that had knitted itself into my chest.

Mother's standards had always been impossible, even for me. Kate would never meet them. She didn't have what it took, and I'd make sure Mother saw that.

Tap, tap, tap.

Tomorrow, I'll call her parents and set the stage for Kate to be sent home. A few carefully chosen words could convince them that Kate didn't belong here. She belongs in the city. Or, if I'm honest, she belongs anywhere *but* here because this lodge is more than a refuge. It's a proving ground. And I've spent too many years upholding my family's legacy to let someone like Kate tarnish it.

Tomorrow, I'll put my plan into motion.

Kate would learn her place. And Mother would have no reason to look at anyone else.

Chapter Sixteen

Rachel

The road to Seeley Lake was a white ribbon of frost, winding through the long river valley. My truck fought the incline, its engine a low, familiar rumble. I gripped the wheel tighter, keeping my eyes on the curves ahead. The sun had just risen, casting the town in a pale light that made the weather-beaten houses and small storefronts look even more frigid than usual.

As I passed the diner, I glimpsed familiar faces through the windows. Heads bent together over mugs of coffee. The usual crowd. They'd glance up if I walked in—polite smiles, but eyes that didn't quite meet mine. I didn't need their pity or their judgment. I had the lodge, and I didn't need them.

The library's parking lot was nearly empty, the snow piled up against the curb. I pulled in, turned off the engine, and sat for a moment. The radio crackled faintly with static, the voices of a talk show host droning on about road conditions up north. I turned it off, letting the silence settle around me.

Inside, the library smelled like old books, aging carpet and stale coffee. The librarian—Mrs. Wheeler—looked up from her desk, her glasses perched low on her nose. She smiled politely, but her eyes told a different story.

"Morning, Norma."

I stiffened. *Norma.* The name coiled around me like a noose. "It's Rachel," I said, sharper than I intended.

Her cheeks reddened. "Oh, of course, Rachel. My mistake."

I nodded and moved past her to the computers. The public access station was tucked in the corner and the screen came to life as I moved the mouse. My fingers hovered over the keyboard for a moment before I began typing.

Winter caretaker needed. Remote location. Must be resourceful, hard-working, and willing to commit through spring thaw, usually late April or early May. Monthly stipend. Room and board included.

I read it over twice before hitting "Post." A weight lifted, just a little. The thought of replacing Kate was satisfying. She wasn't the right fit—not for the lodge, not for me. The next one would be better. Someone less... obstinate.

As I logged off, a familiar voice behind me made me tense. "Rachel? Is that you?"

I turned to see Angie Lawson, her smile wide and brittle. She was bundled in a bright red coat, her arms full of books. Angie used to sing in the church choir when we were younger. She'd been nice to me, once. That kind of niceness that felt like charity.

"It's been so long," she said, shifting her weight awkwardly. "How are things up at the lodge?"

"Fine," I said. "Busy."

She nodded too quickly. "That's good to hear. I—well, I was just telling Jim the other day that we should come up and visit. It's been years since we've been out there."

I smiled tightly. "You're always welcome." A lie, but she wouldn't take me up on it. They never did.

"Well," she said, her tone forced and bright, "it's good to see you. You're still so... normal. I mean, the same as always."

Normal. The word lingered, sour and weighted. I nodded and walked past her without another word. Outside, the cold air bit at my face, but it felt cleaner than the suffocating cheer inside.

Back in the truck, I pulled out my phone and dialed Kate's parents. Her mother answered on the second ring, her voice sunny and warm.

"Hello?"

She was probably the type of mother who had packed all of Kate's lunches; neatly made sandwiches, perfectly sliced apples and a little note with something like, *You're going to ace the math quiz today, sweetie! Love, Mom.*

"Hi, this is Rachel Hedden from the Holland Lake Lodge here in Montana," I began, keeping my tone soft, concerned. "I just wanted to touch base about Kate."

"Oh? Is everything alright?" The worry in her voice was immediate.

"Yes, of course. She's doing ok, but I've noticed she seems a little... withdrawn. I thought it might be good to check in."

There was a pause. Then Kate's mother sighed. "She's always been that way—stubborn as a mule. Especially since her injury and the breakup. She doesn't like to admit when she's struggling."

I hummed in agreement, letting the silence prompt her to continue.

"She and Decker were together for so long. It was hard on her when it ended. I think she saw it as her chance, you know? To settle down. And the end of her tennis career was so hard on her."

Interesting. I made a mental note of that—her desperation, her disappointment, and her vulnerability. Useful details.

Her father's voice came through in the background, muffled but insistent. Kate's mother sighed again. "He's saying we can come get her if it's not working out."

"Oh, no," I said quickly. "Nothing like that. I just thought it might help to understand her better. Sometimes, being up here can be... isolating."

"Yes, I suppose it would be." Her tone shifted, uneasy. "But you think she's alright?"

"She's adjusting," I said. "I'll keep an eye on her."

By the time I hung up, my chest felt tight with irritation. They didn't fully trust me, but they wouldn't come—not yet. That was enough for now.

I started the truck and sat for a moment, watching the quiet street through the windshield. Angie's words echoed in my mind. *Normal.* She thought she knew me. None of them did.

Chapter Seventeen

Kate

The quiet in the lodge was different when Rachel wasn't here. It was softer, less oppressive, like a heavy curtain had been pulled back to let in the light. Her boots weren't clomping across the floorboards, and her tight-lipped presence wasn't suffocating me. It felt, for the first time since I'd arrived, like the lodge was almost welcoming.

I took my time moving through the main corridor, pulling back curtains, flipping on lights and watching the glow expand into the dark corners of the grand space. The lodge always seemed to swallow any light whole, but today it felt a little less greedy.

I grabbed my phone and put on music—a cheerful playlist of my faves. The kind of music you play when you're trying to force yourself into a good mood. It worked. The upbeat rhythm filled the space, bouncing off the high ceilings and settling into the wood-paneled walls. It was strange to hear something so lively in a place like this, as though the walls were too old to hold anything but echoes.

I drifted into the kitchen and started cleaning, more out of habit than necessity. Rachel had me cleaning constantly, but this time it wasn't about meeting her impossible standards. It was about reclaiming the space, even if just for a few hours.

I wiped down counters that didn't need wiping and rearranged things that didn't need rearranging. Cleaning gave me permission to explore, to peek into corners I hadn't dared to linger in before. I opened drawers, flipped through old recipe cards, and even found a dusty silver tray shoved to the back of a cabinet.

In the east lounge, I ran my fingers over the spines of books on the shelves. Most of them were decades old, their covers worn and faded. I pulled one down—a guide to the local area from the 1960s—and as I flipped through it, a folded piece of paper slipped out and fluttered to the floor.

It was a note, handwritten in those familiar, spindly letters: *"The walls have memories."*

I froze, staring at the words. I unfolded the paper, searching for more, but that was all it said.

Who left this? Rachel? Or someone else?

Shaking it off, I slipped the note into my pocket and moved on.

The next one came a little later, when I was dusting the furniture in the library. I tugged at the corner of a chair cushion to straighten it and felt something tucked underneath. Another folded piece of paper, another cryptic message:

"Keep looking."

The music playing in the background suddenly felt too loud, too out of place. I paused it, letting silence fill the room.

For a moment, the lodge itself seemed to breathe, its walls creaking in the stillness. I stood there, listening, trying to convince myself it was nothing more than the aging building settling.

The silence wasn't still. I don't know how else to explain it.

The quiet that filled that space around me felt alive with the tiny, almost imperceptible vibrations of life.

All the fine hairs on my forearms rose at once and I rolled my flannel sleeves down, first one, then the other, before I pressed the play button on my music again. I felt certain that if I didn't force myself to move on, I would stand there frozen, paralyzed, indefinitely. I gathered up my rag and spray bottle and willed myself to focus on the task at hand, exerting all of my mental energies on creating a pattern of cleaning—*spray, scrub, wipe*—that would perfectly match up with the beat of the music. I tried to lose myself in this mental game, but every so often I'd hear something outside of the strange duet I'd created—a faint tapping, a distant creak—and I'd pause the music, straining to hear. The sounds were subtle, just enough to keep me on edge.

The lodge had a way of twisting noise, of turning it into something sinister. Even the cheerful songs I'd chosen, which had seemed to bring a welcome brightness to the space less than an hour ago, now seemed wrong here, their familiar rhythms distorted as though the lodge was swallowing the sound and spitting it back out in pieces.

By early afternoon, I was exhausted, not from cleaning, but from the tension of the day. I sat down on the couch in the den, the feather-light notes weighing heavy in my pocket. I wasn't ready to think about them—not yet.

When the knock came at the door, sharp and sudden, I froze.

For a moment, I didn't move, my pulse quickening as I stared toward the door. It wasn't Rachel—she wouldn't knock.

The knock came again, louder this time.

Chapter Eighteen

Kate

I opened the door cautiously, half-expecting some stranger, or worse, Rachel, returning early for reasons I couldn't guess. Instead, Dominic stood there, his arms loaded with grocery bags and his grin as wide as ever.

"Dominic?" I asked, startled.

"I come bearing gifts," he said, stepping inside without waiting for an invitation. Snow clung to his boots, and his cheeks were flushed pink from the cold.

I closed the door behind him, crossing my arms as I watched him march into the kitchen like he owned the place. "What are you doing here?"

"I saw Rachel drive by in town," he said, setting the bags on the counter. "Figured you could use a little company. Plus, I thought I'd treat you to something special."

I raised an eyebrow as he began unpacking the bags. Out came fresh herbs, wild mushrooms, and a bottle of wine that looked far too expensive for Seeley Lake.

"Okay," I said, leaning against the counter. "What's the catch? You don't exactly strike me as the fine-dining type."

He glanced up, a smirk tugging at the corner of his mouth. "That's because you don't know me yet. I went to culinary school in Seattle; that's where I'm from originally. Worked as a chef and sous chef for ten years before Montana called my name."

"Seattle?" I asked, my interest piqued. "Where?"

He rattled off a few restaurant names, one of which made me pause.

"I've eaten there," I said, surprised. "Years ago. It was... incredible."

"Small world," he said, pulling out a cutting board and a chef's knife. "That place was intense—great food, brutal hours. There's a reason the restaurant industry has so many cocaine users and addicts. Know what I'm saying? Burned out pretty fast."

As he worked, he told me about his life—a story of late nights in kitchens, the relentless pace of fine dining, and the dream that had driven him to Montana.

"I'm saving up to open my own fine dining restaurant," he said, his voice serious as he seasoned venison and scallops. "Something local, but with a touch of the coast. It's not Seattle, but I think Montana deserves better than tough steak and potatoes."

I smiled, his easy confidence disarming. Dominic was more than the two-dimensional ladies' man I'd pegged him as. He was ambitious, talented, and surprisingly thoughtful.

By the time dinner was ready, the kitchen smelled incredible. He'd transformed the dining room into a makeshift fine-dining experience, complete with perfectly plated courses and a bottle of red wine to pair with the meal.

We ate together, and for the first time in weeks, I felt like a normal 26-year-old woman. Dominic's stories of Seattle pulled me out of the lodge's energetic shadow, reminding me of a world I'd almost forgotten. We knew many of the same places and laughed when we realized that we'd grown up only ten miles apart.

We were still chatting about the bakery we'd both frequented growing up, debating the merits of their scones versus croissants, when the front door creaked open.

Rachel's voice cut through the air like an icy wind. "Kate? Dominic?"

I stiffened, my heart sinking as she walked into the room. Her gaze swept over the table, registering the wine glasses, the easy camaraderie between us. Her expression was unreadable, but her eyes lingered on me.

"Looks like you've had quite the evening," she said, her voice even.

Dominic stepped forward, making her a plate with a smile. "Saved you some. Didn't want you to miss out."

She took the plate, her posture relaxing just slightly. "Thanks," she said, glancing between us. "I'll eat upstairs while I work."

Rachel went upstairs, but it felt as though the tension in the room lingered. Dominic didn't seem to notice, his easy demeanor was unshaken, but just seeing her had popped my golden bubble and caused all my relaxed, happy feelings to dissipate.

After a while, our lively conversation became muted and shortly thereafter, he packed up his things. I walked him out to his truck.

"You made my day," I said. "Between Rachel being gone and the wonderful dinner, I felt like I was somewhere else. I really appreciate your thoughtfulness."

"It was nice to cook for someone who appreciates it." He said, piling things into the cab. "Let's do it again."

He hugged me, gave one of his playful, signature winks,

and climbed into the truck. I walked back to the lodge and watched him drive away from the front steps.

As I wandered back through the lodge, the sunshine Dominic had brought with him faded. The shadows seemed to creep and spread, pooling in the corners and the unlit hallways.

Less than an hour ago, I'd been struck by the realization that for the first time in a long time, I'd felt normal. As I'd laughed and engaged in lively conversation, I'd felt balanced and even a bit light-hearted.

I sure didn't feel light-hearted now.

I leaned against the wall behind me with a dejected huff and slid my cold fingers into the pockets of my jeans. My fingertips brushed against paper and I realized I was touching the mysterious notes that I'd received.

Okay, so not only wasn't I feeling light-hearted anymore, I wasn't feeling very balanced anymore, either.

Chapter Nineteen

Rachel

The scallops were perfect—tender, buttery, seared just right with a delicate crust on the edges. I cut into one slowly, savoring the aroma before the flavor melted on my tongue. For a moment, I closed my eyes and let myself drift back.

Back to when the lodge was alive.

The dining room had been the crown jewel in its heyday, bustling with elegance and refinement. Guests would sit at rough-hewn tables dressed in white linen, sipping from crystal glasses as the smell of wild game, fresh trout, and delicate seafood dishes filled the air. My mother had insisted on only the finest—imported wines, cheeses, and scallops flown in from the Pacific Northwest.

Scallops were her favorite.

I chewed, savoring, letting the memory settle over me. Mother would love this meal. Dominic had no idea about the piece of history he'd recreated tonight. The way he plated the dish with such care—it reminded me of the chefs we used to have back then. Professionals, not hobbyists. I imagined Mother sitting beside me now, her eyes lighting up at the sight of the plate. She'd have taken a delicate bite, nodded in quiet approval, and said something like, "This is what the lodge was meant for."

The thought made my arms tingle and my palms sweat. I stopped mid-bite, staring down at the scallops on my plate.

I couldn't eat it all.

I folded a napkin over half the food. Mother deserved to enjoy it, too. Even if... even if it had to wait until tomorrow.

"I need to save this for Mother," I whispered.

I pushed the plate aside and sat back, the fork still in my hand. The warmth of the daydream was fading, replaced by an all-too-familiar irritation. The image of Dominic and Kate downstairs gnawed at me.

The two of them, laughing and eating together like it was their lodge. Dominic, waltzing in uninvited, taking over my kitchen like it was his. And Kate—well, she'd just let him, hadn't she? Smiling, drinking wine, acting like she belonged here.

I gripped my fork tighter.

The lodge wasn't for moments like that. It wasn't a place for casual dinners and lighthearted conversations. It was a sanctuary, a legacy, and they were treating it like a playground.

But Dominic's ambition, his talk of opening his own restaurant—he was already dreaming of something new, something better. I saw it in his eyes tonight, the way he looked at Kate, the way he handled the kitchen space like it was his stage. It was a subtle kind of arrogance, the kind that suggested he believed he could breathe new life into this place.

And Kate. She was too stubborn for her own good, but I could see the spark in her, too. She was younger, stronger, full of that irritating resilience that made her keep going when others would've broken down.

A bitter laugh escaped my throat. "As if they could ever do what I've done here."

I looked at the plate again, the scallops and venison now cold.

I wasn't like Mother. She never had to worry about being replaced. She ran the lodge with grace and authority, never doubting her place at the helm. Guests adored her, the staff respected her. She has lived with the lodge as hers, unchallenged.

But me? My grip felt more tenuous with each passing year.

I glanced at the letter on my desk, the hedge fund's offer staring back at me in bold, overwhelming numbers: $25 million.

It was an absurd amount of money. More than I could've imagined the lodge would ever be worth. The thought of selling it—letting go of the only life I'd ever known—felt like a betrayal of everything I'd worked for.

And yet...

What if they restored it? What if they brought back the elegance, the charm, the vibrancy that had been lost? Maybe the hedge fund could turn the lodge into something Mother would be proud of again. A fine dining restaurant, polished and gleaming, with guests arriving from all over the country, perhaps even the world.

I traced the edge of the letter with my finger, my thoughts racing.

Of course, they'd have to agree to my terms. A clause to ensure the lodge stayed intact. No bulldozers, no modern monstrosities. Certainly no neon. The building would remain as it was—restored to its glory, not transformed into something unrecognizable. And maybe, just maybe, I could negotiate a way for Mother and me to stay. I could oversee the restoration, live on the property, and keep my connection to the lodge.

It wasn't perfect, but it was better than becoming obsolete.

I shook my head, trying to banish the thought. I wasn't ready to make that decision—not yet. For now, I had to focus on keeping things as they were. Keeping control.

I glanced at the plate with the scallops I'd set aside for Mother. She'd love them.

The lodge was still mine. And as long as I was here, no one —Dominic, Kate, or anyone else—would take it away from me.

Not yet.

Not ever.

Chapter Twenty

Kate

The lodge was finally quiet. I'm not sure I could call it a true 'peace', but it was at least a deep silence that only existed after Rachel had gone to her cabin. I moved through the darkened halls, mop in hand, the rhythmic swish of water against wood keeping me grounded. My body was tired, but my mind buzzed, energized by the evening I'd enjoyed with Dominic.

His laughter, the way he spoke about Seattle, his dreams for the future—it all reminded me of life beyond these walls, a world I hadn't thought about in weeks. For once, the work didn't feel so heavy. Tonight, it felt like something I could conquer.

I set my phone on a table down the hall, turning on music to fill the space as I wiped down the walls and stripped old wax from the floor. The melodies mingled with the scents of cleaning products and the lodge's ever-present aroma of aged wood. It was incongruous, hearing something lively in such a solemn place, but the melodies and lyrics kept me company, cutting through the yawning emptiness of the halls.

As I scrubbed, I allowed the music to carry me away, to transport me to a different time when the lodge was bustling with guests, laughter echoing off the walls. Based on the vintage photos I'd seen, the Holland Lake Lodge had hosted musicians and bands, some of them quite well known. Men and women had shown up in their finery to drink, dine, and dance the night away.

The bright and lilting music stopped abruptly, replaced by the sound of deliberate, measured footsteps. I froze, my grip tightening on the mop handle.

Rachel.

She appeared in the doorway, her figure silhouetted against the dim light of the hall holding my phone. Her arms crossed, her lips pressed into a thin line.

"Still at it?" she asked, her tone light but edged with disapproval.

"Just trying to finish up," I said, keeping my voice neutral.

Rachel leaned against the doorframe, her eyes sweeping over the freshly cleaned floor and walls. "You've done plenty for one night. There's no need to overdo it. You always have tomorrow."

I straightened, wiping my hands on a towel. "I don't mind. It helps pass the time."

Her eyes narrowed, her expression softening into something resembling amusement. "Pass the time? Kate, you'll run yourself ragged if you keep this up." She held my phone out, and I stood to take it. "And maybe next time you could use your earbuds? The music... well, it carries more than you think."

I forced a smile. "Sure. I'll keep it down."

"Good. Now, call it a night. You've done quite enough for today."

She lingered for a moment longer, watching me as if waiting to see if I'd obey. Finally, she turned and disappeared into the shadows of the hallway, her footsteps fading into the quiet.

I stayed where I was, staring at the spot where she'd stood.

I cleaned a little longer, though the joy of it had faded. By the time I packed up my supplies and headed back to my room, the very walls around me felt as though they had absorbed Rachel's disapproving energy.

Closing my door behind me, I let out a slow breath. The evening with Dominic felt distant now, overshadowed by Rachel's words. I flicked on the bedside lamp, ready to collapse into bed, but something on my pillow caught my eye.

A small piece of paper, folded neatly.

I stopped in my tracks, my pulse quickening.

No. God, please no.

Picking it up, I unfolded it slowly, the paper crackling in the stillness. The handwriting was the same as the other notes; old-fashioned, precise but shaky, as though written by someone whose hands weren't steady.

"The kitchen was once filled with the smells of fine meals— meat, seafood and herbs, sweets and spices. They ate well here, the guests who came and went. I can still taste the memories."

The words sent a chill through me. I glanced around the room, half expecting to see someone lurking in the shadows, but it was empty. The lamp cast long, jagged shapes across the walls, making the space feel smaller, more confined.

I read the note again, my arms tingling with adrenaline. Someone had left this for me, someone who'd been watching. The phrasing felt intimate, nostalgic, as if whoever wrote it wasn't just imagining the lodge's past but reliving it.

The handwriting didn't look like Rachel's—it was too delicate, thin and almost spidery. Besides, Rachel wasn't the type to leave cryptic messages; she preferred bluntness, her criticisms sharp and direct.

I sat on the edge of the bed, staring down at the note. Was it possible that someone else was in the lodge? The thought was absurd, but the evidence was right in front of me.

The words "I can still taste the memories" echoed in my mind, a strange mixture of wistfulness and menace. Whoever wrote this wasn't just reminiscing—they were here. Watching.

I tucked the note into the drawer of my nightstand. I wouldn't bring this up to Rachel, not this time. She'd dismiss it, call it a prank, or accuse me of letting my imagination run wild.

No, I'd keep this to myself. The notes were pieces of a puzzle, and until I could see the full picture, I would not tip my hand.

I put on my pajamas and brushed my hair in the mirror. My hair had lost its glossy sheen, and the circles under my eyes seemed to darken more with each passing day. I looked tired. This place hadn't been kind to my looks. Getting into bed and pulling the blankets up to my chin, I stared at the ceiling, my heart pounding in the dark.

As sleep claimed me, the note's words followed me into my dreams, twisting them into something I couldn't escape.

Chapter Twenty-One

Kate

I t was late morning on a cold, calm day. I was taking out the garbage when I saw the SUV, parked right there in the clearing, engine humming against the backdrop of snow-covered trees. For a moment, I thought I was imagining it, like my mind had conjured an escape. Then the door opened, and Decker stepped out.

My heart stopped. *Decker. Here.*

He hadn't called, hadn't written since our breakup months ago. Seeing him now, at the lodge of all places, felt like someone had ripped the sutures out of a half-healed incision. I stood frozen, watching him as he scanned the lodge, his hands stuffed into the pockets of that familiar blue jacket, breath puffing in the cold.

"What are you doing here?" The words came out sharper than I intended. The shock of seeing him hit like a punch.

He turned toward me, his expression softening when he saw my face. "Hey," he said, voice low but steady. "I hadn't heard anything after you left. Got worried. Decided to check on you."

Worried. The word tugged at something deep inside. Relief, maybe. Comfort in a familiar face, even if it was him. Even if we hadn't spoken since everything fell apart.

"I'm fine," I said, though the words felt hollow. "You didn't need to come all this way."

Decker stepped onto the porch, eyes searching mine, and I felt the old familiar pull, the one I'd spent months trying to forget. "You're not answering your phone," he said, frowning. "No one's heard from you. No service here?"

I shook my head, trying to collect myself. "No signal. I haven't had service since I went into town a couple of weeks ago."

Decker's eyes lingered, a mixture of concern and something else I couldn't place. It felt like too much, too fast—him trying to push his way back into my life when I wasn't ready. When I wasn't sure I wanted him there at all.

Before I could respond, I heard footsteps. *Rachel.*

She walked up the pathway from her cabin. Her face was placid and unreadable. She had her eyes locked on Decker, assessing him. That smile—forced but almost warm, at least on occasion—was gone, replaced by something colder, sharper.

"My goodness, Kate. You didn't tell me you were expecting company," she said, her tone polite and controlled... but there was an edge to it.

I swallowed, trying to gauge her reaction. "I wasn't," I said, meeting her gaze. "He just... showed up."

Rachel's eyes darted between me and Decker. "Well," Rachel said, clearing her voice primly, "it's not every day we get visitors out here."

Decker offered her a smile, but she didn't return it. "Yeah, I just wanted to make sure Kate was okay. Didn't mean to surprise anyone. Decker Thomas." He held out his hand.

Rachel hesitated, then shook it. "How do you do?" Her

voice was cool. "We're... remote, Mr. Thomas. Folks usually don't come without some notice."

The tension between the three of us hung in the air. This wasn't just about Decker showing up unannounced—it was something more.

Rachel's eyes passed to me again, and this time, I saw it clearly—something possessive in the way she looked at me. *Decker's presence was an intrusion. I was hers, and he had no business being here.*

I forced a smile, trying to ease the tension. "It's fine," I said, voice tight. "I wasn't expecting him, but... he's here now."

Rachel's lips pressed into a thin line. For a moment, I thought she might argue, but she didn't. She just nodded, her eyes cold as they moved back to Decker. "Right. Well, I'll let you two catch up." Her words sounded more like a dismissal than anything else.

Decker gave her a quick nod, sensing the undercurrent between us. Rachel turned and walked back inside the lodge, but I could still feel her there.

I turned back to Decker, a familiar sense of conflict tugging at me. Part of me was glad to see him, to have someone from my old life here. But another part of me was uneasy, knowing Rachel wouldn't let this go. She'd seen how Decker looked at me, how I reacted to him. And she didn't like it.

"So," Decker said, breaking the silence, "are you gonna tell me what's going on here?"

I shook my head, still trying to process everything. "Nothing's going on," I said, but even I could hear how my voice lacked conviction

Decker frowned, looking at the lodge behind me. "Something doesn't seem right, Kate. I know you. You wouldn't be out here if everything was fine."

I opened my mouth to argue, to push him away again, but the words didn't come. Because deep down, he was right. *Nothing was fine. Nothing about this place, this isolation, my life, felt okay anymore.*

Chapter Twenty-Two

Kate

Rachel didn't waste any time distancing Decker from me. She gave him the best room at the far end of the lodge, with a view that stretched over the frozen lake and the mountains beyond. The room could have been the presidential suite long ago.

"It's a little nicer than the employee wing, don't you think?" she'd said, her voice soft but the jab clear. She could've stuck him in the staff quarters, but she didn't and she wanted me to know it.

Decker stood at the window, looking out at the snow-covered wilderness. His face lit up like a kid seeing the world for the first time. "I can't believe this place," he said, his breath fogging the glass. "It's absolutely stunning. We should've left Seattle years ago."

His words hit me as shortsighted. He hadn't seen the darkness yet—the weight of the lodge, the isolation that pressed in at night when the wind howled. All he saw was the view. The dream of something better.

I forced a smile. "It's beautiful, isn't it?" I said, but my voice lacked the enthusiasm he wanted to hear.

Decker nodded, still glued to the mountains. "You're lucky to be here. I think I'm starting to understand."

There was nothing lucky about this place.

After Decker got settled into his room, Rachel had become even more present—hovering, scrutinizing, inserting herself into our conversations. At first, I tried to tell myself it was her way of being welcoming, but it wasn't. It was control.

She took over the tasks I was supposed to handle that day— maintenance checks, cleaning projects, chores she hadn't bothered with before. She offered no explanation, no conversation. At first, it felt like less work for me. But then I saw what she was doing. It wasn't help—it was about making me irrelevant. *A way to make Decker wonder what I even did to earn my salary.*

I found Rachel in the storage closet, restocking supplies I'd said I would handle.

"I was going to take care of that," I said, trying to keep my tone even.

Rachel didn't look at me right away, just kept stacking shelves like I hadn't spoken. Then she turned, her tight smile in place. "I thought you'd appreciate a break," she said, voice syrupy sweet.

I bit my tongue. "I'm managing fine. I'm just taking a couple of hours to catch up with Decker. I can finish this evening." I said, though I could hear the strain in my voice.

Her smile widened, like she'd won. "Of course you can," she said, looking toward Decker's room. "But I like to be thorough."

She brushed past me, leaving me standing there. This wasn't about chores. She wanted me to feel small, unnecessary, redundant. And with Decker here, the dynamic had shifted. No longer was *I* the outsider, out of place and slightly unwelcome. No, now there was another outsider and, based on the way she watched him with narrowed eyes and a calculating gaze, he wasn't just unwelcome; he was an active threat. A threat to what exactly, I couldn't say, but as the afternoon wore on, the tension grew and eddied around us like the dangerous rip currents Decker and I had been so careful to avoid every time we'd take a trip to the beach.

We were in the mountains now, but the sensation of being pulled under, of drowning, felt very real.

Chapter Twenty-Three

Rachel

I set the lantern down on a crate and surveyed the cluttered storage room. Shelves of forgotten tools and old paint cans lined the walls, and a few broken chairs leaned haphazardly in the corners. At the far end, partially hidden behind a stack of firewood, was the tunnel entrance—a narrow door, barely visible unless you knew where to look.

I exhaled sharply, rolling up my sleeves.

Mother had always insisted the tunnel be kept secret. It was a lifeline during storms, a private passage between the lodge and my cabin. But now, with Kate nosing around and Decker showing up unannounced, I couldn't risk it.

As I started moving the firewood, I muttered to myself, the words breaking the oppressive silence.

"Decker," I hissed, the name bitter on my tongue. "Why is he even here? He has no business showing up like this, disrupting everything."

The logs were heavy, rough against my hands. I stacked them carefully, layering them higher, creating a solid wall in front of the door. My arms ached, but the physical work was grounding, a welcome distraction from the thoughts swirling in my head.

"This changes everything," I said aloud, as if the tunnel itself needed to hear my frustration. "I had a plan. Mother would've seen soon enough that Kate wasn't up to the task. A few more days—just a few—and it would've been obvious. But no, he had to show up and throw it all off balance."

Decker's presence had unsettled me more than I cared to admit. He was a distraction, a disruption. Worse, he brought energy into the lodge that didn't belong—an energy that could complicate it all.

"And Mother won't like it," I added, my voice rising slightly. "She won't like it at all. Fornication in the lodge is forbidden. Always has been."

The word hung in the air, heavy and accusing.

I turned to grab more firewood, stacking it higher, obscuring the tunnel entrance completely. Mother had been firm on this rule, perhaps more than any other. When the lodge was open in the summer, with young men and women working side by side, it had been a constant battle to keep them in line.

"Late teens, early twenties," I muttered, recalling their faces. "The boys with their cocky grins, the girls giggling at every little thing. Mother saw it all, every glance, every whisper. She always knew."

Keeping them celibate had been exhausting. Mother's rules were clear—no fraternizing, no sneaking into each other's rooms. She had a way of enforcing discipline, her sharp words cutting through the flirtations like a knife.

"She was right," I said, my voice steady now. "This place isn't for that. It's sacred. It's not a playground for hormones and foolishness."

The thought of Decker staying overnight sent a fresh wave of anger coursing through me. His presence would only embolden Kate, give her some misplaced sense of normalcy or security. That wasn't what the lodge was about.

I paused, wiping sweat from my brow, and leaned against the stack of firewood.

"Mother will be furious," I whispered, staring at the hidden door. "If she knew he was here... if she knew I allowed it..."

But did I allow it? What choice did I have? Decker had shown up uninvited, with that easy smile of his, charming Kate as if the lodge were some romantic getaway.

"It's not his place," I said sharply. "And it's not hers, either. She hasn't earned it."

My fingers curled into fists. Kate's every move had been under Mother's scrutiny, every task an unspoken test. The notes Mother left—praising her resilience, her effort—were daggers in my heart. Those words used to be mine.

I straightened, my resolve hardening.

"I'll fix this," I said, my voice firm. "Decker won't stay long. He'll leave, and then I'll set things right. Kate will see what's required, what's expected. And when she fails, Mother will understand. She'll see that I'm still the only one worthy of this place."

I grabbed an old tarp and draped it over the firewood, further obscuring the tunnel entrance. The storage room looked like nothing more than a forgotten corner of the lodge now, a place no one would think to investigate.

Stepping back, I surveyed my work.

"Good," I muttered. "That'll do."

But the unease lingered. Decker's arrival had delayed my plans. The impossible challenges I'd devised for Kate—tasks designed to expose her shortcomings—would have to wait. And the longer he stayed, the more comfortable she'd become, the more emboldened she'd feel.

That couldn't happen.

Mother's rules weren't just rules. They were the foundation of the lodge, the principles that kept it pure, untarnished by outside influences. Decker's presence, his connection to Kate, threatened all of that.

I turned off the lantern and stepped into the hallway, the darkness of the lodge painting blackness all around me.

"This is my home," I whispered, the words steady and resolute. "It's not theirs. It never will be."

As I made my way back to my cabin, I could almost hear Mother's voice in the back of my mind, sharp and unwavering.

She was watching.

She always was.

And I would not fail her.

Chapter Twenty-Four

Kate

The next morning, I was up early and made a quick breakfast for Decker. The smell of coffee filled the kitchen, a small comfort against the cold seeping through the cracks. Decker wandered in, yawning and stretching, his hair messy, eyes soft with sleep.

"Slept like a rock," he said, running a hand through his hair. "This place is solid. Not a squeak, not a creak. They sure knew how to build them back then."

I forced a smile, handing him a mug. "Yeah, they don't make them like this anymore," I replied. The lodge didn't feel solid to me at all—it felt unstable, like it was barely standing against the elements. Decker took a sip, his eyes on me, but before I could respond, the sound of an engine broke the moment. Dominic's truck. I frowned. Rachel hadn't mentioned needing him, and the generator had been working fine.

A few minutes later, Dominic walked in, snow caking his boots. "Morning, Kate," he said with a grin, his eyes passing from me to Decker. "Rachel called. Said I should check the generator." I blinked, thrown off. "The generator's fine. There haven't been any issues."

Dominic shrugged, grabbing his tools. "Guess she wanted to do a little preventative maintenance.. I'll take a look, make sure everything's running smoothly." He looked at Decker, a grin tugging at his mouth.

Decker leaned back, watching Dominic without emotion, catching the too-familiar tone. Dominic was always friendly, but now, with Decker here, it felt like something more—a little too friendly.

"I'll be outside for a bit," Dominic said, heading toward the door. "Might be a minute. Snow's piling up."

I nodded, still wondering why Rachel had called him. Dominic slipped out, the cold gusting in as he left, and I turned just in time to see Rachel glide into the kitchen.

She glanced toward the door, her smile tight, her eyes unreadable. "Why is Dominic here?" I asked, not able to stop myself.

Rachel turned to me, her face calm. "Just a precaution," she said, like she'd rehearsed the answer. "Better safe than sorry."

I opened my mouth to ask more, but before I could, Rachel shifted her attention to Decker. Her face softened, but there was something calculated behind her smile.

"How did you sleep?" she asked, her voice too polite.

Decker looked up, unaware of the tension. "Great," he said, leaning back. "This place is incredible. Slept like a baby."

Rachel's smile widened, and she crossed her arms. "Did you know Charles Lindbergh slept in your room back in 1927?"

Decker's eyes widened. "No kidding? That's incredible."

Rachel nodded, pleased with his reaction. "He stayed here three days on a national tour after crossing the Atlantic. We've had some famous guests over the years."

Decker seemed impressed, falling more in love with the lodge by the second. The history, the stories behind the walls, fascinated him. And for a moment, I saw how easily Rachel could pull him in, the way she had with me when we'd spoken on the phone months ago. I forced a smile, but couldn't shake the feeling that Rachel was using these moments to deepen her hold, to create connections that would somehow give her more leverage and make her feel more in control.

The tension shifted when Dominic came back inside, brushing snow from his shoulders. "Everything's running fine," he said, his eyes once again lingering on me. "No problems. Won't need an oil change for a couple of months."

I nodded, still unsettled by Rachel's behavior. *Dominic shouldn't have been here today.*

Decker stood, setting his mug on the counter. "I'll help Kate with the floors," he said. "Got to earn my keep."

Rachel's disapproving look was immediate. "I don't think that's a good idea," she said, her voice clipped. "I can't pay you, and I have a very particular way I want it done."

Decker didn't flinch. "No problem. Kate can school me."

Dominic could sense the tension and gave a salute as he turned and walked out the door to the parking lot.

Rachel's lips thinned, but she said nothing. She watched Dominic get into his truck.

Decker wasn't backing down, and Rachel didn't like it. I could feel the quiet battle between them as she turned and left the room. Once she was gone, Decker got to work with me. For a moment, the tension lifted as we worked in silence, stripping the old wax from the floors. But even with Rachel out of sight, her presence lingered, the unease settling back in.

Chapter Twenty-Five

Kate

B y the time dusk began settling outside, Decker and I had spent hours working on the floor. We had worked together efficiently, but we hadn't yet broached any subjects beyond the high pH of floor strippers, logistics of applying the chemicals and the inherent beauty of the natural wood grain. I hoped dinner with Decker would let us reconnect on a more personal level and sort some things out.

We hadn't really talked since he arrived, let alone since I'd checked into rehab, and part of me wanted to feel like things between us could still be as easy as they'd been once upon a time. And maybe we could forget, just for a little while, the events that had led up to all the drama in Seattle and the tension that had settled over everything since he'd shown up at the lodge.

Decker had brought a case of wine from his parents' vineyard. My favorite, of course. It brought back memories I wasn't quite ready to face, but I pushed them aside, determined to keep the evening light.

But just as we sat down, plates in front of us, Rachel

appeared in the kitchen's doorway. No knock, no pause. Just Rachel, pulling up a chair beside Decker like she'd been invited.

"Mind if I join?" she asked, but it wasn't a question.

I glanced at Decker. His face stayed neutral, but I could see the way his shoulders tightened. The warmth of the room vanished the second Rachel sat down.

Rachel poured herself a generous glass of wine without asking, taking a slow sip. "This is excellent," she said, her eyes landing on Decker. "You have good taste."

Decker tried to smile. "It's from my parents' winery," he said. "Brought a few bottles for Kate."

Rachel stared at him, her face tight. "How thoughtful,"

Rachel took another sip of wine before she started asking questions—sharp, probing ones. It wasn't a conversation; it was an interrogation.

"So, what exactly do you do, Decker? I didn't catch that before."

"I work in tech. Corporate job," he answered.

"Tech. Must be stressful."

Decker shrugged. "It has its moments. But it's not so bad."

The questions kept coming, each one more pointed than the last. Rachel wasn't trying to get to know him—she was trying to make him uncomfortable. And it was working. Decker, for all his calm, was feeling the weight of Rachel's resentment and tireless scrutiny. Our food was getting cold as she continued her line of questioning.

At one point, he mentioned why he'd come. "I hadn't heard from Kate in a while," he said, his voice soft. "I was worried."

"Worried?" she said. "Why would you be worried? Kate's fine here."

My grip tightened on my wine glass. The way she said it,

like she was speaking to me, grated on my nerves. I could feel the irritation building, creeping up my spine.

"He was just concerned. He cares about me." I said.

A flash of hurt crossed Rachel's face, but it disappeared quickly, replaced with a tight smile. "Of course," she said, her tone controlled. "But you don't need to worry about Kate. She's perfectly capable of taking care of herself."

Decker looked at me, his eyes searching mine, but I couldn't meet them. I was too busy trying to figure out what game Rachel was playing, why she was speaking on my behalf, why I was letting her. Why did she need to assert control over every part of my life?

Rachel turned back to Decker, her smile sharpening. "How long do you plan to stay?" she asked.

"Not sure yet," he said. "Depends on how things go."

"We don't get many visitors out here. It's a long way from the city."

The way she said it, like Decker didn't belong, set my teeth on edge. Rachel was making sure Decker knew his place. The rest of the meal was quieter as Rachel sat back and watched us eat, drinking a second glass of wine. Jealousy simmered just beneath the surface, visible in her pursed lips and clenching jaw. Decker held his ground, but I could see he was irritated. The battle between them was unspoken, but real. By the time Rachel excused herself, the atmosphere in the room snapped with electricity.

As soon as she was gone, Decker turned to me. "What the hell was that?"

I shook my head, the knot of tension in my chest tightening. "That's just Rachel," I said.

"She doesn't seem like *just* anything, Kate. Something's seriously off about her."

Chapter Twenty-Six

Kate

The blizzard arrived, snow piling against the windows, erasing everything beyond the lodge. Rachel had left for her cabin hours ago, with parting words: "We'll have plenty of shoveling in the morning."

Inside, the storm felt distant. The fire crackled and, for once, a small part of the lodge felt warm and cozy. Decker and I sat on the couch, the second bottle of wine nearly gone. The tension of the day was finally softening, the edges blurring with each sip.

"Your boss is a piece of work," Decker said, glancing over his shoulder as if expecting her to appear. His voice was low, almost conspiratorial.

I stayed quiet, taking a long drink of the red wine. I knew what he meant. But agreeing with him would mean admitting that maybe I'd made a mistake coming here. And I wasn't ready for that.

"She acts like she owns you," Decker said, his eyes on me. "It doesn't seem healthy."

The wine had loosened my tongue. "She's a serious bitch to

work for," I muttered, setting my glass down. "And she's creepy."

I said it louder than I meant to, but I didn't care. Rachel was in her cabin, far from us, the storm keeping her there. Decker's grin widened, his gaze softening as he leaned in.

"There's my old Kate," he said, smiling, his voice warm. "God, I've missed you."

Before he could say anything else, my lips were on his. The kiss started out gentle, almost hesitant, before it quickly developed its own gravity, pulling me back into something familiar, something I hadn't realized I'd missed so desperately.

We stumbled down the halls, stopping to kiss again against the rough log walls, hands tangled in each other's clothes. A button popped off his shirt, pinged against the wall, and rolled down the hallway. The cold of the storm vanished, the year we'd spent apart falling away like it never happened.

By the time we made it to his room, we were breathless. The antique bed stood like a relic, a reminder of when this place had been full of life. We fell into it, everything else disappearing.

Lying there afterward, with him beside me, I felt like I'd finally come home. The feel of him, the familiarity—it was like going back to a time before everything had fallen apart. I'd missed human touch, but, more specifically, I'd missed *his* touch.

We stared up at the ornate ceiling; the firelight flickering across the room, casting long shadows. Decker's voice broke the silence. "Be careful around her," he said, his words cutting through the stillness. "I don't trust her and I'm worried about you working here."

The warmth of the moment faded. I couldn't deny that he was right. The way Rachel watched me, the way she inserted herself into everything—it wasn't just coincidence anymore. It felt calculated.

I turned to look at him, but he was already asleep, his breathing steady, his arm draped over me.

But I couldn't sleep. I stared at the ceiling. *I have to be careful around her.*

Rachel was trying to isolate me. I could see that now. She controlled the space, the tasks, even the people around me. She'd pushed Decker to the far end of the lodge and taken over jobs that weren't hers. She tried to drive him away with her relentless and uncomfortable questions.

I laid there, the cold creeping back in despite Decker's warmth, listening to the storm raging outside.

Chapter Twenty-Seven

Rachel

The fire crackled in the cast-iron stove, its warmth spreading through the cabin's close quarters. I stood over it, sleeves rolled up, watching the flames dance and lick the cast iron walls. The stove had always been a comfort—steady, predictable, an anchor in the chaos of the world. Tonight, it was more than that.

The old-fashioned non-electric clothes iron rested on the stove's surface, its spring handle glinting faintly in the light. I'd found it years ago in one of the storage rooms at the lodge, a relic of a time when people relied on more than electricity and convenience. It was heavy, solid, real.

I picked up a log and added it to the fire, ensuring the flames stayed steady, feeding them just enough to maintain the heat. The iron needed to be perfect—not too hot, not too cool. My movements were meticulous, almost reverent, as I adjusted the air vent on the stove, letting the fire breathe.

When the iron's surface glowed, I reached for it, testing the handle. The spring had always fascinated me, the way it allowed the iron to be handled even when the metal was searing. I lifted it, feeling its weight in my hand, and placed it back down. Not yet.

I pulled a chair closer to the stove, rolling up my sleeves as I sat. The skin of my forearms was pale around the pink and ropey scars, the faint blue of veins visible beneath. They were strong arms—arms that had scrubbed floors, chopped wood, built fires, and carried the weight of the lodge for decades. But they were also arms that carried memories.

I reached for the iron again, its heat radiating through the air, and positioned it above my forearm. My pulse quickened, my breath steadying as I brought the tip of the iron down.

The sizzle was sharp and immediate, the smell of scorched flesh filling the cabin. Pain bloomed bright and fierce, but I didn't flinch. Instead, I pressed the iron with deliberate precision, holding it just long enough to leave a clean, tidy triangle.

I lifted the iron and set it back on the stove, exhaling as the pain settled into a dull throb. The endorphins followed, rushing through me like a wave, steadying my mind in a way nothing else could.

The act was familiar, practiced. It had been years since I'd done this, but the ritual came back to me like an old habit. A therapy of sorts, though most wouldn't understand. The pain was grounding, a reminder of control, a release from the chaos that churned inside me.

I picked up the iron again, ensuring it stayed hot, and moved to the next spot on my arm. Another triangle, aligned with the first. The sizzle, the pain, the release—it was all the same, each mark as deliberate as the last.

Decker. Kate. The names simmered in my mind, feeding the fire in more ways than one.

The two of them, with their whispers and stolen glances, their brazen disregard for the rules of the lodge—it was intolerable. Fornication in the lodge had always been forbidden.

Mother had made that clear, drilling it into me from the time I was old enough to understand. The lodge was sacred, not a place for indulgence or recklessness.

But they didn't understand that. Decker, with his sincerity and casual presence, and Kate, so willing to follow his lead. They thought they could do as they pleased, that their little romance didn't matter.

The iron came down again, this time a fraction higher on my arm. The pain seared through me, sharper than the last, and I let it linger, letting the heat drive out the anger.

It wasn't just their actions that bothered me. It was what they represented. Youth. Desire. The things I no longer had.

There had been flings, once. Summers when the lodge was full of young employees—handsome boys who flirted with me in their clumsy, eager ways. Forest rangers with their rugged charm, their boyish smiles. But that was decades ago.

Now, my body felt like something separate from me, a vessel I carried rather than lived in. The softness of youth was gone, replaced by the aches and stiffness of age. The skin I burned tonight would scar, just like the rest of me.

I set the iron down and leaned back in the chair, the high of the endorphins settling over me like a warm blanket. The pain was still there, but it felt distant now, muted by the rush that followed.

I tipped my head back, staring at the ceiling. The firelight flickered, casting faint shadows on the wood above, but in my mind, the roof gave way to the night sky.

I imagined the stars—sharp, cold points of light against the darkness. I wondered if Mother could see me now, if she was watching as she always seemed to be. Would she approve of this? Would she understand?

The cabin was silent, save for the crackle of the fire. The

marks on my arms throbbed, but the ache inside me was quieter now, dulled by the ritual.

Decker and Kate would learn, one way or another. They didn't belong here, not in the way I did. They didn't understand the rules, the sacrifices, the weight of this place.

But I would make them understand.

I closed my eyes, the warmth of the fire lulling me into a strange, peaceful, half-dozing dream state. Tomorrow would come soon enough, and with it, the task of restoring order. For now, I let the stillness of the cabin wrap around me, my mind quiet for the first time in days.

Chapter Twenty-Eight

Kate

The morning light glowed through the snow-covered windows, rendering everything around me in varying shades of pale grey. Decker was still asleep beside me, sprawled on his back, his rhythmic breathing slow and steady. For a moment, I watched him, taking in his presence and trying to absorb some of his steadying energy, but it was no use. Any peace I received from him was overshadowed by the skittish unease and restless anxiety I almost always felt these days..

I slipped out of bed, grabbed my clothes, and looked outside. Four feet of fresh snow blanketed the ground, untouched. No footprints. If Rachel had come to the lodge from her cabin overnight, it would've been obvious. The snow would have shown me.

The lodge was even colder than usual as I made my way back to my room in a distant wing of the building. Empty hallways echoed under my footsteps, and something felt off, something beyond the massive snowstorm and pale, watery half-light. I couldn't put my finger on it, but it gnawed at me. This sense of...wrongness.

I took a long, hot shower, letting the steam fill the bathroom as I tried to clear my mind. Rachel was becoming more difficult by the day, her moods darker, her desire to control tightening. Part of me wanted to leave, to pack up and head back to Seattle with Decker. But another part—the stubborn part—pushed back. I'd committed to this job for the winter, and I wasn't about to let Rachel's mind games run me off.

I wanted to show the people in my life, and most importantly myself, that I could see a commitment through until the end. That I could endure and overcome.

My breakdown after a last brutal argument with Decker had sent me into a deep hole emotionally. I still can't believe that I ended up hopelessly addicted to opioids. Almost a year ago now, my sudden and spiraling addiction rocked my parents. Their fear, and my own, really, had convinced me to commit myself to psychiatric care and rehab. I had hated it, but had to admit the time in the hospital had done me a lot of good.

But I wasn't going back to Seattle, not yet at least, and I needed to protect myself here. The simple fact that Decker came to see me was further evidence that my addiction, unpredictable behavior, and the horrible things I had said to him hadn't scared him off. And if last night was anything to go off of, he would be willing to wait for me for just a bit longer.

After I dressed, I scanned my room and sensed it immediately. Something was wrong. My laptop was gone. I'd left it on the nightstand.

Frowning, I checked everywhere: the dresser, under the bed, even my bags. Nothing. Panic flickered through me, but I shoved it down. Maybe I'd left it somewhere else. But deep down, I knew I hadn't.

I searched the lodge, going from room to room, even the kitchen. It wasn't until an hour later that I found it—in the third-floor lounge, a place I never went. There it was, sitting on a table, like someone wanted me to find it.

A chill ran through me. Someone had moved it. Someone had been in my room. The realization made my skin crawl.

Rachel's voice echoed in my mind, dismissing me like always: "You're just misplacing things, Kate. You're letting this get to you." Her words had stung before, but they were starting to feel like more than a dismissal. They felt like a taunt, like gaslighting.

I wasn't going to tell her about the laptop. Not this time. I'd mentioned the notes and the missing scarf before, but she always brushed it off, making me feel like I was losing it. But this—this was different.

I took the computer back to my room, my thoughts racing. Rachel had to be behind this, right? Who else, if not her? Was she trying to make me doubt myself, to break me down? Because if that was her goal, it was starting to work.

I went downstairs and made a cup of coffee. I made another for Decker and walked it up to his room, moving carefully so I didn't spill a drop. He was still asleep, his face peaceful. I set the cup down beside him and left quietly. Until I arranged my thoughts, I didn't want to talk. I needed space to think.

Stepping outside, the cold air hit me like a slap. But the bite of it helped clear my head as I grabbed a shovel and started clearing the snow around the lodge. The rhythm of shoveling grounded me, but the questions wouldn't stop. Every heave of snow brought me back to Rachel. Was she torturing me? Testing me?

I thought about Decker's warning from the night before, his suspicion of Rachel. He'd felt it too—the way she was always watching, always too involved. Was she trying to push me into a corner until I doubted everything? Until I went crazy? *Again?*

As I kept shoveling, the snow pressed into footprints under my boots. The stress drilled down on me.. If Rachel was trying to make me feel trapped, she had succeeded.

Chapter Twenty-Nine

Kate

Later that morning, after what felt like hours of shoveling, Decker and I had finally cleared a path to Rachel's cabin. He had joined me after getting up and donning his winter clothes.

The cold burned my lungs, but the physical effort felt good —like each shoveled pile of snow helped clear the negativity that had been building inside me. Decker and I worked in sync, as if no time had passed since the old days in Seattle. We didn't talk about last night—the way we'd slipped back into something familiar—but there was a spark between us, an electricity that hadn't been there before.

I felt it and I knew Decker did, too.

Decker grinned, leaning on his shovel. "Feels good, doesn't it? Being out here, doing real work."

I nodded, smiling back. "Yeah, it does."

Afterward, I headed toward the lodge while Decker wandered toward the woodpile. He seemed to love the physical labor up here, the chopping of wood, the shoveling of snow—it was as if being out here in the wilderness had reignited something in him. He was thriving.

But the moment I stepped into the lodge, the sense of peace slipped away because Rachel was there in the kitchen, waiting. *How did she get here? How had she slipped past us on the trail to her cabin? She must have circled around through the woods on snowshoes or cross-country skis.*

She was standing by the window, her back to me. It was silent, except for the coffeepot, which hissed and bubbled by the stove. I hesitated in the doorway, unsure of what to say. Before I could leave, she spoke, her voice trembling.

"I feel you're pulling away."

I stopped, surprised by the emotion in her voice. I stepped inside. "Rachel, it's not like that," I started, trying to keep my voice calm, but the intensity in her eyes when she turned to face me stopped me cold.

"You've been spending so much time with Decker," she said, her voice tight. "I thought we were getting close."

I opened my mouth to respond, but she cut me off, her words rushing out. "I have been here alone for so many years." She took a breath, her shoulders slumping as she wiped at her eyes. "But you don't know what it's like to be left behind."

"I'm not pulling away," I said, though I wasn't sure I believed it. "Decker just... showed up. I wasn't expecting it either."

"I just don't want to lose you," she said as a tear slid down her cheek. Her words, her emotion, they should have elicited my sympathy, but after the events of the past month, I couldn't shake the feeling that this was yet a new tactic, a new way to manipulate.

"Nothing is changing from how it had been these past two months," I said, taking a step back. "But I need space. I need to do my job. I need to spend time with Decker, too."

"Of course," she said, her voice soft. "I understand."

But I knew she didn't. The look in her eyes told me everything. And the more I tried to pull away, the harder she'd fight to keep me under her thumb.

I nodded, not trusting myself to say anything else, and turned to leave. But as I walked away, Rachel's words echoed in my mind.

"I just don't want to lose you."

I shivered.. Rachel might not want to lose me, but if her odd behavior continued, I was afraid I'd lose my mind.

Chapter Thirty

Kate

I wasn't trying to eavesdrop. I was just walking through the lodge, heading toward the storage closet, when I heard Rachel's voice. Low, hushed, like she didn't want anyone to hear. Curiosity pulled me closer to the half-open office door. Her tone was sharp, tense.

"No, she hasn't signed it—I haven't had a chance," Rachel was saying. "But I'll keep working on her."

My pulse quickened. I froze in the hallway, my mind racing. Who is she talking about? She wasn't talking about Decker, so that meant she was talking about me. *Signed what?*

I held my breath and listened. Rachel's voice dropped lower, but I strained to hear more. The creak of the floor under my foot gave me away. I winced, my heart pounding as the murmur of her conversation abruptly stopped.

The office door swung open. Rachel stepped out, phone still in hand. Her eyes locked onto mine instantly.

"Need something?" she asked. Her voice was calm, but her gaze was shrewd.

I forced a smile, though the tension in my chest made it

hard to breathe. "No, just... passing through," I said, trying to sound casual. I turned quickly and walked away, trying not to move too fast, even though my legs felt shaky.

Why was she keeping an eye on me? The question echoed in my mind. Something bigger was going on here, something I wasn't seeing yet.

That evening, Rachel walked to her cabin, leaving Decker and me alone in the lodge. We ate dinner by the fire, the warmth doing little to ease my nerves after overhearing Rachel's telephone conversation earlier. Unsurprisingly, Decker was more relaxed. He leaned back, watching me over the rim of his wineglass, a soft smile on his face. "You know, I've been thinking," he said, setting his glass down. "Maybe you should come back to Seattle with me."

I blinked, caught off guard.

He nodded, leaning forward. "I have to get back to work, but I don't like the idea of leaving you here with her. And, I thought maybe...we could give it another try."

I sat back on the leather sofa. *Back to Seattle and back together?* I had come here to show myself that I could make bold decisions and regain my independence. I wanted to set out to do something hard and follow through by finishing it. I wanted what Decker was offering, but I needed to finish what I'd started. Rachel's bullshit was tough, but I could get through it and prove it to myself.

I smiled, shaking my head. "I appreciate it, but I'm not ready to go back. I need more time away from the city, away from everything. I've committed to stay for the winter, and I want to see it through."

Decker's smile faded a little, but he nodded. "I get it. I respect that. You've always been stubborn, or should I say dedicated?" he said, smiling. "I just don't like the idea of you being here alone with her. Something's not right."

I sighed, glancing at the fire, still unsettled by what I'd heard earlier. "She's got her quirks, that's for sure." I admitted. "But I can handle her. And you'll come back, right? Once you can take more time off?"

Decker grinned, brushing a strand of hair from my face. "Of course. I'll be back as soon as I can. You couldn't keep me away from this old place if you tried."

There was a solid spark between us again, more than just a flicker of that old connection. Before I knew it, we were kissing, the fire casting a glow over us as we fell into each other's arms.

Later, lying in bed beside him, I stared out the window at the winter sky, trying to push the earlier conversation with Rachel out of my mind. But Decker's words, *"Something's not right,"* stayed with me.

I was just drifting off when Decker's hand gently shook me awake. "Kate," he whispered, his voice low. "Do you hear that?"

I blinked, disoriented, before I registered the sound. The lodge was groaning, the wood shifting in the cold. But there was something else. Footsteps. Faint but distinct, moving through the hallways. I sat up, my pulse quickening. The sound was faint but rhythmic - *shuffle, pause, shuffle, pause* - moving slowly down the hallway outside the door. My heart pounded, and I glanced at Decker, his face mirroring my unease.

"Did Rachel come back?" he whispered.

I shook my head, my throat tight.

We sat there, listening as the footsteps, or whatever they were, faded into the distance and the soft eerie sounds were replaced by creaks of the log beams around us.

Footsteps? Surely not. Surely the storm was causing all kinds of slight structural shifting and the mysterious sounds were nothing more menacing than that. My imagination, already overactive, was in hyper-drive after the stress of recent weeks, but, for once, it wasn't just me. I could see from Decker's expression that he was uneasy as well, and that made me feel less crazy.

"Maybe it's just the building," Decker said, trying to reassure me, but I could see the doubt in his eyes.

I nodded, though the knot in my stomach wouldn't loosen. "Maybe."

But as I lay back down, I couldn't shake the feeling that Rachel wasn't just keeping an eye on me. She knew more than she was letting on. And whatever it was, it was getting harder to ignore.

Chapter Thirty-One

Rachel

I paced the small cabin; the phone pressed to my ear. Snow outside blanketed everything in silence, but inside, my mind raced, alive with anticipation. The fire in the wood stove crackled faintly, the sound grounding me as I listened to Mr. Campbell's crisp, condescending voice on the other end.

"Yes, Mr. Campbell, I understand the need for expediency," I said, forcing a calm professionalism into my tone. I hated feeling rushed, hated being prodded into decisions, but I couldn't deny the significance of his offer.

A buyout. The lifeline I'd dreamed of in fleeting, desperate moments over the years. The New York firm's offer to buy the lodge wasn't just substantial—it was transformative.

"Good," he replied, his voice sharp and efficient. "Our investors are enthusiastic, but before we proceed, we'll need proper documentation proving your legal authority over the property."

I stopped pacing, my grip on the phone tightening.

"Authority?" The word tasted sour, though I knew exactly what he meant. "You mean the inheritance paperwork?"

"Exactly," Campbell confirmed. "We'll need a clean chain of title passing directly to you. That means your mother's signature transferring ownership. No gaps, no loose ends. Standard procedure."

I glanced at the door, as though expecting someone to be listening. The room was empty, of course, but the weight of his words felt oppressive.

"Mother is... not well," I said, choosing each word as though they might betray me. "Getting her to sign will require some finesse."

There was a pause on the line, and when Campbell spoke again, his voice had softened, though impatience lurked beneath. "We understand that family matters can complicate things, but this is critical. Without a clean title, the deal won't move forward. Our timeline is short—investors are considering properties in Big Sky as well, so if you're serious about this, we'll need you in Bozeman on Friday of next week to finalize the details."

Big Sky. The word flared in my chest like a spark. Competition. I couldn't let this opportunity slip away.

"I'll be there," I said, my tone firm. "But let's be clear—this lodge is a historic property. If your investors have any plans to alter its layout or heritage, I'll need that explicitly stated beforehand. No modern remodeling. No tearing down walls."

There was a pause, and I imagined Campbell holding back a sigh. "Of course, Ms. Hedden," he said smoothly, though his tone carried a practiced neutrality. "We'll prioritize preserving the lodge's charm where feasible. However, profitability is our investors' primary concern. Compromises may be necessary."

Compromises. The word grated against me. This wasn't about profitability—it was about legacy. My legacy.

"I expect full transparency on any changes," I replied, my voice cold. "I won't see this lodge gutted for the sake of some investor's spreadsheet."

"Understood," Campbell said, his tone careful. "We'll need those signatures in place by next week. Once the paperwork is in order, we'll be ready to proceed. We'll see you in Bozeman."

"Thank you, Mr. Campbell," I said, forcing politeness into my voice. "I'll see you then."

I hung up and stood there for a moment, the quiet of the cabin pressing in around me. The inheritance, the signatures—it all seemed so simple when spoken of in legal terms, but the reality was far messier.

Mother's grip on the lodge was unrelenting, even now. She had refused to relinquish control, holding onto it as tightly as she had held onto everything else in her life. Now, her mind was lost in a haze of memory and time, far from the present moment, but her legal authority still loomed over me like a shadow.

The irony of it stung. After all my years of sacrifice, of devoting myself to the lodge, I still wasn't officially in charge. I still needed her approval. Even now.

I crossed to the window and stared out at the falling snow. The world outside was blanketed in white, a soft silence that belied the storm brewing in my chest. The thought of Bozeman, the meeting, the papers—it felt like a dream I'd rehearsed a dozen times but had never dared to live.

This wasn't a betrayal, I told myself. This was survival.

The lodge needed me, not her. Not anymore. It was my time to take full ownership to ensure its future. The buyout would give me the leverage to preserve the lodge's history while securing my own financial stability.

I closed my eyes, leaning my forehead against the cold glass. Above me, I could almost feel her presence, as though she were watching from the corners of the ceiling, her disapproval palpable.

"Mother," I whispered, the word barely audible. "This is the way it has to be."

The snow continued to fall, the fire continued to pop and crackle and the world continued to turn.. I turned away from the window, the weight of the upcoming week settling over me. The inheritance, the sale—it all rested on my ability to navigate the fine line between the past and the future.

For now, I could only hope that the line didn't blur beyond recognition.

Chapter Thirty-Two

Kate

The recreation storage room smelled of aged wood and mildew, its shelves lined with relics of a bygone era. Wooden cross-country skis, leather-strapped snowshoes, and faded sleds were piled haphazardly alongside a few tarnished trophies and brittle winter coats. Decker reached up and pulled down a pair of wooden snowshoes, their varnish cracked but still sturdy. He turned to me with a grin.

"These might actually hold up," he said, holding them out for my inspection.

I ran my fingers over the woven leather bindings. "They look ancient. But I guess we don't have many other options."

Decker grabbed another pair, testing the straps for strength before handing them to me. "Vintage charm, right? Besides, it's better than post-holing through eight feet of snow."

We strapped the snowshoes onto our boots, the bindings creaking with age. The wide frames felt awkward at first as we clomped out of the lodge, but soon we found a rhythm, trudging through the pristine blanket of snow stretching toward the woods.

The world around us was a hushed cathedral of white, the snow absorbing every sound except for the crunch of our steps and the occasional creak of the wooden frames beneath our feet.

"It's beautiful," I murmured, my breath visible in the cold air.

"It is," Decker agreed, his voice soft. He glanced over at me, his brow furrowing slightly. "I've missed this, Kate."

My heart skipped, but I kept my eyes on the trail ahead. "You mean snowshoeing?"

"No," he said with a quiet laugh. "I mean you. Us. Being with you like this."

We moved in silence for a few moments, his words settling over me like freshly fallen snow—light, but impossible to ignore.

"Do you think we could do this again? You know, us... together?" Decker finally asked.

I hesitated, my snowshoes crunching against the frozen surface as I thought. "I don't know. It feels... complicated."

"Complicated doesn't mean impossible," he said. He glanced at me again, his expression serious. "What would it look like? For us, I mean, once this winter is over?"

I sighed, my breath fogging in the air. "I don't know, Decker. I'm still trying to figure out who I am right now. After everything..."

He slowed his pace, letting me walk a step ahead before asking, "Is this about your recovery? About rehab?"

My stomach tightened. The questions were direct, almost clinical, and defensiveness flickered inside me. "Why do you ask?"

"Because I need to know," he said, his voice calm but unwavering. "I need to know if you think being 'better' is some kind of prerequisite for us getting back together. Because it's not. It never has been."

I stopped and turned to him, my snowshoes sinking slightly into the powder. "You mean that?"

Decker nodded. "I mean it. I loved you then, and I love you now. You don't have to fix yourself for me. I just want you to be okay—for you."

The words hit me harder than I expected, my eyes stinging against the cold. "I don't even know what 'okay' looks like anymore."

"Maybe we figure it out together," he said, taking my gloved hand in his.

We reached Holland Falls just as the sun began dipping lower, casting the frozen cascade in hues of orange and gold. The waterfall stood fifty feet high, a towering sculpture of ice, its ridges glittering like crystal.

"It's incredible," I whispered, feeling small in the face of something so vast, so untouched.

"It really is," Decker said, but when I turned toward him, his eyes weren't on the falls. They were on me.

I'd always thought he had kind eyes, a warm chocolate brown with golden flecks near the pupil, visible only up close. They crinkled a bit at the edges when he smiled at me, which was often.

I tilted my head, our breath mingling in the cold air. He leaned in. The kiss started tentative, then deepened, its warmth cutting through the chill.

When we finally pulled apart, we lingered in the moment, holding onto each other as the frozen world around us seemed to stand still.

"We should head back," Decker said reluctantly.

I nodded, and we turned toward the lodge, our snowshoes crunching through the snow.

As we neared the lodge, the cliffs along the lake loomed to our left, their jagged edges stark against the pale snow. The underbrush rustled, and both of us froze.

"What was that?" Decker asked, his voice low.

I scanned the shadows, my pulse quickening. "I don't know. Maybe a deer?"

Then came the sound of snorting, deep and guttural, followed by a low growl that sent a shiver down my spine.

"That's no deer," Decker said, his voice tight.

We moved quickly, our snowshoes dragging against the snow, but running was nearly impossible. I risked a glance back and felt my stomach drop.

A massive grizzly bear emerged from the underbrush, its hulking frame moving with surprising speed despite the deep snow.

"Decker!" I shouted, panic lacing my voice.

He turned and froze for a split second before grabbing my hand. "Go! Keep moving!"

The lodge was still a distant speck, and the bear was closing the gap, its furious growls echoing across the lake.

The grizzly's roar shattered the stillness, its massive paws punching through the snow as it charged forward. My breath came in sharp gasps as I glanced back, heart pounding. The bear was gaining, its powerful frame plowing through the drifts. But then it hit a patch of snow too deep even for its power, and its movements slowed. Each step became a struggle, the beast growling in frustration.

"Keep moving!" Decker shouted, his voice hoarse. He yanked me forward as we dodged through the trees. The snowshoes gave us just enough of an advantage to stay ahead, though our strides were awkward and panicked. Branches whipped against my face as we zigzagged, trying to put as much distance as possible between us and the bear. My legs burned, my lungs screamed, but I didn't dare stop.

Then a gunshot cracked through the air, startling us both. The bullet struck a tree nearby, spraying bark and snow.

We ducked instinctively but kept moving, our heads swiveling as we tried to track both the bear and the source of the shots.

Another shot rang out, this time hitting the snow just feet from us.

"Who's shooting?" Decker yelled.

"I don't know!" I shouted back.

The shots rattled the bear, and it slowed, snorting angrily before retreating toward the cliffs, its massive frame disappearing into the shadows.

We stumbled into the lodge's clearing, gasping for breath, our legs trembling beneath us.

Rachel stood near the entrance, calmly sliding a long rifle into its case.

"Winchester Model 70," she said, almost conversationally. ".300 H&H Magnum. A literal elephant gun."

I stared at her, still panting. "You could have shot us."

Rachel gave a tight smile, her eyes glinting. "You should talk to me before going on romantic walks. This isn't Seattle. It's dangerous here."

Her gaze lingered on both of us, unreadable, before she turned and disappeared into the lodge.

Decker looked at me, his face pale. "What the hell was that?"

I didn't have an answer. All I knew was that the lodge had just become even more dangerous—and not just because of the bear.

Chapter Thirty-Three

Kate

The smells coming from the kitchen were rich and comforting, a welcome distraction from the stressful few days. Marta had returned to cook, and the scent of her huevos rancheros filled the lodge. The sizzle of the skillet and the occasional clatter of dishes should've made me feel more at ease. But my gloomy thoughts were focused on the impending goodbye.

After a quick breakfast, Decker started packing, tossing his things into his duffel. The county plow had finally cleared the road from the highway all the way to the lodge parking lot. I lingered by the door, watching him zip up the bag, emotions rising as I watched. Part of me felt relieved—our time together had stirred up a few things I wasn't ready to face. But I wasn't ready for him to leave either. His company had been a comfort; a familiar warmth in a place that still felt foreign to me. Yet with Decker here, Rachel's behavior had become more unpredictable. And dangerous.

We walked out together in silence. Decker caught my eye

as he tossed his bags into the back of his SUV. "You sure you don't want to come with me?" he asked.

I forced a smile. "I'm sure. I need to stick it out here. See it through. I'll see you soon, though."

He nodded, but the worry in his eyes was clear. He didn't want to leave me. "I get it," he said. "But if you change your mind—"

"I know," I cut in, my voice firm. "I know how to reach you

As we stepped outside into the biting cold, I pulled my jacket tighter, trying to fend off the chill that had settled deeper than my skin.

Decker turned to me. His big hands found my waist, and we kissed—a lingering goodbye that felt more bitter than sweet. He'd be back. I knew that. So why did it feel like I was watching him walk away for the last time?

When we pulled apart, I forced a smile. "Drive safe,"

"I'll be back soon. Be careful," he said.

I stood there, watching as he climbed into the Jeep. My breath fogged in the air as the engine started and tires crunched over the snow. I didn't move until his taillights disappeared down the road.

An ache settled in my chest, a sinking feeling I couldn't shake. I should've been relieved. Our visit had gone well, and he'd be coming back soon. This wasn't a permanent goodbye. But as I watched his vehicle disappear into the distance, something about it felt final.

As I turned to go back inside, I saw her. Rachel stood in the doorway, watching me. Her face was nearly expressionless, and perhaps I would have thought it completely neutral months or even weeks ago, but I was getting attuned to her subtleties and there was a definite smile on her lips, though the curve was so subtle it was almost invisible, and the gleam of satisfaction in her eyes was unmistakable. She was glad Decker was gone. I swallowed, forcing myself to meet her steady gaze. My skin prickled under her stare, and for a moment, I felt the urge to say something—anything—to break the tension hanging between us. But before I could speak, Rachel stepped forward, her smile widening, just enough to make my heart race.

"It'll be just us again," she said, her voice soft but deliberate.

There was no comfort in her tone. No reassurance. Only possession.

I nodded, stiff, moving past her into the lodge. My hands shook a little as I unwrapped my scarf and pulled off my gloves. The lodge felt darker and colder, despite the fire burning in the hearth. Rachel followed me inside, closing the door behind her. She lingered just behind me as I walked through the lobby.

As I made my way toward my room, Rachel's words echoed in my mind. *"It'll be just us again."*

Chapter Thirty-Four

Rachel

The lodge was too quiet.

I sat at the kitchen table, the sound of the clock ticking grating against my nerves. Kate hadn't come down for breakfast, hadn't lingered in the hallways or loitered near the fire. For weeks, I'd known where she was, what she was doing, but now she was pulling back.

Withdrawing. It wasn't like her.

I tightened my grip on the coffee mug, my mind racing. She was up to something; I could feel it. Her behavior had shifted— small, almost imperceptible changes that anyone else might dismiss, but not me. I'd spent years watching people, reading them, anticipating their next moves.

Kate was hiding something.

I pushed the chair back and stood, my bare feet cold against the tiled floor. The lodge creaked around me, its weight settling like it always did, but today the sound felt different. Ominous. As though the building itself was holding its breath.

Mother's words echoed in my mind, as they always did.

"Pay attention to the details, Rachel. They'll tell you everything you need to know."

And I had been paying attention.

Kate was avoiding me. Oh, her tasks were still getting done —floors scrubbed, furniture dusted, sheets changed—but she no longer lingered to ask questions or seek approval. Her silences felt deliberate, calculated, as if she were trying to keep me out.

I moved into the great room, the heels of my hands brushing over the back of the sofa as I surveyed the space. The wood floors gleamed under the faint morning light filtering through the windows, but I knew where to look for mistakes and oversights.

Kneeling, I pressed my fingers to the floorboards near the hearth. The faint scratches I'd left the night before were still there, subtle but just visible against the polished surface. Kate either hadn't noticed—or she hadn't bothered to fix them.

That wasn't like her.

I stood, the knots in my stomach tightening. Had she been distracted? Or was she testing me, too?

Mother had always been exacting about the floors. She'd inspect them daily, running her hand along the grain to check for scuffs or dirt. "The lodge reflects who we are," she'd say, her tone sharp. "If it's imperfect, then so are we."

I could almost hear her voice now, disapproving and cold, and it sent a familiar shiver down my spine.

The bear had been an opportunity.

I thought of the look on Kate's face when she'd stumbled into the lodge, her cheeks flushed with cold and fear, her breath coming in short gasps. Decker's wide-eyed panic had been almost comical, though I'd kept my expression neutral, as always.

The Winchester had felt heavy in my hands, its weight grounding me as I'd aimed down the scope. I could still hear the crack of the shot splitting the air, the satisfying sound of snow exploding where the bullet hit.

They'd ducked, of course, their heads swiveling in panic. The bear had turned back, lumbering toward the cliffs, but not before they'd gotten the message.

I'd saved them. I'd reminded them that this place, this landscape with all of its inherent dangers, could kill them—and that I was the only one experienced enough to stand between them and the wilderness that surrounded us.

But it wasn't just about the bear.

Those shots had been deliberate. Close enough to frighten them, to make them understand that I wasn't just some aging caretaker in the background of their story. I was capable. Serious. Necessary.

They needed to know that I was watching, that I could protect them—or choose not to.

When I'd put the rifle back in its case, the click of the latches had been the loudest sound in the room. I'd watched them both, their faces pale, and said the words I knew would linger: *Talk to me before going on romantic walks. This isn't Seattle. It's dangerous here. You don't understand.*

Kate hadn't looked at me the same since.

I wandered into the kitchen, the tension mounting. But my frustration wasn't just about the floors. Kate had started finding the notes—Mother's notes—and I couldn't stop thinking about them.

Those notes—those words—meant for me once were now being left for her. Resilience. Dedication. I'd built my life around those virtues, spent decades proving myself, and now Mother was turning her attention to Kate.

The coffee mug shook in my hand and several dark drops splashed onto the counter below. I set it down before I dropped the whole thing.

Does she see something in Kate that I don't?

The thought turned sour in my mind. Kate's independence, her growing confidence—it was dangerous. She was becoming too comfortable here, too bold.

I moved to the sink and grabbed a damp cloth, running it over the counter. My movements were slow, deliberate, as I mulled over my options.

If Kate was going to act like she didn't need me, like she could handle this place on her own, then I'd show her just how much she didn't understand.

The sabotage was simple at first.

A muddy footprint left on the entryway rug after she'd cleaned it. A smudge of dirt on the window she'd just wiped. The scratches on the floor. I wanted to see how she'd react, if she'd catch the imperfections or let them fester.

But it wasn't enough.

By the second day, I started leaving chairs askew, opening drawers she'd closed, pulling threads loose from the curtains. Small things. Petty things. But they were mine, and they were deliberate.

Each night, I'd inspect her work, leaving my own silent marks as a reminder that this lodge would never belong to her.

The paranoia grew with every step she took away from me.

When I passed her in the hallway, her eyes no longer lingered on me, no longer flickered with the hesitance I'd come to expect. She looked past me, her expression calm, indifferent.

She was hiding something—I knew it.

In the kitchen one afternoon, I opened the drawer she'd been using for cleaning supplies and found a crumpled piece of paper shoved in the corner. My hands trembled as I unfolded it.

"Keep steady, Kate. Your efforts don't go unnoticed."

The words blurred for a moment as a deep, hollow ache opened in my chest.

Mother had written this.

My knuckles whitened as I crumpled the note into my fist. "Not unnoticed," I muttered. "Not by her. Not by me."

The thought of Mother watching Kate, leaving her those messages—it wasn't merely encouragement. It was judgment. Kate wasn't just being praised; she was being measured.

That night, I prowled the halls long after Kate had gone to her room. The lodge creaked beneath my weight, the familiar sounds soothing and maddening all at once.

Kate's door was closed, her light out. She was probably asleep, oblivious to my fury.

I knelt in the hallway, wiping the baseboards with a damp cloth. I left a faint smear behind—my own quiet challenge. Would she notice tomorrow? Would she fix it?

Mother would see. Mother always saw.

And I would make sure she understood. Kate might be resilient, she might be dedicated, but she wasn't ready.

She wasn't worthy.

Chapter Thirty-Five

Kate

As the snow fell outside, the lodge felt lonely, with Decker gone. He'd only stayed for three days, but I'd grown accustomed to his comforting presence. Marta, who always hummed when she worked and frequently mumbled to herself in Spanish, had finished cooking and departed for her home in Seeley Lake.

In the afternoon, a truck arrived with a logo of Emerson Engineering and Development on the doors. Two men started working around the lodge with surveying equipment and a fancy GPS antenna. I asked Rachel about them and she dismissed it as a check of the property lines for tax purposes. She seemed evasive. Regardless, it was nice to see other humans on the property. But within a few hours, they were gone, too.

Now it was just Rachel and me, alone in the quiet building. I tried to find solace in the routine of stripping the floors. There was something calming about it—the steady motion, the rhythmic scraping of wax coming off the old wood. It kept me grounded in a place that felt like it was constantly shifting under my feet.

Decker had left me his old iPod, a relic from our past, loaded with music that brought back memories I'd forgotten. With the earbuds in, I let the world outside fade away. But the peace never lasted long. Rachel's visits had once again become more frequent and more invasive. She'd show up at my door unannounced, sometimes walking in without knocking. Her strange, unsettled energy filled the room the moment she stepped through the door. It was like she was always watching, always hovering, as if she needed to remind me she was in charge. This was her space, her room, as much as mine.

She started bringing little gifts—books, snacks, things I didn't need or ask for. I felt obligated to accept them, but there was always an unspoken expectation. She wanted my attention, my time. I had just finished work for the day and was just settling in with a novel when I heard the door creak open. Rachel again. She walked in. I pulled out one earbud, trying to keep calm. "Hey," I said, forcing a smile. "What's up?"

She didn't answer right away, just moved to the window and adjusted an armchair, pulling it closer to the wall. "Looks better this way," she said casually, like she was doing me a favor.

I stared at her for a moment, irritation flaring. "I liked it the way it was," I said.

"Of course," she said. "It's your space."

I turned back to my book, anything to avoid engaging further. The silence between us stretched, with her looking around the room and me waiting calmly, pretending to read. I didn't want to give her the satisfaction of knowing she was getting to me.

After a long pause, Rachel spoke again, her voice softer, almost coaxing. "You've been working so hard," she said, glancing at my bucket of wax removal supplies. "I thought you might want a break."

I forced a smile, though it felt strained. "I'm fine. I like keeping busy."

Rachel moved closer, her gaze still on me, like she was studying my reaction. "You don't have to do everything yourself," she said. "You're not responsible for everything here. We're in this together."

The way she said "together" made my skin crawl. It was subtle, but there was an edge to her voice, something dark and possessive lurking underneath. I felt the knot in my stomach tighten.

"This is my job," I said, keeping my voice steady. "For the season. In exchange for my salary and room and board. I've got it under control."

Rachel's smile stayed in place, but her eyes darkened. She lingered for a moment before stepping back toward the door. "Of course," she said again, her voice smooth but cold. "But don't forget—this lodge is our haven, our little world. Yours and mine."

Her words sent a shiver down my spine. She said it like it was a fact, like I should just accept it. But hearing her claim the space as *ours* made something snap inside me. I didn't respond, not trusting myself to speak. I just nodded and watched her leave, her footsteps echoing down the hall until the lodge fell silent again.

I sat there for a long moment, trying to shake off the strange, possessive energy she'd left behind. My breathing was shaky. This wasn't about Rachel being overbearing or helpful. She was trying to take ownership of me, to claim me along with the lodge. The gifts, the visits, the rearranging of my space—it wasn't generosity. It was ownership. And no matter how hard I tried to ignore it, her words echoed in my mind: *our little world.*

Chapter Thirty-Six

Kate

I was restless. The trip to town had helped a bit, but my uneasy feelings and my futile desires to resolve them and find some tranquility wouldn't fade. Decker's messages lingered in my mind, offering a way out, a return to normalcy. But I was still here, trapped in the lodge by my own stubbornness, working my fingers to the bone and stuck in Rachel's orbit.

I decided to clean my room, hoping that staying busy would help. I hadn't scrubbed my own floor in weeks, and the dusty, tracked wood needed attention. Maybe tidying my little hideaway would distract from the conflict that had been building between Rachel and me.

I started with the usual—sweeping, scrubbing the floors. The sound of the bristles against the floor was oddly calming. But when I got to the space under the bed, I dropped to my hands and knees, wiping the cloth along the floorboards. My sleeve snagged on something. Curious, I leaned under the bed and spotted a small wooden box wedged beneath the bed frame. It wasn't mine. I'd never seen it before. I pulled the box out and saw that it was a wood cigar box with a little metal latch.

My pulse quickened as I opened the latch and lifted the lid. Inside were items that didn't belong here at all. A journal, a pair of leather gloves, and a photograph.

I picked up the photo first. It was a color photo, fairly recent, and the young woman in it looked familiar, though I couldn't place her. She was wearing a purple rain slicker, her dark hair plaited into a braid that fell over her shoulder, and she was smiling at the camera. Her smile was wide, but not Duchenne. It didn't quite reach her eyes and there was a marked tightness in her posture.

Turning the photo over, I saw a date—last winter. And a name: Lydia Forsythe.

Lydia. She must have worked here before me. But why were her things hidden under my bed? Had this been her room? Why had Rachel not mentioned her?

I flipped through the journal. The handwriting was cute and feminine, the capital letter big and curving. Aware that I was overstepping but unable to help myself, I started reading and immediately broke into a cold sweat. Lydia had been here, living in this same room, feeling the same things I was. She wrote about Rachel—how her presence grew weightier and more oppressive over time, how Lydia had felt watched, then followed. She described the doors left open, belongings moved, that constant neck-prickling sensation of being observed. Of being judged.

It was eerie reading Lydia's words. It was like she had lived my days, like we were trapped in the same parallel story. I kept reading, my pulse quickening.

Then I saw it.

"I know there's someone else here besides Rachel. Last night, I went to her cabin during the storm, but she wasn't there.

Where was she?"

An icy shiver ran down my spine. Lydia had felt it too—that unsettling sense that the lodge held more than just the two of them. And Rachel—why hadn't she been in her cabin during a storm? It was too far to town, especially with the roads snowed over. Where else could she have been?

I flipped through the journal faster now as the desperation in Lydia's writing grew. What had happened to her? Why had she left?

The last entry hit me like a punch.

"I need to get out of here before it's too late."

The words leapt off the page, a warning from someone who had stood exactly where I was now. Even her handwriting had changed. It was more sprawling with strange empty spaces between lines. The fear in her writing was raw, urgent, like she knew her time was running out. But I didn't know if she'd managed to leave. Did she escape, or had something—or someone—stopped her?

My stomach ached. I couldn't stop picturing Lydia packing in a rush, looking over her shoulder, feeling the same dread that now clung to me.

Had Rachel done this to her? Had she driven Lydia to the edge? And if she had—what had kept Lydia from leaving?

The silence in my room felt suffocating. I slammed the journal shut, my heart racing. I needed air. I needed to think.

I stood too quickly, knocking over the cigar box as I backed away from the bed. Lydia's warning ringing in my ears. Before it's too late.

I had to find out what happened to Lydia. And I had to figure it out fast—before it happened to me.

Journal Entries of Lydia Forsythe

. . .

January 3

I thought this would be good for me. Quiet, fresh air, time to think. But I don't feel peaceful here. I feel...I don't know? Unsettled, I guess. It's hard to explain.

The lodge is beautiful, but it feels almost too quiet. I've been jumpy. I jump at every little noise. Rachel is nice enough, but she has this way of looking at me, like she's waiting for me to mess up. Or maybe I'm imagining it. I'm probably just being overly sensitive.

I hope it gets better.

January 10

A weird thing happened today. I came back from the kitchen, and my door was open. I always close it, but maybe I didn't this time? I don't know.

Rachel said it was the wind. She didn't seem bothered, but it's hard to tell with her. She has this calm way of talking that makes me feel like a kid getting scolded, even when she's being nice.

It's probably nothing.

January 14

The generator went out last night. Rachel went out to fix it and wouldn't let me help. She was out there a long time.

When she came back, she barely said a word and went straight to her cabin. I wanted to ask her if everything was okay, but she didn't seem like she wanted to talk.

This morning, I saw footprints leading into the woods. Not to the shed, not to her cabin. Just... into the trees.

. . .

January 20

I woke up to footsteps last night. They were slow, like someone walking in circles outside my door. I wanted to get up and look, but I froze.

When I finally opened the door, the hallway was empty.

Rachel brushed it off this morning. "It's an old building," she said. "It makes noises." But these weren't just noises. I know what I heard. I feel like I'm going crazy.

January 25

Rachel wasn't in her cabin during the storm.

I went to check on her because I was worried, but the cabin was dark. Her truck was still there, so where was she?

When I asked her about it today, she just smiled and said, "I have my places." I don't know what that even means, but I KNOW I saw her walk out to her cabin last night.

February 2

Something's not right here.

Last night, I heard whispering. It wasn't Rachel—her cabin lights were off. I followed the sound down the hall, but it stopped before I could figure out where it was coming from.

This morning, I found scratches on the windowsill. Rachel said it was squirrels, but they were too deep.

February 8

I found a note in my dresser. It wasn't there before.

It said, "You're not safe here."

I wanted to pretend it was a joke, but who would leave that? Rachel? Someone else?

I hid it here, in my journal. I don't know why, but I couldn't just throw it away.

February 12

Rachel asked me today if anyone knew I was here. She made it sound casual, but it didn't feel casual.

She asked me if I have family nearby, like she was just curious. I said no. She said that was good and made for less to worry about.

It gave me chills.

February 15

I noticed scratches on the floor by the fireplace. Big ones, like something heavy was dragged across it. I asked Rachel, and she said, "It's just the log walls shifting."

I don't think it is.

February 20

I can't stay here.

I packed a bag and put it under my bed. I'm waiting for the next clear day to leave. I'll tell Rachel I'm going to town for supplies, but I won't come back.

I have to get out of here. I don't know what's wrong with this place, but it's not safe.

Chapter Thirty-Seven

Kate

The storm had returned with a vengeance, hammering the lodge with icy wind and snow that piled high against the doors and windows. The howling wind sounded alive, like it was trying to claw its way inside. Trapped again.

I spent the day dusting, though it felt more like pacing with a purpose. My hands moved automatically, swiping cloth over old furniture while my mind spun in frantic circles. The lodge was massive, and the task endless, but the work kept me moving, kept me from sitting still and thinking too much.

Thinking about Lydia.

Her journal entries were burned into my mind now, the words flashing in front of my eyes every time I blinked. Her fear, her sense of being watched, her growing certainty that she wasn't alone here—all of it mirrored what I'd been feeling since the day I arrived.

Knowing that someone else had felt the same things I'd felt, had actually wondered if she'd been going crazy too, gave me a sense of intense validation. Intense but unsatisfying, because I couldn't help but wonder and worry about what had happened to her.

I'd started dusting the sitting room when I froze mid-swipe. A window latch was unfastened, the glass rattling against the frame. I didn't remember leaving it that way. But then, I didn't remember leaving my door open the other night either. Or misplacing my gloves. Or hearing faint whispers in the dead of night.

Lydia had written about this—the little things that added up to something too big to ignore. She'd thought Rachel was behind it. That Rachel was trying to drive her mad. But now I wasn't so sure.

Maybe Rachel wasn't the only one in this place.

I shivered and glanced over my shoulder, moving slowly, but nothing and no one was there. As usual.

I went to my room to drop off my dusting supplies and there was a tray waiting for me outside my door. A full breakfast, though it was well past noon, complete with folded napkins and a handwritten note:

For my favorite person.

I crouched to pick it up, but my hands hovered over the tray. The handwriting wasn't Rachel's. It was messier, uneven, like someone was trying to disguise their usual style.

Thinking of you. Can't wait to see your smile. I'd seen notes like this before. They'd appeared on Rachel's lists of chores, scrawled at the bottom like afterthoughts. But whose thoughts?

I carried the tray into my room, setting it on the table by the window. The eggs were cold, the toast stale. I didn't touch the food. I couldn't. My eyes kept flicking to the note, my pulse thudding in my ears.

Lydia had written that Rachel blurred boundaries. That she made herself the center of everything. But what if this wasn't just Rachel? What if Lydia had been right about something—or someone—else in the lodge?

The storm that had been building up since yesterday increased in volume and began to howl, shaking the windowpanes. The sound was tortured, moaning low before rising up in pitch and volume like a child in a tantrum. I looked at the snow piling against the glass and imagined trying to leave in it. The roads would be completely buried. I was stuck here, no matter what I'd found or how much my gut told me to run.

Without any other feasible options, I forced my body back into motion, cleaning the last guest room of the day. I was finishing up when I heard footsteps in the hall—Rachel's distinct, deliberate stride. She appeared in the doorway before I could pretend not to notice her.

"There you are," she said, her voice sweet, honey masking poison. Her hands fidgeted with the hem of her sweater, a nervous tic I hadn't seen before. "How's the dusting?"

"It's fine," I said, turning back to the dresser. "Almost done."

She stepped closer, her shadow falling over me. "You've been working so hard. Maybe I could help more. We're practically family now, after all."

I stiffened. *Family.* The word rang in my ears like a warning. Lydia had written about Rachel using that word too, about how it felt more like a trap than an offer.

I set down the duster and turned to face her. "We're not family," I said.

Rachel blinked, her smile faltering for just a moment before sliding back into place. "Of course," she said, her tone softening. "I didn't mean to overstep. I just felt we'd gotten closer. You've been here a while now. I thought maybe you'd see it that way too."

My heart pounded. She was testing me, just like Lydia said

she would. I bit the inside of my cheek, forcing myself to stay calm. "I appreciate the help," I said. "But the work's fine. I'm fine."

Her smile thinned, her eyes darkening as she studied me. "Good," she said again, almost in a whisper. "I just want to make things easier for you. I care about you, Kate."

Her words crawled under my skin, setting off alarms. Lydia had written about Rachel's "care." How it started small, a kindness here, a gesture there, and then grew into something suffocating.

"Thanks," I said, stepping back and pretending to busy myself with the dresser again. "I should finish this."

Rachel hesitated, watching me for a moment longer before nodding and stepping out into the hall.

The storm blew even louder that evening, the wind battering the lodge like it wanted to tear it apart. I sat by the window in my room, staring at the snow piling higher, listening to the wind wailing, wondering how much longer I could stay here before the walls closed in.

My thoughts circled back to Lydia. She had planned to leave, but her last entry didn't say if she'd made it out. What had stopped her? The storm? Rachel?

The wind rattled the glass, and I flinched at the sound. My eyes drifted to the tray on the table, the cold eggs untouched, the note still sitting beside it. I didn't know what Rachel wanted from me. But I was terrified of what would happen if I couldn't give it to her.

And even more terrified of what she might take if I tried to leave.

Chapter Thirty-Eight

Rachel

The storm was unrelenting, roaring through the trees and rattling the lodge's ancient bones. It didn't bother Mother, though. She liked storms. She said they made her feel alive, as though the chaos outside mirrored something within her.

I balanced the dinner tray as I climbed the stairs to the third floor, my hand trembling just enough to make the silverware rattle. I paused at the top, steadying myself. I couldn't let her see my nerves. Not tonight.

I paused outside the nondescript door at the end of the dim hallway. Just a plain, unmarked door like the ones that hid storage closets and mechanical rooms. Most people who worked in the lodge never even noticed it. But I knew better. Behind this door was the third-floor suite—a secret I had carried for years. A secret I had built my entire life around.

I took a deep breath, my fingers trembling slightly as they grasped the key ring clipped to my belt. The brass key slid into the lock, and the soft click sounded louder than it should have in the silence. I pushed the door open, stepping into the narrow corridor beyond. A single bulb flickered overhead, casting jittery shadows on the walls. The air smelled of lavender, mixed with the dampness that seemed to seep into the top floor of the lodge from the ceiling above.

At the end of the corridor was the heavy oak door. It loomed there, waiting. I knocked once, then twice, before turning the knob and stepping inside.

The suite was enormous. Even now, after all these years, its size felt absurd. Ornate wallpaper, once jewel-toned and now faded to pale pastels, covered the walls. Heavy velvet drapes hung over tall windows that overlooked the frozen lake. A fire crackled in the hearth, weak but steady, and beside it sat Mother.

"Mother," I called as I stepped inside, the word catching in my throat. "It's me."

Her voice drifted out from the shadows, smooth and warm. "You're late."

I swallowed hard. "The storm," I said, closing the door behind me. "It's been a busy day."

She was sitting in her usual chair, a fringed shawl draped over her thin shoulders. The storm's light cast her in silhouette, making her seem larger than she was.

I crossed the room and set the tray on the small table near her. "Soup," I said, straightening the silverware and napkin carefully, precisely, as if my very life depended on it. "And bread. I checked your refrigerator—it's stocked. I also brought fresh towels for the bathroom."

"Hmm," she murmured, leaning forward to inspect the tray. "You're always so thorough, Rachel."

I moved to the bathroom, stacking fresh towels on the shelf, restocking her soap, checking the cabinet for anything out of place. Everything had to be perfect. Everything had to be ready.

"You've been walking the halls at night again," I said as I returned to the sitting room. My voice was as light as I could make it. Casually, though, my stomach churned with every word. "You really shouldn't. It's... not safe."

She laughed. "The night is when this place belongs to me," she said. "You know that. It's quiet. It's mine. Why would I give that up?"

I bit the inside of my cheek, forcing myself to stay calm. "I just think—maybe it's better for you to keep a daytime schedule. You'd feel more rested."

"Rested?" she repeated, amusement threading through her tone. "Don't be ridiculous, dear. I don't need rest. And I certainly don't need your advice."

Her smile was sharp, even as her words remained sweet. "But I appreciate your concern. You're always so thoughtful."

My hands clenched into fists at my sides, but I nodded, keeping my face neutral.

"You've been spending time with her," she said suddenly, her tone changing.

I knew who she meant, and my heart sank.

"Kate," she said, her voice almost reverent.

"She's doing fine," I said quickly. "She works hard. She doesn't complain."

"She's extraordinary," she said, her smile widening. "So capable. So resilient. I like her."

The words burned. I forced my hands to relax, clasping them in front of me. "She has her flaws," I said tightly.

"Don't we all?" she replied, leaning back in her chair. "But she's strong. More so than the others. Don't you think?"

I hated how she looked at me then, as though Kate had

already outshone me in her eyes. My chest tightened. "She's fine," I said again, my voice clipped.

She tilted her head, studying me the way one might study a piece of furniture—deciding whether to keep it or throw it away. "Don't be jealous, dear," she whispered. "It doesn't suit you."

"I'm not jealous," I snapped, then immediately regretted it. I lowered my voice. "I just don't think she's as perfect as you seem to think."

Her smile faltered briefly, and I felt a flicker of relief. But then it returned, softer, more cutting. "Hmm." She picked up the soup spoon and stirred the bowl. "You were like her once. When I found you. So much potential."

The word "found" hit me like ice water. I felt small again, the way I always did when she reminded me of how this had all started.

"You've done well for yourself," she said, her tone almost condescending. "But you shouldn't let your insecurities get the better of you. It's unbecoming."

"I'm not insecure," I said quietly, though the words felt hollow.

She sighed, as though tired of me, and waved her hand dismissively. "You've done enough for tonight. Go. I'll see you tomorrow."

I stood, my heart pounding, and moved toward the door. But I couldn't resist looking back at her, just once. She sat there, framed by the storm outside, her smile faint but still in place.

"Goodnight, Mother," I said, the words heavy in my mouth.

"Goodnight, Rachel," she replied, her voice as soft as silk.

I stepped into the hall and shut the door behind me, leaning against it for a moment as I caught my breath. The storm howled around the lodge, the sound pressing against the walls like a living thing.

Kate was becoming a problem. Mother's attention, her praise—it was shifting. And if Kate became too important...

No. I wouldn't let that happen.

Mother was *mine*. She had always been mine.

And I would not let anyone take her away from me.

Chapter Thirty-Nine

Kate

The storm buried the lodge under six more feet of snow, with no end in sight. I couldn't even see the lake anymore—just drifts piling higher with every gust of wind. The power had been out for hours; the lodge sinking into a bottomless cold.

Rachel and I dug our way out the front door and around the side of the lodge to the generator building. We tried to start the engine, but it sputtered and died. She crouched by the fuel lines, her breath hanging in the cold.

"Frozen," she muttered. "Too cold for this grade of diesel without heated lines."

My stomach tightened. "What...? What does that even mean? Can we fix it?"

Rachel stood, wiping her hands on her coat. "Not in these temperatures. We'll need Dominic to install new line heaters when the storm clears. "

Rachel called Dominic on the satellite phone, but he couldn't come until the roads were plowed. Could be days, maybe a week.

"We're stuck," Rachel said flatly.

I nodded, my chest tight. Stuck didn't feel like the right word. Imprisoned was closer.

We had plenty of lanterns, kerosene, and firewood. There was no immediate danger, but the weight of being snowed in with Rachel, of being held hostage by both the elements and her unpredictable, manipulative behavior, felt like its own kind of threat.

"We've got the small generator," Rachel said. "It'll keep the refrigerators and the satellite phone going, at least."

I nodded again, relieved for the backup, but my mind kept circling back to the phone. I wanted—needed—to call Decker, hear his voice. It wasn't just the storm keeping me isolated, it was her.

We stood by the door when I asked. "Can I use the sat phone? Just for a few minutes. I want to call Decker."

Rachel's face hardened immediately. "No."

The word cut through the room like ice. I blinked, caught off guard.

"No?" I repeated, my voice rising. "I know it's a dollar a minute. I'll pay for the call."

"It's not about the money," Rachel said. "The phone's for emergencies, Kate. We don't know how long the storm will last. We can't waste minutes on personal calls."

I swallowed hard, frustration rising. *Emergencies only?* Rachel used it for personal calls all the time. I'd overheard her chatting with people in town. Now, when I needed it, she was cutting me off?

"Rachel," I said, forcing calm into my voice. "You've used it before—for yourself."

Her eyes flashed, but she just smiled, a tight, controlled smile that made my skin crawl.

"I know what I'm doing," she said, her tone condescending.

"We need to save the minutes. The weather could get worse, after all."

I clenched my jaw, biting back my response. We were already snowed in. What could be worse? But I knew better than to argue. Rachel controlled the phone. She controlled everything. And she knew I couldn't reach anyone—not even Decker—without her permission.

Her gaze, when it turned towards me, was assessing, daring me to push back. I didn't. Why would I? There was no reasoning with her, no winning. Pushing the issue further would only rock the boat and add to the existing tension between us. I just nodded, frustration gnawing at me as I turned away.

"I'll be in my room," I said, walking away before I said something I'd regret.

Back in my room, the wind slammed so hard against the log walls of the big building that I could feel tiny vibrations on the floorboards below. It was mind-boggling to think of a structure so imposing, so seemingly rock-solid, being affected by an invisible element, but Mother Nature was nothing if not powerful.

The fireplace blazed but struggled to keep the chill at bay. I sat on the edge of the bed, Rachel's refusal weighing on me. I wanted to scream, punch something, but instead, I grabbed my earbuds and plugged in Decker's old iPod.

His playlists were all I had left. His voice, even through the music, was my only connection to my old world, to the life I'd left behind. I closed my eyes, letting the music drown out the silence.

Outside, the snow swirled. The wind howled, and the isolation settled deeper into my bones.

I was trapped here. And Rachel was making sure I knew it.

Chapter Forty

Rachel

"**M**other," I said, my voice softer than I intended. She turned to look at me, her expression one of expectation. Her white hair was swept into a loose bun, a few cottony wisps loose around her ears. She looked smaller than I remembered, almost frail tonight. Her body seemed to be shrinking more with every passing year, but her eyes were sharp, as sharp as they'd ever been, and they cut through me like glass.

"Rachel," she said, her voice light with surprise. "What are you doing here, dear? Is the lodge all right?"

For a moment, I couldn't answer. The folder in my hands felt impossibly heavy. The words I needed caught in my throat. Then I forced myself to move closer, clutching the leather binder to my chest.

"Everything's fine, Mother. The power is out, but you have plenty of kerosene and firewood, just like always."

"I know that. I don't need electricity," she snapped.

"I just need you to sign some papers," I said, my voice quavering.

"Papers?" Her brow furrowed, and she reached for her glasses on the side table. "What sort of papers?"

"Just routine documents," I said, keeping my tone even. "For the lodge. Legal things. Nothing important."

I unclipped the pen from the folder and extended it to her. "I just need your signature, here, at the bottom."

She squinted down at the papers but didn't take the pen. "Oh, sweetheart, you know I can't sign anything without my husband looking at it first. He handles all the legal and business matters."

My chest tightened. I gripped the folder so hard my knuckles ached. "Mother, Father isn't here anymore."

She didn't remember that her husband and three children had been dead for thirty-two years. Didn't remember that as she watched from the lodge, they had fallen through the ice on Holland Lake.

She looked up at me, her face calm but resolute. "Then you'll just have to wait until he is. Or better yet, why don't you go find my daughter? She's been so helpful lately. She can fetch your father and get this sorted out."

I froze. "Mother, I am your daughter," I said, my voice strained. *Please believe that I'm your daughter. I am everything a daughter should be.*

She smiled, a light, dismissive smile that made my stomach churn. "Oh, darling, you're confused. My daughter is young and pretty, and she's been working so hard, scrubbing the floors and keeping the lodge in such wonderful shape. Such a good girl, my Rachel. Not like these caretakers they bring in every winter."

She's talking about Kate.

Her hand patted mine absently, as though I were some stranger trying to comfort her. "You're sweet, but you're much too old to be my daughter. You're just the winter caretaker, dear."

Her words hit me like a slap. My breath caught, and I felt the room tilt, as if the firelight was playing tricks on me. "Mother, look at me," I pleaded. "I've been taking care of you for years. I've managed the lodge, kept everything running. You know who I am."

She tilted her head, studying me with that faint, indulgent smile, as if I were a child telling a story she didn't quite believe. "You're a hard worker. I'll give you that. But my daughter is a treasure. You should meet her. She's the most devoted young woman I've ever seen."

I felt the edges of my control fraying. My throat tightened, and tears stung the back of my eyes. I wanted to shake her, to scream the truth into her face, to force her to see me. But I knew better. I had learned long ago that there was no reasoning with her when she slipped into these delusions.

"Mother, please," I tried again, my voice breaking. "Just sign the papers."

"Not without my husband," she said, turning back toward the fire. Her gaze was distant now, her attention slipping away. "Why don't you run along and ask Rachel? I'm sure she'll be able to help."

I stood there, trembling, watching as she pulled the shawl tighter around her shoulders and settled deeper into her chair. I was dismissed, a stranger in her life. A stranger in the life I had sacrificed everything to build.

When I stepped out of the suite and closed the door behind me, the cold air of the corridor hit me like a slap. My hands shook as I fumbled with the key, locking the door again. My chest felt tight, like it might split open from the pressure of everything inside me.

One thought burned in my mind as I walked back down the hallway, the sound of my boots echoing in the emptiness: *Kate had to go. She was a threat, a usurper, and I would do whatever it took to reclaim what was mine.*

Chapter Forty-One

Rachel

T he office was cold. I hadn't lit the fireplace, and the overhead light cast a sickly glow over the room. My desk, usually a place of meticulous order, was cluttered with papers, most of them irrelevant, arranged as a decoy should anyone wander in. But at the center, under the weight of my trembling hands, sat the documents that mattered most.

The sale of the lodge.

The folder lay open, the papers inside crisp and pristine, except for the glaring absence of a signature. I stared at the blank line that demanded her name, my mother's name, the name that still carried weight even if the woman herself didn't remember who she was.

I could still feel her dismissal like a fresh wound. *"You're just the winter caretaker, dear."* The words echoed in my head, twisting and tightening until I thought I might scream. My teeth clenched as I gripped the pen, my knuckles white. She would never sign it. Not now, not ever. She was lost in her fantasies, her mind caught in a web of memories that didn't even include me anymore.

But I had no choice. Without this signature, everything I'd worked for—everything I'd sacrificed—would crumble. The lodge would remain frozen in its endless winter, a monument to her grief and my servitude. And Kate...would win.

My chest burned at the thought. She was young, clever, and resilient, everything my mother now believed her daughter to be. It was as though Kate had stolen the life I had worked so hard to build, and she didn't even know it. But this was something Kate couldn't take. This was mine.

The papers rustled under my fingertips as I turned to the last page, the place where her signature was required. My hand shook as I gripped the pen, hovering over the line. For a moment, my breath caught in my throat, and the room seemed to go silent, as though even the lodge was holding its breath.

"Mother would want this," I whispered, the words almost inaudible. "She would understand, if she could. This is what's best for the lodge."

But even as I spoke, I knew it was a lie. This wasn't about what was best for the lodge. It was about survival. My survival.

I lowered the pen, pressing its tip to the page. My hand moved slowly, deliberately, forming the loops and curves of her name. I'd practiced it enough times, watching her write checks and notes, copying the way she tilted the letters just so. The ink bled onto the page, transforming the empty line into something final, something irreversible.

Norma Hedden.

The name stared back at me, stark and damning. My stomach boiled, and for a moment, I thought I might be sick. But then I sat back, letting the pen drop onto the desk with a dull clatter. It was done. The lodge was mine now, in every way that mattered.

I sat there for a long time, staring at the signature as though it might come alive and condemn me. The room felt colder, the shadows darker, pressing in around me. The fire I hadn't lit seemed like an accusation, the frost on the window a warning. But I couldn't stop now. This was my only chance, my only way forward.

As I gathered the papers and slid them back into the folder, a strange calm settled over me. The fear, the guilt, the doubt— they were still there, but muted, buried under a growing sense of purpose. The lodge would sell, and I would be free. Free of her. Free of Kate. Free of this place that had consumed me for so long.

I locked the folder in the bottom drawer of my desk, then stood, smoothing my hands over my shirt. My gaze lingered on the window, where the lake gleamed faintly in the moonlight, the snow-covered ice still and silent. For a moment, I thought I saw a figure moving across the ice, a shadow slipping into the darkness. But when I blinked, it was gone.

"It's over," I said to myself, my voice steady. "It's finally over."

But as I turned off the light and stepped into the hallway, a chill ran down my spine. Deep down, I knew the truth: nothing was ever really over in this place.

Chapter Forty-Two

Kate

The power had been out for nearly a day; the lodge growing colder by the hour. The storm outside didn't ebb and flow. It was relentless, swallowing the landscape and holding us hostage.

Rachel found me in the kitchen, standing by the wood stove as I stirred a pot of Marta's chicken soup. Her voice, sharpened to a point, broke the quiet.

"The boiler's out. If we don't keep fires going, the pipes are going to freeze." She crossed her arms, the tension in her posture matching her tone. "We need the fireplaces burning. Kitchen, lobby, east lounge, west lounge and five other rooms. I've written them down for you. If these stay burning, the pipes won't burst and flood the building." She set a sticky note on the counter with the room numbers.

I turned to face her, the weight of her words sinking in. "Okay," I said, already feeling the exhaustion creeping in. "I can help. Maybe we can take shifts—maybe four on, four off?"

Rachel's eyes narrowed, her lips curving into a smile that didn't reach her eyes. "Shifts?" She almost laughed. "You've had it easy, Kate. Practically getting paid to live here. And now you want shifts?"

Her words stung, the way she dismissed everything I'd done since arriving. "Rachel, I *have* been working—doing everything you've asked."

She waved me off, her expression hardening. "Dusting? Cleaning? That's nothing. It's time to earn your keep. You'll manage the fires. If the pipes freeze, it's on you."

I felt a knot tighten in my chest. Rachel wasn't interested in helping. She was making it clear that this was now my burden to carry.

Without waiting for a response, she turned back to the counter, packing up a box of food. "I'm going to ride out the storm in my cabin," she said, her tone light, like she was heading off for a mini-vacation. "Keep the fires going. Don't let them go out."

I stared at her, disbelief swirling in my gut. "Rachel, that's a lot—"

"You'll figure it out," she said, cutting me off. She grabbed the box and smiled, a satisfied look on her face. "After all, Kate, this is your job."

And with that, she was gone, leaving me standing there, her words echoing in the empty kitchen. My job. My responsibility. My failure if I couldn't keep it all going.

The storm outside sounded like a freight train as I stood there, my frustration building. I needed to move, to get the fires going before the cold got any worse, but between my shock and anger, I felt almost paralyzed.

This was an absolute nightmare. I was here as a caretaker, not a miracle-worker. Keeping all the fires going in a place this large, under these conditions, wasn't so much a chore as it was a Sisyphean task. How could Rachel possibly expect me to do this alone?

I thought of the last time I'd wanted to give up, the last time I'd felt overwhelmed by life, and how I'd wound up in the rehab hospital, possessed by an opioid addiction. The nurses and staff had helped me recover and then rebuild, but *I* had done the work; the endless rounds of doctor's appointments, med checks, counseling, group therapy. I had done those things because I had recognized that the only way I was going to get well, get healthy and then get out was by doing the work. The only way out was through.

A sudden creaking in the rafters above me shook me out of my stupor. I huffed out a gusty sigh and raised my chin. *The only way out was through.*

Stoking the kitchen's wood stove, I piled in more cordwood and watched the flames rise. At least this one was under control. I moved next to the lobby, stoking the fire in the large stone hearth. The blaze swallowed the wood quickly, filling the room with warmth. For now.

Room by room, I worked. The two lounges, then the rooms Rachel had noted. Each fireplace came to life, crackling with the sound of burning wood. By the time I'd lit the last one, my arms were sore. But the fires were just the beginning. I still needed wood—lots of it.

I bundled up and trudged outside, the cold biting at my face. First, I had to shovel a path to the covered woodshed, two hundred feet around the building. Then I hauled armload after armload of firewood inside to the racks that sat beside each fireplace.

The snow piled higher with every trip, making the trek more difficult. But I didn't stop. I couldn't. Rachel's words played on a loop in my head: *Don't let them go out.*

Back and forth, I moved through the storm, stacking wood in the kitchen, the lobby, and each room. Hours passed, my muscles screaming for rest, but I kept going. By the time I'd stockpiled enough to last the night, darkness had already fallen. The lodge was still, except for the dancing flames, rising sparks and occasionally shifting log.

After many, many hours had passed, I sank into a kitchen chair, finally allowing myself a moment to breathe. The storm was still raging. Its fury had not abated, but at least I didn't have to deal with Rachel's intensity tonight. That was something.

As I stared into the flames, the reality of the night ahead sank in. I'd be up all night, moving from one fireplace to the next, stoking the flames, making sure the fires stayed burning. Endless rounds of retrieving firewood, stacking it, and then piling it onto the existing blazes. Maybe I could find a rhythm, a way to manage it all without losing my mind.

Either way, I couldn't let the fires die.

Chapter Forty-Three

Kate

Night felt endless. The storm had settled in for the long haul, snow piling up against the windows, white and heavy. The entire landscape was unrecognizable as every familiar boulder, tree or hill was blanketed by snow.

I couldn't help but wonder how long it would take for Dominic to reach us, or if the plows would come before we were completely snowed in. It could be days.

I made endless rounds, moving from one fireplace to the next, feeding them cordwood, stoking the flames. After thirty-two, I lost count and allowed myself to get lost in the rhythm— haul the wood, stoke the fire, move on. Over and over. The heat in the rooms held, with the cold still seeping in from every crack and crevice. I'd hoped for at least an hour or two of rest between rounds, but the most I could manage was half an hour every three. I was careful to set my alarm because I knew if I allowed myself to fall asleep, I'd sleep for days without waking. The alarm went off with a cheerful *chirp-chirp* and then it was back to the fires, keeping the lodge from turning into a frozen tomb.

After many hours of hauling wood, I lowered my aching body into the deep leather couch in the lobby. The massive stone fireplace roared in front of me, a gratifying testament to my efforts, throwing waves of warmth into the room. More heat than I'd felt in days. I set the alarm on my phone for thirty minutes and sank into the cushions, exhausted. The moment my eyes closed, I drifted off into a dream.

In my dream, I was alone in one of the long hallways of the lodge. People from the past—decades, maybe a century ago—walked past me, laughing and talking as they moved toward the lake. They didn't seem to notice me, caught up in their own world. It was a cheerful scene, full of life and color, a stark contrast to the cold, empty lodge I knew.

Then, I felt a hand on my shoulder. I turned to see a woman—beautiful, older, with long gray hair and kind blue eyes. She wore a simple white dress that flowed around her as she stood there, smiling.

"Hello," she said, her voice gentle. "Nice to meet you, Kate."

This woman radiated warmth and lightness. I reached out a hand to introduce myself. She smiled, benevolent and gentle, before turning to join the others, disappearing into the crowd of guests dressed in clothes from the 1920s.

I woke with a start, my heart still racing as my alarm went off. The dream clung to me, her voice echoing in my mind. "Nice to meet you, Kate."

The warmth of the lobby fire had done little to ease the chill settling over me. I sat up, blinking against the soft glow of the flames, my head still spinning from the dream. But something was wrong.

There was a draft.

I looked around, my eyes scanning the room. The hairs on the back of my neck stood up, and a sudden, sharp coldness cut through the air. I turned, and my breath caught in my throat. The front door of the lodge was wide open.

Panic hit me. I jumped to my feet and ran to the door, my boots skidding on the wood floor. I leaned out into the night, my eyes scanning the snow-covered ground.

No footprints. Just a perfect, undisturbed sheet of white stretching as far as I could see. Whoever—or whatever—had opened the door was inside the lodge with me.

I slammed the door shut, locking it with trembling hands. My mind raced. The dream was still vivid in my thoughts. The woman—her voice had been so clear, so kind.

I pressed my back against the door, staring into the empty lobby, the fire casting flickering shadows across the walls. The lodge felt too quiet, too still, the crackling of the flames the only sound breaking the silence.

Whoever had opened that door was still here. Somewhere.

Chapter Forty-Four

Rachel

The storm was a symphony tonight, wind howling through the pines, snow battering the cabin like a drumbeat. I sat in my favorite chair by the wood stove, its iron belly glowing red with heat. The storm made the air outside sharp and bitter, but inside it was warm enough to make me drowsy. I pulled a wool blanket tighter around my legs and smiled to myself.

Kate would be busy by now.

I pictured her scurrying through the lodge, struggling with her arms full of firewood, sweat dripping down her neck as she tried to keep every fireplace stocked and roaring. The lodge was massive, with more rooms than she could hope to manage during a storm like this. It was a test of endurance, patience, and strength.

Most people broke under the strain.

The fire popped, and I stirred my tea, savoring the quiet comfort of my cabin. The radio hummed softly in the background, a jazz station out of Missoula that I kept on during storms. My little generator purred steadily outside, providing just enough power for the essentials. Unlike Kate, I wasn't at the mercy of the lodge's ancient wiring or its temperamental generator. I'd planned well for nights like this.

Mother always said storms were when you found out what you were made of.

I could still hear her voice, sharp and confident, echoing in my head. "You don't need anyone," she would say, as she lit the kerosene lamps in her suite. "Not when you have your wits about you."

She loved storms. Loved the chance to prove, if only to herself, that she didn't need the world. The pantry in her suite was always stocked—canned goods, dried meats, tea. The heavy quilts on her bed could ward off the cold of the deepest Montana winter, and her fireplace kept the suite as warm as any sunlit room.

When the power went out, as it often did during storms like this, it was almost a delight for her. She would light her lamps, settle into her chair by the fire, and disappear into one of her books. It made her feel self-sufficient, she said. Independent.

Once, early on, I had checked on her during a storm. I'd thought I was being thoughtful, that she might need help.

She'd been livid.

"Do you think I can't manage?" she'd snapped, her eyes blazing. "Do you think I'm weak?"

I'd learned my lesson that night. Now, when the storms came, I left her alone. She didn't need me to stock her woodpile or refill her pantry. She didn't need anyone.

And yet, here I was.

The snow lashed against the windows, but I ignored it. I leaned back in my chair, letting the heat from the stove soak into my bones. I had everything I needed—food, water, warmth. I'd built my life to withstand storms like this.

But Kate?

I grinned to myself, imagining her red-faced and frantic, darting from one room to the next in the freezing lodge. The fireplaces were all she had to keep the place warm, and there were too many for one person to handle. Her muscles would ache by now, her nerves fraying with every gust of wind rattling the windows.

Storms were crucibles. They burned away weakness, leaving only the strong.

Or nothing at all.

I thought of Mother upstairs, enjoying this as much as I was. She'd taken to Kate well—too well, if I were honest. Her compliments about Kate were pointed, almost like barbs.

"She has resilience," she'd said the other night. "I admire that."

Admire. The word sat uneasily in my chest.

Mother rarely admired anyone. She'd shaped me into who I was, molded me with her sharp words and impossible standards. For years, I'd worked to earn her approval, to become the person she wanted me to be. I wasn't about to let Kate take that away from me.

The fire crackled, and I sipped my tea, trying to push the thought aside. Mother's opinion of her didn't matter. What mattered was that I was here, warm and comfortable, while Kate fought to keep the lodge from freezing over.

This storm would be a crucible for her. A test.

And if she failed, well... that was her weakness, not mine.

Chapter Forty-Five

Kate

I moved through the lodge in a daze, my heart pounding. Rachel had left for her cabin hours ago, and if she'd returned, there would've been footprints in the snow. But there weren't. The front door was the only entrance besides the kitchen, and I had checked both. The snow outside lay smooth and untouched, like a white duvet over a perfectly made bed.

I carried wood to the fireplaces on autopilot, running on nothing more than adrenaline and willpower, my mind spinning. The scarf, the notes, my laptop, the doors swinging open —none of it made sense. I'd convinced myself that Rachel was behind it all, playing some sick game, hazing me for her own amusement. Maybe she was a sociopath, getting her kicks from tormenting the winter caretakers. The idea wasn't far-fetched. She could easily manage my work along with her duties as lodge manager. Reading Lydia's journal had confirmed that someone else had experienced this before, and somehow, that made me feel less crazy.

But I still felt alone.

Sawdust and pine pitch clung to my clothes, and the smell

of smoke and ash lingered in my hair. I was filthy, exhausted, and on edge. After loading wood into the last fireplace, I decided to make a call to Decker. Maybe hearing his voice would ground me. Rachel's office was locked, but that didn't matter. The door had an old-fashioned knob, the kind I knew how to pop open with nothing more than a credit card. It took me less than two minutes to slip inside. I went straight to the filing cabinet where Rachel kept the satellite phone. It wasn't there.

She must've taken it to her cabin.

Frustrated, I stood in the dark office, my flashlight casting a narrow beam over the room. I flashed the light across Rachel's desk and saw a file labelled *Holland Lake Lodge Buy/Sell Agreement*. I flipped it open and read the cover letter from a New York real estate hedge fund. The lodge was being sold for nearly twenty-five million dollars. I'm still not even sure what possessed me to do so, but I used my phone to shoot photos of the papers in the file and closed the folder. *The lodge was being sold. What hadn't Rachel mentioned it?*

That's when I heard it—a rhythmic creaking, like someone walking upstairs on the third-floor balcony overlooking the lobby. The lodge shifted and groaned in the storm, but this wasn't the usual sounds of the building settling. This was different. It was too regular, too deliberate.

I stepped out of Rachel's office and closed the door quietly. I turned off my flashlight and stood still, listening. The snow outside had stopped, the wind was quiet for the first time in hours, but the creaking continued. My throat tightened.

"Hello?" I called out, feeling foolish as the word echoed through the empty lodge. "Who's there?"

The creaking stopped.

My pulse thundered in my ears. The silence that followed

was thick and oppressive, but I could still feel it—someone was here.

I crossed the lobby, every board creaking under my weight. The grand staircase loomed ahead, and I hesitated before climbing. Each step felt heavier, my breath shallow and quick. At the landing, I stopped to listen again.

I forced myself up the next flight of stairs, my flashlight darting back and forth across the darkened hallway as I reached the third floor. The hallway stretched out in both directions, but nothing moved. The creaking had stopped.

I exhaled a long, shaky breath. I hadn't realized I'd been holding it. My chest felt tight, my head light. I stood there for a moment, trying to convince myself I'd imagined it all—just another trick of the mind after days of isolation.

Then, below me, I heard it.

The front door downstairs swung open.

Chapter Forty-Six

Kate

I raced down the stairs, my flashlight casting frantic beams of light across the lodge's dark walls. I took three steps at a time, fueled by anger more than fear. Whoever kept opening the doors was about to get a piece of my mind. My terror had given way to fury, and I didn't care what I found at the bottom of the stairs—I was ready for a fight.

But I wasn't ready for what happened next. As I hit the last step, I slammed full force into a solid figure. We both went down hard. My flashlight spun away, clattering across the floor, and we landed in a heap. I was on top of whoever I had just barreled into. My breath was knocked out of me. The fire in the lobby was burning low, casting the room into near darkness, and panic surged up, fast and wild. I screamed and struggled, but strong arms locked around me.

"Hey, hey, Kate! It's me, Dominic!" His voice was calm and steady, but I was too panicked to register it. I thrashed harder, desperate to break free. His grip tightened, and then, out of nowhere, he kissed me. Deep and firm, his lips stopped my panic cold.

For a moment, I leaned into it, surprised by how quickly the terror melted into something else entirely. But then reality snapped back in, and I pulled away, breathless. He was grinning at me now, his flashlight illuminating his face. "Surprise!" he said, like this was all some kind of joke.

I rolled off him and scrambled to my feet, my heart racing, but not from fear anymore. I was tingling from the kiss, but anger flared hot. "Have you ever heard of knocking?" I realized how ridiculous I sounded. "You scared the shit out of me!"

Dominic got to his feet, brushing himself off. "Sorry, Kate. I didn't think anyone was here. I figured you'd be with Rachel at her cabin—with power and light."

"No, I've been here all night keeping the fires going." I rubbed my eyes, exhaustion settling in. "I'm on edge. I've been hearing things, hallucinating, maybe." I let out a shaky breath. "But I'm really glad you're here."

Dominic nodded, his grin fading into something more serious. "Rachel called me on the satellite phone, said the generator was down. I drove to the turnoff and snowmobiled the rest of the way. Even that was dicey."

I was shaking a little from the lingering adrenaline as I put my snow gear on and helped him get to work on the generator. Together, we heated the frozen fuel lines and added additional insulation and heating tape. Within an hour, the lodge hummed back to life. The lights flickered on, and warmth began to seep from the radiators. As we worked, Dominic talked, filling the silence with stories.

"Ever since I moved to town," he said, tightening a bolt. "I've heard the rumors about this place. No caretaker stays for a second year—ever. Between Rachel, the isolation, and the weird vibe of the lodge, no one comes back." He glanced at me. "That's if they make it through the winter at all."

I forced a laugh, but his words settled in my chest. "Well, I'm still here."

Dominic's eyes lingered on me for a moment. "What about your boyfriend? Decker, right? Couldn't take it?"

"Decker's back in Seattle," I said, my tone defensive. "And he's not exactly my boyfriend."

Dominic smirked. "Could've fooled me."

We finished up, the lodge finally became warm and alive again. As we gathered the tools, Dominic hesitated. "Do you mind if I crash here tonight? Riding back now wouldn't be smart. And there's gotta be a spare room somewhere."

"Of course," I said, trying not to sound too relieved. "But now that the boiler's working and the lights are on, I'm going to bed. Alone," I added, giving him a pointed look.

Dominic grinned, holding up his hands in mock surrender. "Believe me, I have ideas, but they can wait for another time. Once you know me a little better." He winked, then turned and walked down the hallway toward the guest rooms.

I watched him go, feeling a strange mix of gratitude and tension. He was cocky, sure, but he had made the trek out here in the middle of a storm to help me. As I headed back to my room, exhaustion settling in, I realized how glad I was that he was here.

Chapter Forty-Seven

Kate

In the morning, after coffee and a massive breakfast, Dominic and I snowshoed to Rachel's cabin. It was mid-morning, and we hadn't seen any sign of her. Usually, she was in the lodge before dawn. The trek through the morning sun and powder snow was so pleasant and reviving that the toils of the night felt like a distant nightmare. We approached Rachel's log cabin with its stone chimney. It looked like a postcard.

We trudged onto the little covered porch and knocked on the door. There was no answer. Dominic and I glanced at each other. We knocked again and then peeked in the front window. No movement.

"Let's make sure she hasn't fallen and hurt herself," said Dominic, turning the old brass doorknob. "Hello? Rachel?"

We stepped into the entry hall and listened. There were no sounds except the last embers crackling in the cast iron wood stove. The cabin was warm and cozy and had its own generator. No wonder Rachel preferred to stay here rather than at the lodge. No wonder she wanted a winter caretaker on-site.

"Where is she?" Dominic asked, looking around.

I didn't answer because I was staring at a faded color photo framed on the wall just inside the door. It was Rachel, maybe twenty-five years ago, standing on the beach down at the lake in front of the lodge. Her arm was around an older woman with long hair. The woman from my dream. I stared at it in disbelief. "Take a photo of this for me," I said to Dominic.

He snapped a photo and started to ask why when a voice from behind us made us both spin.

"What are you doing?" asked Rachel as she walked up the path from the lodge, her parka pulled tight. Her expression was livid, her eyes narrow as she glared at us.

"Checking on you," I said, trying to keep my voice steady. "Did you spend the night in the lodge?"

Rachel's lips twisted into a sneer. "I wasn't sure you could handle it," she snapped. "But I guess you had help, from the looks of it," she said, glancing at Dominic.

Dominic stepped forward, unimpressed. "That's pretty unprofessional," he said, his voice calm but firm. "Kate was up all night keeping the place warm. She could've used help."

"You're a hired hand. Mind your own business," she snarled.

"He's right," I said, my patience frayed. "Last night was hell, and I heard you walking around. It wasn't professional to leave me hanging like that."

"Watch your tone, both of you. Don't forget who runs this place and signs your checks," Rachel said.

Rachel's eyes blazed as Dominic and I turned away and started the trek back to the lodge. She didn't say a word, but I could feel her eyes on us, that vicious look burning into my back.

I stopped thirty feet down the path. I'd had enough, and I turned to face her. "Rachel, we need to talk."

Her expression shifted, caught between anger and something else. I pressed on, my voice firmer than I expected. "I need some space. I feel you're interfering with my ability to do what I was hired for. I need you to back off and be professional. I'm not here to be friends. I'm here to keep the lodge clean and handle the maintenance tasks listed in the job description."

"You're being ridiculous," she snapped, her voice sharp. "I'm just trying to be supportive. You don't appreciate anything I do for you."

"Supportive?" I couldn't believe what I was hearing. "This isn't support. It's control."

"You'd be lost without me," she said, her voice fragile.

Dominic shook his head, snorting in disbelief. "You've been out here too long, Rachel. You're lucky Kate's still here. I would've quit months ago."

His words made me smile, a moment of warmth cutting through the tension. Rachel's face was unreadable as Dominic and I turned and headed back toward the lodge.

As we walked, Dominic's tone shifted. More serious now. "Kate, I want to see you again," he said, his voice low. "I could snowmobile in and pick you up. No funny business. I'd love to cook you dinner at my place in town."

I glanced at him, surprised by his sincerity. "That sounds nice," I admitted. "But things with Decker... they're complicated. We've got stuff to work out."

He nodded, not pushing. "I get it. Just know I'm here whenever you're ready."

I smiled, appreciating his honesty. "I'd love to have dinner with you," I said. "Let's see where things go."

Before he left, I asked Dominic to send me the photo of the two women from Rachel's cabin—the one with the mysterious woman who looked like she walked straight out of my dream.

"Can you show it to some of the old-timers in town?" I asked. "See if they know who she is?"

He nodded, not questioning why. "I will," he promised. "I'll be back in three days, 5 PM sharp, to pick you up for dinner."

I watched as he gathered his things, then hopped on his snowmobile and fired up the engine. "You can thank me later," he called out over the noise of the engine. He handed me a plain cardboard shoebox. With a playful wave and a blown kiss, he roared off, disappearing into the snow.

I opened the shoebox and saw a sleek package inside. It was a mini Starlink terminal—satellite internet and Wi-Fi. I could communicate with my phone and laptop. I closed it and looked around for Rachel.

As the sound of the snowmobile faded, I stood there, alone with the quiet of the lodge again. Rachel's presence still lingered in the back of my mind like a sour aftertaste, but Dominic's gift felt like a glimmer of something normal—a life-line to the outside world.

Chapter Forty-Eight

Rachel

I paced the small confines of my cabin. The satellite phone sat on the counter, useless after a series of calls that had only confirmed what I already knew. The county plow wouldn't make it out here. Not on a day like today. Not for me.

I clenched my jaw, my mind racing. The meeting in Billings, eight hours away on a good day, wasn't optional—a lifetime of work hinged on it. Lawyers, investment bankers, men who didn't reschedule just because the weather turned. A $25 million deal would not wait for the storm to clear.

My SUV wouldn't make it past the first mile of unplowed road. I'd driven it enough winters to know its limits. And a helicopter? Ridiculous. The noise alone would wake Mother and draw Kate's attention. If Kate saw a helicopter landing in the middle of a snowstorm, the questions wouldn't stop. I couldn't afford questions.

I turned to my bag, half-packed on the bed. Inside were a change of clothes, my laptop, and the carefully organized file of documents I'd need tomorrow. I pressed my fingers to my lips in consideration before I added a few more items—a heavy

176

sweater, thick socks, and my warmest gloves. It wasn't enough. Not for Montana in winter. I grabbed a blanket from the closet, folding it before shoving it into the duffel. Then came a flashlight, a pack of batteries, and an emergency radio. I hesitated, then added a few protein bars and a water bottle. I'd learned long ago that winter travel here demanded preparation. Being caught off guard could mean the difference between life and death.

Some of us live, while others must die.

I glanced out the window at the endless snowy forest, my breath fogging the glass. I needed a plan, and I needed it now.

I stepped back inside, peeling off my gloves and tossing them onto the counter. I grabbed the hot iron from the fireplace, its insulated handle warm. Rolling up my sleeve, I exposed the pale skin of my forearm, needing to focus my mind in the chaos that threatened to overwhelm me. The heat from the iron radiated as it sizzled against my skin, the pain sharp and immediate, anchoring me. I sucked in a breath, held it, then exhaled slowly. The tension in my chest eased.

I didn't pull the iron away immediately. Instead, I kept it pressed against my skin, letting the pain linger. My mind cleared, the impassable road outside forgotten. The crackling of the fire filled the room, steady and calming. I let the iron's weight ground me; the pain sharpening my thoughts until everything else fell away.

Better, much better.

I set the iron back on the hearth, flexing my fingers as the sting pulsed in my arm. I pulled my sleeve down, savoring the clarity that came with the pain. My thoughts were sharper now, cutting through the fog of panic.

Kate could handle the lodge in my absence. I had trained her well enough. But she could never know about the tunnel or Mother's third-floor suite. The thought made my stomach jump. What if she stumbled upon them while I was gone? What if she explored and found the secrets buried beneath the lodge?

My eyes darted to the clock on the wall. Time was slipping away. I ran through my options again.

I returned to the duffel, meticulously rearranging its contents. I added another layer of clothing, a thick scarf, and my insulated boots. Then I tucked in a small first-aid kit and a thermos of coffee I'd brewed earlier. The bag was heavy, but it would keep me prepared for whatever lay ahead.

I stopped, my hands resting on the duffel as I stared at the packed contents. A sense of pride flickered in my chest. I was ready. Whatever the storm threw at me, I'd prepared for it. As usual, after engaging in my ritual, I'd gained near-immediate clarity and my plan had come together, sharp and solid. It wasn't conventional, but it would work. I'd made sure of that.

I glanced at the fireplace, the iron resting on the hearth cooling in the dim light. The pain still pulsed in my forearm, a reminder of my resolve. I tightened the straps on the duffel and stood tall, my mind set.

A small, determined smile crept across my lips. I knew exactly how I was going to get to Billings. I'd worked too hard, risked too much, to let anything—not even a Montana snowstorm—stand in my way.

Chapter Forty-Nine

Kate

I hurried back to my room, heart pounding, keeping an eye out for Rachel. She was nowhere to be found, probably stewing in her cabin after our confrontation. Once inside, I closed the door behind me, releasing a shaky breath as I pulled the small Starlink device from my bag. If Rachel knew I had this, she'd lose it. I couldn't risk her finding out—not now.

I set the little rectangular satellite antenna in the window, following the setup instructions with trembling hands. My fingers fumbled with the cords, but within minutes, I was online. A flood of messages appeared on my phone, and I scrolled through them. Decker had written several times, his texts a mix of apologies and heartfelt messages, each one softer and sweeter than the last. Reading his words, I felt a pang of longing. He was a good man, despite everything we'd been through. I hadn't realized how much I missed hearing from him until now.

Then there were messages from my parents, short and simple, asking how I was. They missed me, sent pictures of our family dogs, happy and playful. For a moment, I almost felt the warmth of home. I shot off a quick reply, telling them I was doing well. I fibbed, texting that I was enjoying the job and having fun. I didn't want to worry them.

The silence in the hotel was eerie. I listened, holding my breath, but the hallway remained quiet. Taking a deep breath, I dialed Decker's number. Butterflies fluttered in my stomach as I listened to the ringing, but my excitement turned to disappointment when it went straight to voicemail. My heart sank.

"Hey, Decker," I said, my voice barely above a whisper, hoping Rachel wouldn't hear me through the walls. "I finally have service, but it's over Wi-Fi. We can call or text when Rachel's not around." I paused, trying to gather my thoughts. "I think I'm ready to give up. I've tried, but this place... Rachel... It's too much. I just needed to hear your voice. I miss you."

I talked until the voicemail cut me off, and even then, I wished I could say more. Just as I was about to tuck the phone away, footsteps echoed in the hallway. My blood ran cold as the doorknob rattled. Panic surged through me.

"Just a minute!" I called out, scrambling to unplug the Starlink antenna and shove it out of sight. My hands fumbled with the cords as I kicked the device under the bed, hiding it just as the key rattled in the lock and the door swung open. She didn't even wait for me to open my door.

Rachel stood there, her face unreadable, but her presence felt heavy, charged. "We need to talk," she said, her voice clipped.

I straightened up, trying to act casual. "Yes, we do," I replied, meeting her gaze. My heart raced, but I kept my voice steady.

"Could we meet in your office or in the lobby? These are my quarters and I'd like to keep things professional from here on out." I said.

Rachel stood in the doorway, her eyes cold and sharp, like

she had been waiting for this moment. Her arms crossed over her chest, her posture stiff. "No, we cannot. I know what you've been doing," she snapped, her voice cutting through the room. "Sleeping with Dominic. Sneaking around behind Decker's back like the tramp you are."

My cheeks burned, shock and anger rising in me. "What are you talking about?" I managed, my voice tight.

"Oh, don't play innocent," she spat, stepping closer. "I saw the way you looked at him. The way he looked at you. Unprofessional doesn't even begin to cover it. And cheating on Decker? Does he even know what kind of person you really are?"

I opened my mouth to defend myself, but Rachel wasn't done. Her words came like a flood, each one more venomous than the last.

"I should fire you on the spot," she continued. "But that's not even the worst of it, is it? Breaking into my office. Stealing three thousand dollars in petty cash. I should've known you were trouble the moment you got here."

My heart raced, my mind spinning. "I didn't take anything," I said, my voice shaking. "Yes, I went into your office, but I was looking for the satellite phone. I didn't touch any money."

Rachel's eyes narrowed, her lips twisting into a cruel smile. "Three thousand dollars is missing. And you were in my office. Coincidence? I don't think so."

Panic surged through me. She knew I'd been in her office—she might have even watched me pick the lock last night. But I hadn't stolen anything. "I swear, I didn't take any money," I said, my voice low.

"The deputy sheriff will be here as soon as the roads are clear," Rachel said, her tone almost gleeful. "They'll dust for fingerprints, interview you, and when they find out you were there, what do you think they'll believe? That you were just looking for the phone?"

My heart pounded in my chest. *If they fingerprinted the office, they would find proof I had been inside.*

Her eyes bore into mine, unblinking. "If you come clean now," she said softly, her voice low and calm, "and return the money, I won't press charges. You can stay, and we'll move past this. But if you don't, you're going to jail."

I stared at her, my pulse thundering in my ears. This was it —her trap. She wanted to pin this on me, to force me into a corner where I couldn't escape.

"I didn't take it," I whispered, shaking my head. "I didn't steal from you."

Rachel's smile faltered, replaced by a cold, calculating look. "Then I guess we'll see what the sheriff finds, won't we?" she said.

She turned and left the room, the weight of her threat hanging heavy in the air. My legs felt weak, my mind reeling. How did it come to this? How had she turned everything around so completely?

I sank onto the bed, my thoughts racing. I didn't take the money. But I'd broken into her office. And now Rachel had me exactly where she wanted me.

Chapter Fifty

Rachel

The wind howled as I secured the last strap on the bag slung over the back of the snowmobile. My gloves fumbled against the buckles, and the icy air stung my cheeks, but I didn't stop. Every second counted, and I needed to put as much distance as possible between the cabin and me before Kate noticed the sound of the snowmobile—if she could even hear it over this storm. She was probably sobbing into her pillow after the tongue lashing I'd given her.

The machine roared to life beneath me, a steady growl that I hoped was swallowed by the wind. Snow swirled in the headlights as I eased out of the shed beside my cabin, the snowmobile crunching through the deep drifts. The path was familiar, and I'd traveled it enough times to know where to avoid the deeper pockets of snow. I leaned forward, gripping the handlebars as the snowmobile surged ahead.

Four miles of road, I reminded myself. Just four miles. The unplowed terrain was rough, the snowy ruts deeper than I'd expected, but I kept the throttle steady, my eyes fixed on the line of trees in the distance. My fingers ached from the cold despite my gloves, and the steady vibration of the machine sent a dull throb up my arms.

When I reached the highway, a mix of relief and tension settled over me; one leg of my journey had been successfully completed, but I had many miles to go, and many hurdles to overcome, on my way to reach Billings and the liberation the lawyer's paperwork represented.

The road ahead was barely visible, buried under a thick layer of snow, but I could just make out the reflective markers on the outside of each lane. I stayed between them and proceeded cautiously; the snowmobile handling the snowy surface well enough. The wind was relentless, but I ignored the needling pain in my exposed cheeks and nose and focused on the task at hand.

Turning onto Old Barn Road, I felt the first flicker of genuine hope. Dale's house was just ahead, a dark shape barely visible through the snow. The old dog wouldn't return from Mexico for another two months. His driveway was covered, but I'd been here before to pay him for firewood and knew the layout well enough to navigate. I parked the snowmobile near his woodshed, cutting the engine and listening as the storm filled the silence. My legs wobbled as I dismounted, the weight of the bag pulling at my shoulders.

I moved quickly to the back door of the house, pulling a small hammer from my bag. With a quick glance to ensure no one was watching, I swung it at a small pane of glass near the lock. The sound of shattering glass was muted by the wind, and I reached my gloved hand through, unlocking the door from the inside.

The house was cold and quiet, the faint scents of Pine-sol and wood smoke lingering in the air. I stepped inside, my boots leaving wet prints on the floor as I moved toward the door where the keys hung. Just as I'd expected, they were right there, dangling from the hook. I chuckled quietly. It was so satisfying when people were as predictable as they seemed. My fingers wrapped around the keys, and I allowed myself a brief moment to exhale. So far, so good.

I didn't linger. The big, jacked-up truck sat in a lean-to shed, sheltered from the snow. The diesel engine roared to life as I turned the key, a low, reassuring rumble that sent warmth flooding through the cab. I cranked up the heat and adjusted the vents, letting my frozen fingers thaw against the stream of warm air.

Reversing out of the driveway was slow work, the tires struggling against the drifts, but the truck's four-wheel drive handled it better than I'd expected. I turned onto the highway, the heavy vehicle carving a path through the snow with ease. The wind buffeted the truck, but I barely noticed now, my focus locked on the road ahead.

A small victorious smile tugged at the corners of my lips. I'd done it. The storm, the snowmobile, the break-in—all of it had worked. I was on my way to Billings, and nothing was going to stop me now.

But the thought of Dale lingered. He'd find out eventually, and when he did, he'd want compensation. I'd either pay him off or have sex with him, fulfilling a decades-long desire on his part.

I'd deal with that later. One problem at a time. For now, I concentrated on the road; the truck cutting through the snow as the storm raged around me.

Chapter Fifty-One

Kate

I sat in my room, Lydia's journal in my hands. I needed to calm down but also needed to understand Rachel and her motivations if I was going to defend myself to the police. The lodge was quiet now; the fire crackling in the hearth, yet another storm beginning outside. But inside, I felt an even deeper chill. I flipped through the pages, reading Lydia's words again, this time more carefully, searching for something I might have missed before. Her handwriting was neat but growing more frantic and markedly sloppy toward the end.

The entries started innocently enough. Lydia wrote about her excitement to work at the lodge, the hope of saving enough money over the winter to allow her to travel over the spring and summer. Soon, she mentioned the isolation, the work. The early pages could have been my own diary, describing the same routines, the same walks through the empty halls. But then things shifted. The tone of her writing darkened, her words growing heavier, more anxious.

Rachel. Always Rachel. Lydia wrote about her constantly.

How Rachel had been kind at first, welcoming, even friendly. But then, like a shadow creeping across the floor, Rachel's presence dominated. Lydia wrote about the way Rachel inserted herself into everything, how she blurred the lines between friendship and control, how she hovered, watched, and manipulated.

"She doesn't let me have a moment alone," Lydia wrote in one entry. *"She's always there. Always watching. I don't have a moment alone."*

I swallowed, my pulse quickening. The words felt too familiar, too close. It was like Lydia had been living my life. The same uneasy feeling, the same sense of being trapped, of Rachel pulling the strings.

As I read further, the entries became even more unsettling. Lydia described how Rachel twisted their relationship, how she went from being a helpful presence to something much darker. *"She's trying to control me, and succeeding,"* Lydia had written. *"She makes it seem like she's helping, but she's trying to keep me here. I feel like a prisoner. I haven't been allowed to go to town for months. Rachel says the truck is broken, but I know it isn't. My little car can't make it over the rutted roads here."*

My hands trembled a bit as I turned the pages. The parallels were undeniable. Rachel had done this before. She'd latched onto Lydia the same way she'd latched onto me, slowly tightening her grip into a chokehold, making it impossible to leave. Lydia had felt trapped, just like I did now.

Then I reached the final entry, dated only a few days before Lydia disappeared—or left. I didn't know which. The words were scrawled hastily, the writing shaky.

"I need to get out of here before it's too late. I'm not sure if Rachel will let me."

I stared at the words, my heart hammering in my chest. Lydia had tried to leave. She'd known something was wrong.

And now I was following the same path, living through the same nightmare.

I didn't know if Lydia had escaped, or if Rachel had forced her out—or worse. But I couldn't ignore the warning in Lydia's final entry. It felt like she was speaking directly to me, urging me to pay attention, to get out before it was too late.

I snapped the journal shut, the sound loud in the silence of the room. My hands trembled, my mind racing. I needed to leave. I needed to get away from Rachel, from the lodge, from whatever this place was turning me into.

I connected the Starlink terminal again and Googled Lydia's full name. Her Facebook profile was first. She was young and pretty with a photo of her with a little brother and a scruffy dog. The next search results were all news stories about Lydia going missing. She had gone missing a year ago and had never been found. I raced through the articles, scanning the text. Lydia had never come back from her caretaking job at the lodge. Rachel was quoted as saying that Lydia had quit midwinter and had driven away into a storm. The police had investigated, searched the lodge and surrounding wilderness. Lydia and her car were never found.

I sat in front of the laptop, dumbfounded. Lydia had disappeared after working my same job, living in my same room, working for my same boss.

I had to be careful. I had to make a plan. And I had to get out—before it was too late.

Chapter Fifty-Two

Kate

I couldn't wait any longer. What once felt eerie now felt truly dangerous and the very air around me felt electrically charged., I had questioned my own instincts for so long, doubted my own observations, but learning about Lydia's mysterious disappearance had finally galvanized me into action. There was no time to waste. Keeping my movements quiet, I started packing my bags, trying not to make a sound. Every creak of the floorboards seemed deafening in the empty halls. My heart pounded, adrenaline rushing through me, making my hands shake.

Dominic. He was the only way out. His snowmobile was the only hope with the roads buried under snow. Walking wasn't an option—four miles of deep, unplowed snow separated me from the highway and I wouldn't make it half that distance in these conditions.

I dialed Dominic. Straight to voicemail. My stomach knotted as I hung up and typed out a message: *Things are bad. I need to leave. Please come get me ASAP. This is an emergency.*

I sighed, finger hovering over the send button, ready to

shoot off the message when everything around me went black. The power cut out. The message hadn't been sent. Panic surged through me.

I yanked the Starlink terminal out of the window, shoving it into my bag. I couldn't leave it where Rachel could find it. Then I stepped into the hallway. The lodge was draped in somber shades of grey and black, shadows stretching out across the walls and pooling in the far corners. The last light of day was fading fast, but once my eyes adjusted in the sudden darkness, I realized that there was still enough contrast to see for now. I listened, straining for any sound, any sign of Rachel. Silence. I moved toward the stairs.

The large staircase creaked under my weight as I descended, my breath shallow, trying to stay calm. The lobby was quiet, darker than before. The fires had all gone out, and the cold was creeping in fast. I called Rachel's name, but the emptiness swallowed my voice.

No answer.

I grabbed my coat and stepped outside, the biting cold hitting me immediately. The sun had just set, leaving a gradient of deep purples and blues bleeding into the night sky. It was beautiful, but unsettling—a calm backdrop to the chaos brewing inside the lodge. I followed the path to Rachel's cabin, my boots crunching against the snow.

I walked around the side of the lodge, feeling the weight of its silhouette against the darkening sky. Something pulled at my attention, and I glanced up. There—on the third floor—a flicker of light. It disappeared almost as quickly as it appeared, leaving me wondering if I'd imagined it.

But I didn't have time to dwell on it. I needed to check the generator. The maintenance panel was open, wires and fuel lines sticking out at odd angles. Not cut cleanly, but shredded, torn apart as if something had ripped through them.

My heart sank. There was no easy fix for this. The lodge was going to stay dark, and the cold would only get worse.

I glanced back at the looming building, the sense of danger tightening around me. I needed to haul firewood again. It was going to be a long night.

And I wasn't sure how much longer I could last.

Chapter Fifty-Three

Kate

I pulled my hat low and wrapped my scarf tighter around my neck, bracing myself as I stood at the front door of the lodge. I had already checked Rachel's cabin three times that evening, but I couldn't shake the feeling that she was still somewhere nearby. The old pickup truck was parked right outside, and it wouldn't have made it over the road anyhow. She hadn't left. So where could she be?

Just one more time, I told myself. One more look, just to make sure. Maybe Rachel was hiding, waiting for the right moment to reappear. Or maybe she was already watching, lurking somewhere in the shadows. Either way, I had to know.

The cold stung as I stepped outside. The wind sliced through my layers, cutting straight to the bone. Every breath turned into a cloud of frost, swirling in front of my face before vanishing into the dark. I forced myself forward, the crunch of snow under my boots the only sound in the dead silence of the night. The sky was pitch black—no stars, just a void that pressed down on me as I made my way toward the cabin, its faint outline faintly visible through the snow and darkness.

She had to be there. I clung to the thought, trying to steady the panic rising in my chest. That Rachel could be hiding inside the lodge itself, watching my every move, was too much. The notes, the noises, the sense of being stalked—it all led back to her.

By the time I reached the cabin, my heart sank. It was dark and silent, just like before. No lights, no movement. Not a solitary sign of Rachel. I knocked on the door anyway, hoping against hope that something had changed.

"Rachel?" My voice cracked as it cut through the cold. "Are you in there?"

Silence. Nothing but the howl of the wind.

I tried the door, but it was locked, just like it had been before. Pressing my face against the frosted window, I squinted through the thin layer of ice covering the glass. The cabin was empty, just as dark and cold as it looked from the outside. No Rachel, no clues. Just the same maddening silence.

With a heavy sigh, I turned and started back toward the lodge. My body was stiff, my bones chilled from the frigid air that seemed to settle deeper and deeper the longer I was out there. The lodge seemed impossibly far now, each step slower than the last, the snow dragging at my boots. I pulled my coat tighter and forced myself to keep moving.

Finally, I reached the lodge, relief flooding me—until I pushed on the front door. It was locked tight. The same door I knew I had left unlocked a few minutes ago. Adrenaline buzzed through me as I twisted the big handle, twisting and pushing on it with all my might. It didn't budge. I tried again, rattling it harder, but it was no use. It was locked.

"What the hell?" I muttered, my voice shaky with panic.

Desperate, I ran around to the kitchen entrance, praying it was still open. My fingers were numb, barely able to grip the handle as I tried to turn it. Locked.

"No. No, no, no," I whispered, my voice growing frantic. This couldn't be happening. I had been gone for minutes—there was no way someone could have locked me out. Unless—

The realization hit me like a punch. Rachel wanted me out here. She was trying to trap me.

The cold bit harder now, sharper than before, searing my exposed skin. My hands were trembling so badly I could barely move them, and the panic only made it worse. I needed to get back inside now. My eyes scanned the snowy ground, desperate for anything I could use. A rock caught my eye, half-buried in the snow. Without a second thought, I grabbed it and hurled it at the nearest window. The glass shattered with a loud crash, shards scattering across the snow like glittering ice. The sound was too loud, echoing in the silent, frozen night.

I didn't care. I clambered through the broken window, ignoring the jagged edges that caught at my coat, scratching my skin. The cold air followed me in, creeping through the broken window, but at least I was inside.

My breath came in ragged gasps, my heart racing as I leaned against the hearth, still shaking. The lodge felt different now—less like an empty vessel filled with threats and more like a threat itself, menacing and alive. The fire was burning low, casting long, flickering shadows that made the space feel foreign and hostile. I threw more wood onto the pile of coals, watching the fire roar back to life. The heat scarcely registered. I was numb, inside and out.

She had locked me out. She was playing with me, pushing me to the edge. I could feel it deep in my gut, a fear that wouldn't let go.

I sank into the armchair by the fire, hugging my knees to my chest, watching the flames. My mind raced, but there was no clear thought, just a swirl of questions and fears. I wasn't safe here. Not in the lodge. Not anywhere. The place I'd once hoped could be a refuge had turned into a trap, and I had no way out.

And Rachel—wherever she was—was at the center of it all.

Chapter Fifty-Four

Kate

I stared at the broken window; the glass scattered across the floor like tiny, glittering daggers. The wind blasted through the hole, biting cold, and I shivered—not just from the chill, but from the fear simmering just below the surface. This needed to be fixed. Now. I couldn't let the cold—and whatever else was out there—creep back inside.

Focus. I took a breath, steadying myself. I knew what to do. Dad had taught me enough over the years in his wood shop. I was a mess mentally, barely holding it together, but physically, I knew I could handle this. After rummaging around in the lodge, I finally found a dusty piece of plywood and a hammer with a handful of half-rusted nails in the storage room.

With fingers still numb, I propped up the plywood as best I could and started hammering it over the broken glass. The sound of each blow echoed through the lodge, and I clung to that noise—it gave me something solid, something real to focus on. Each strike of the hammer felt like a step toward taking back control of my time at the lodge.

Finally, I stepped back, looking over my work. It was rough, but it would keep the worst of the cold out, at least for now. The wind howled, rattling the broken glass, but inside, it was calm. Eerily so.

One problem solved. Too many left to count.

So don't, my mind reasoned. Don't even count the problems, just take this one step at a time.

I made my way back to the lobby and collapsed again in front of the fire, my lifeline in this freezing cavern. I had limited energy and an endless night of work ahead. I needed to be smart and strategize.

The pile of wood I had carried in earlier was almost gone. I estimated that I'd need to make between twenty and thirty trips outside for enough wood to last the night and keep the pipes from freezing. I hauled myself to my feet, pulled on my heavy jacket, gloves, and boots, and headed toward the door.

Why did I even care if the pipes froze? It wasn't my problem. This goddamn stubborn work ethic and a deep need to prove myself.

The labor began—back and forth for the next three hours— eighty steps out the door, around the lodge to the woodpile. Pick up five or six pieces of cordwood. Eighty steps back to the lodge and then into each of the eight rooms to drop the wood. It was after 3 a.m. when I finally finished fully stocking the stacks beside each fireplace. I curled up in a ball on the sofa in front of the lobby fireplace, still in my thick winter gear.

My body screamed for sleep, every inch of me heavy with exhaustion, but I sat up and grabbed another piece of cordwood and tossed it into the flames. For a moment, the warmth settled over me, and I poked at the embers, muttering to myself just to break the silence.

"You wouldn't believe the mess this place has become, would you, Decker?"

I glanced over my shoulder, half-expecting her to be there,

watching with that look on her face. But it was just me. Shadows and silence.

At that moment, I heard a distant sound. Outside the lodge. A booming, resonating crack.

I paused, straining to hear anything else that could help me identify the sound. Maybe I was hearing things.

"Figures. It had to happen sooner or later. Maybe it's the lodge caving in and ending all of our misery."

I sighed, tossing another piece of wood into the fire. Talking to myself felt ridiculous, but I'd rather hear my own voice than nothing at all.

"You too," I murmured, picturing the woman with the white hair from my dreams. "I know you're around here somewhere."

I let out a hollow laugh, more to keep myself awake than anything.

"Alone, not alone. Pretty funny."

The fire crackled, offering little comfort, but I kept talking anyway, letting the words fill the emptiness. I was rambling, maybe acting a little crazy, but it was better than the silence. It kept me company, anchoring me somehow, keeping me from descending into total despair.

Eventually, exhaustion pulled me under, and I drifted off to sleep. That's when she came to me again—the woman with the white hair. The dream was clearer this time, every detail sharp and vivid. She stood at the edge of the frozen lake, her face stern, her eyes filled with something close to pity. Or was it a warning?

"Leave," she whispered, her voice echoing across the snow and ice. "You're not safe."

The crackling of the fire pulled me out of the dream. My eyes flew open, and for a moment, I couldn't tell where I was.

The warmth of the fire in the lodge's lobby wrapped around me, but the howl of the storm outside sent a shiver through my body. Shadows from the flames flickered across the high ceiling, and I realized I had fallen asleep on the couch.

And that I wasn't alone.

Chapter Fifty-Five

Kate

I froze. A figure stood over me, staring down with calm, piercing eyes. Long white hair framed her face, and for a moment, I felt like I was still dreaming—like she'd stepped out of my subconscious and into the real world. My breath caught as recognition slammed into me. She was the woman from the photograph in Rachel's cabin.

"Hello, my sweet Rachel," she said, her voice trembling but strangely steady. "You've been sleeping too much. You always did that when you were little."

My throat went dry. I sat up quickly, my heart hammering, and scrambled to put distance between us. "Who—who are you?" I stammered.

The old woman smiled, her lined face softening with what seemed like affection. "Why, I'm Norma Whitaker,, silly. Don't you recognize your own mother? I've missed you so much."

I couldn't speak. I couldn't even think straight. She leaned closer and brushed a cool hand over my forehead. The touch was so gentle it sent chills down my spine. I flinched but didn't move away, too stunned to react.

"You feel warm," she said softly, her expression shifting to concern. "Are you catching a chill from the storm? You've been working so hard, keeping the fires going. I'm so proud of you."

Her words hit me like a bucket of ice water, snapping me out of my paralysis. "I—what?" I croaked. "Who are you? How did you—how are you here?"

She tilted her head, her smile never faltering. "You've always been such a curious child. I've been here all along. This is our home. Don't you remember?"

"No," I whispered, shaking my head. "I'm not Rachel. Rachel is—Rachel is my boss. She runs the lodge."

Her smile wavered, a flicker of confusion crossing her face before she chuckled. "No, no, that's not right. She's just a hired hand. A caretaker. She's been with us for a long time, yes, but you—you're my daughter. My youngest. My heart."

I stared at her, my chest tightening as her words settled over me like a heavy blanket. "How long... how long have you been here?" I asked, my voice barely above a whisper.

Her chuckle deepened, as though my question amused her. "Oh, a very long time. Decades, I suppose. Time moves differently here. I've always been here, watching over the lodge, keeping it as it should be. Just like my father and his father before him."

My stomach churned. "You've been living here, in the lodge? Wandering the halls at night?"

"Of course," she said, as if it were the most natural thing in the world. "Someone has to make sure everything is in its place. I tidy up, leave little reminders, play my games. It's how I keep busy."

My mind spun. The notes. The scarf. My missing books. "That was you," I said, my voice shaking. "You've been moving my things."

She nodded, her smile widening. "I knew you'd figure it

out, my clever girl. It's all in good fun. You always loved my little games when you were younger."

I swallowed hard, the room spinning as I tried to process what she was saying. "I don't understand," I said, gripping the edge of the couch. "None of this makes sense."

"It will," she said gently, reaching out to take my hand. Her grip was surprisingly strong. "In time, it will. You've always had such a good heart, Rachel. Look at all you've done to keep this place warm and safe. Your father and brother would be so proud."

My legs felt weak, and the air seemed too thick to breathe. "Let me take you back to your room," I said, struggling to steady my voice. "It's cold here, and you shouldn't be wandering around."

Her face lit up like a child hearing a bedtime story. "Such a thoughtful girl," she said. "Come, I'll show you. It's not far."

She led me up the grand staircase, her steps sure and light despite her frail appearance. The nightgown she wore trailed behind her like a ghostly veil. At the end of a dim hallway, she opened the door to a maintenance closet and revealed a hidden staircase tucked behind the shelves.

"Right this way," she said with a conspiratorial smile, as if sharing a precious secret.

At the top of the stairs, she opened another door, and I gasped. The room was warm—warmer than anywhere else in the lodge—with a roaring fire in a stone hearth. The air smelled of chamomile and lavender, and a teapot steamed over the fire. The bed, piled high with quilts and comforters, looked impossibly cozy. Heavy drapes covered the windows, and the soft glow of kerosene lanterns bathed the space in a golden light.

"This is my sanctuary," she said, her voice filled with pride. "Everything I need is right here."

I couldn't speak. My throat was too tight. I felt like I was standing in the middle of a dream—or a nightmare.

"You've been living here all this time," I finally said, the words barely audible.

"Of course," she said, settling into a chair by the fire. "This is our home, Rachel. Our legacy. And you—you've kept it alive."

My legs trembled as I backed toward the door. "I'll keep checking on you," I said, my voice hollow. "You shouldn't be alone in this storm."

Her smile softened, her eyes glistening with what looked like genuine emotion. "My sweet Rachel," she said. "You've always taken such good care of me."

I nodded, numb, and slipped out of the room, closing the door behind me. As I descended the hidden staircase, my mind raced. The pieces were falling into place, but the picture they formed was more horrifying than I could have imagined.

Chapter Fifty-Six

Kate

T he kitchen was alive with sound—the low hum of the small generator powering the Starlink terminal, the hiss of eggs frying in the skillet, the steady crackle of bacon crisping in the pan. My hands moved on autopilot, but my mind raced, electrified by the adrenaline coursing through me. I had just discovered a secret no one should have been able to hide: the old woman upstairs.

She shouldn't have been here—not in this freezing lodge, not in that hidden room, not in the state she was in. Her frail frame, the way she confused me for her daughter—it all screamed that she needed care. Real care. A memory care unit, a retirement facility, somewhere warm and safe, not this cold, drafty lodge in the middle of a Montana winter.

I flipped the bacon, the grease spitting and popping. She had to be starving. She'd said she had everything she needed, but could that possibly be true? Food, warmth, companionship —how could she have survived up there, alone, for so long?

Had Rachel been helping her? Keeping her here? By either force or manipulation? Keeping her hidden? The questions churned in my mind as I plated the eggs and bacon; the steam rising like a faint promise of comfort.

I turned off the burner and stared at the plate, gripping the edge of the counter to steady myself. What was I going to do? I couldn't leave her here. And I couldn't just pretend this wasn't happening.

The sound of the storm outside had died down, leaving a heavy silence that pressed against the walls. I glanced toward the stairs, half-expecting her to shuffle down in that thick night-gown, her long white hair catching the early light filtering through the windows.

She needed me now, and as much as the thought terrified me, I couldn't abandon her.

I grabbed my phone from the counter and texted Dominic again. *Please answer me. I need your help.*

The screen stayed stubbornly silent. I let out a shaky breath, grabbed the plate of food, and carried it to the lobby. The fire in the great hearth still burned, the warmth radiating out in waves, but it wasn't enough. The cold crept into my bones, an unwelcome reminder of just how fragile this place was against the harsh winter.

How fragile we all were against the forces larger and more powerful than us.

I set the plate on the coffee table by the fire and sat down, my mind spinning with everything that had happened. The adrenaline was still there, buzzing under my skin, but now it was joined by a growing sense of dread.

What if Rachel came back?

What if she found out I'd discovered the woman? Would she try to hurt me? Hurt her?

The fire crackled, the only sound in the cavernous room, and I pulled out my phone again, scrolling through my messages. Nothing from Dominic. I couldn't wait any longer. I dialed 911, my heart racing as the line connected.

"911, what's your emergency?"

I struggled to find the words. "I—I'm at the Holland Lake Lodge," I began, my voice shaky. "There's an elderly woman here who needs help. She shouldn't be living here. It's—it's freezing, and she's not safe."

The operator's tone shifted, a hint of confusion creeping in. "Ma'am, is she injured? Are you reporting a medical emergency?"

"No," I said, fumbling for the right words. "But she's in her late eighties. She has dementia, I think, and she's been living in a hidden room in the lodge. She's not safe here. I think my boss has been keeping her here."

There was a pause. "Do you believe she's being held against her will?"

"I don't know," I admitted, my voice rising in frustration. "But she needs help. She's confused. She thinks I'm her daughter."

"Ma'am, this doesn't sound like an emergency. I'm going to transfer you to the non-emergency line at the Missoula County Sheriff's Department. Please hold."

The line clicked, and I gritted my teeth, gripping the phone tighter. After what felt like forever, a man's voice came on the line.

"This is Deputy Price with the Missoula County Sheriff's Department. How can I help you?"

I stumbled through the explanation, trying to piece together the situation in a way that made sense. I told him about the storm, about Rachel's disappearance, about the old woman upstairs and her hidden room.

"She's not safe here," I finished, my voice trembling. "And I don't know what happened to Rachel. She's either missing or hiding, but I don't feel safe."

The deputy listened patiently, but his tone remained calm, almost detached. "The roads out to Holland Lake are still snowed in," he said finally. "We're working on getting them cleared. In the meantime, do you feel safe staying there?"

Do I feel safe? The question hung in the air, almost laughable in its simplicity. "I—I'm not sure," I admitted. "But I can't leave her alone. She needs help."

"We'll prioritize getting someone out there as soon as possible," the deputy said. "If anything changes, or if you feel like you're in immediate danger, call us back, okay?"

"Okay," I said, though the word felt hollow. I hung up and stared at the phone, my frustration bubbling up. They didn't understand. How could they? I could barely explain it to myself.

The fire crackled in the hearth, the warmth no longer reaching me. I texted Dominic again. *Please, Dominic, call me back. I need your help.*

The screen stayed dark.

The light outside grew stronger, the pale dawn giving way to a cold, gray morning. The day stretched out before me, long and uncertain. I was trapped in this lodge, in this silence, with no choice but to keep going—and no idea how to escape the maze I'd found myself in.

Chapter Fifty-Seven

Kate

B alancing the tray, I climbed the stairs. The hot coffee sloshed in the mug, and I adjusted my grip to steady it. My heart thudded in my chest, and I couldn't help but think about how surreal this all was. Less than twenty-four hours ago, I did not know the woman upstairs even existed outside of my dream. Now, I was bringing breakfast to a woman I'd found living in a hidden room, a woman who believed I was her daughter.

My boots creaked against the stairs as I made my way to the maintenance closet. The hidden staircase beyond it also felt like something out of a dream—or a nightmare. How long had she been living up here, tucked away like some forgotten relic of the past? And Rachel—my boss—what part did she play in all this? Was she helping the woman? Hiding her?

I reached the top of the stairs and nudged the door open with my shoulder. Warmth enveloped me immediately. The fire in her stone hearth was roaring again, and the room was bathed in the golden glow of kerosene lanterns. She was sitting in the armchair near the fire, wrapped in a quilt that hung over her thin shoulders.

Her face lit up the moment she saw me. "Rachel, my sweet girl," she said, her voice trembling with joy. "You're here! Oh, my heart—my sweet baby of the family."

I froze for a moment, thrown by how genuine her happiness seemed, and then forced myself to smile. "Good morning," I said, crossing the room. "I brought you some breakfast."

She clasped her hands together, her expression delighted. "You've always been such a thoughtful girl, Rachel. Just like your father. He was always so kind. And your brother and sister, how they love their baby Rachel."

I swallowed hard, the knot in my stomach tightening. "Thank you," I said, setting the tray down on the small table near her chair. She gave no sign she recognized me as anything other than the daughter she thought I was.

"Here," I said, trying to keep my voice steady. "You should eat while it's hot."

She smiled at me, her eyes glistening. "You've made this for me? My darling girl. I always said you'd grow up to be someone special." She picked up the fork, her frail hands trembling, and began eating.

I perched on the edge of a chair nearby, watching her carefully. After a few bites, she glanced up. "This is delicious," she said. "Just like the meals your grandmother used to make in this very lodge. She loved cooking for everyone, keeping us all fed and happy."

My chest felt tight. "I'm glad you like it," I said.

She nodded, then looked around the room. "Where's the caretaker?" she asked, her tone casual. "She's been with us for so long. Always running around, working so hard. Have you seen her?"

For a moment, I wasn't sure how to respond. "I—I haven't been able to find her," I said finally. "She's not here."

The old woman frowned, her expression thoughtful. "Hmm. She's probably playing around in the tunnel again," she said, almost dismissively.

I blinked, thrown. "The tunnel?"

She nodded, taking another bite of eggs. "My grandfather had it built when he owned the lodge. He also owned mines, you know—he was quite the entrepreneur. His workers blasted a tunnel from the lodge to the caretaker's cabin so the caretaker wouldn't have to go outside in the winter."

"A tunnel," I repeated, skepticism creeping into my voice.

"That's right," she said, pointing her fork toward me. "The entrance is in the east wing storage room. It's hidden, of course. My grandfather was a practical man, but he always loved his secrets."

I nodded, unsure of what to believe. She seemed so certain, but the idea of a secret tunnel sounded more like the stuff of legends than reality. Still, I played along. "Thank you for telling me," I said.

She finished her meal and gave me a warm smile. "You're such a good girl, Rachel. I'm so proud of you. Your father and grandfather would be proud, too."

"Thank you," I said softly, standing and gathering the tray. Her words felt like a weight pressing down on me as I made my way back down the hidden staircase.

When I reached the kitchen, I dropped the dishes into the sink and stood there for a moment, staring at the wall. A tunnel? It couldn't be real. There was no way. And yet, this information had come from a woman who had been living in a secret room in the lodge, so perhaps I wasn't the greatest authority on what was and wasn't possible in this space.

Might as well check it out, I thought as I dried my hands on a towel and grabbed a flashlight from one of the drawers. If the tunnel existed, I needed to find it.

The storage room in the east wing was packed with old furniture, dusty crates, and piles of forgotten equipment. It took me several minutes to even find the back wall, let alone anything resembling a hidden entrance. But then I noticed a narrow seam in the wood paneling, almost invisible beneath layers of dust and cobwebs. Had I not been actively looking for irregularities, I never would have spotted it.

I set the flashlight on the ground and began clearing the junk away, shoving aside a heavy trunk, then a stack of chairs that toppled noisily to the floor. My breath clouded in the cold air as I worked, and my hands trembled, though I wasn't sure if it was from the effort or the adrenaline.

Finally, I uncovered a small door, low and unassuming, set flush against the wall. My heart pounded as I pulled it open, revealing a steep set of stairs leading down into the darkness.

The air that wafted up was damp and cold, carrying a faint metallic tang.

I clicked on the flashlight and pointed it down, but the beam barely seemed to penetrate the blackness below.

The lights didn't work. Of course.

My pulse quickened as I straightened and looked around the storage room, searching for a brighter flashlight or something better suited for what lay ahead. My gaze landed on a bright yellow handheld flashlight mounted on the wall near the door.

I grabbed it, tested it, and felt a jolt of relief as its powerful beam cut through the shadows.

Taking a deep breath, I stepped back to the small door and descended into the tunnel, the flashlight's glow lighting the way.

Chapter Fifty-Eight

Kate

The air in the tunnel was damp and bitterly cold. My flashlight's beam carved a narrow path through the darkness, illuminating rough walls hewn straight out of the granite. The ceiling was low and forced me to hunch as I descended, my breath visible in front of me with each exhale. The uneven stone scraped against my hand as I steadied myself, and I kept my free arm bent, shielding my head from the jagged ceiling above.

Every step down felt like a journey into another world—one I wasn't sure I wanted to enter.

The walls narrowed, and I turned the flashlight's beam ahead, the shadows writhing against the walls.

That's when I saw them.

At first, they seemed almost cheerful. Tissue-paper streamers in bright pinks and purples hung from the walls, their colors vivid against the gray stone. Bunches of fake flowers—roses, daisies, carnations—were pressed into the cracks, creating bursts of color that seemed absurdly festive. It reminded me of decorations for a child's party or a makeshift wedding, a strange, joyful touch in this damp and claustrophobic tunnel.

But the farther I walked, the more the decorations felt wrong.

My flashlight's beam caught on something up ahead, and my steps faltered.

Long, narrow wooden benches lined both sides of the tunnel, leaving only a slim path in between. They were covered with lumpy piles of silk cloth, taffeta, and lace, the materials shimmering faintly under the flashlight's glow. On top of the mounded fabric, artificial flowers had been arranged in careful, deliberate patterns, reminding me of decorated wedding cakes..

Something deep and animal inside me told me to stop, to turn, to flee, but my feet carried me forward, my heart pounding so loudly I was sure it would echo off the stone walls. As I approached, the truth revealed itself, and my blood turned to ice.

Bodies.

There were eight of them, one on each bench. Human bodies, their heads the only part visible, their faces staring upward into the darkness. Their skin was shrunken and pulled tight over their skulls, their empty eye sockets hollow and staring, their grimacing mouths frozen in grotesque silence.

Their hair, in varied lengths and shades, was immaculately styled—glossy and smooth, adorned with ribbons, bows, and delicate pins. Someone had decorated them like dolls, their dehydrated, mummified faces framed in what could have been a grotesque parody of love and care.

My stomach turned, the bile rising in my throat. The air felt heavier here, thick with decay and the weight of secrets too dark to comprehend.

"These were caretakers," I whispered, my voice barely

audible over the pounding of my heart. "These were Rachel's caretakers."

My flashlight trembled in my hand as I swept it across the benches, each body a frozen monument to some horrifying ritual. And then my breath caught in my throat.

Lydia.

One of these women was Lydia. I was sure of it. I could feel it in the marrow of my bones, a certainty that felt as though it had been etched into my soul. Lydia, the caretaker before me, who had vanished without a trace.

Rachel did this.

Rachel, who had always seemed so in control, so steady, had been hiding this. Rachel, who lived in the caretaker's cabin, had used this tunnel to slip back and forth without leaving tracks in the snow. That's why I'd seen her in the lodge, but never outside. She'd been using this tunnel—this hideous, hidden world—to move unseen.

The old woman upstairs knew about the tunnel. She'd told me about it with a faint smile and a wistful look, as if it were nothing more than an old family story. But an old woman like that wouldn't—couldn't—kill healthy young women.

No. This was Rachel's doing.

I was supposed to be here. I was supposed to be one of them.

The thought hit me like a hammer, my knees nearly buckling under its weight. My breathing came fast and shallow, the air feeling thinner with each gasp. I turned, ready to run, when a faint sound reached my ears.

A noise from above.

My body went rigid. Someone—or something—was outside the lodge.

My flashlight flicked toward the ceiling, my hands trembling. The sound came again, faint but distinct: the crunch of snow under tires. A vehicle.

Rachel. It had to be Rachel.

I bolted, adrenaline coursing through my veins as I stumbled back through the tunnel. The rough stone tore at my coat and scraped my hands as I scrambled up the steps and into the storage room. Daylight filtered through the window, the pale light casting long shadows across the cluttered space.

I crouched low, peering out the window, but the snow-covered driveway was empty. The sound of the vehicle had stopped. My mind raced, torn between relief and terror.

I placed the flashlight back where I'd found it, my movements quick and deliberate. If it was Rachel, I couldn't let her know I'd been down there. I had to erase every trace of what I'd just done, every hint that I knew about the tunnel, the benches, the bodies.

I pressed my back against the wall, my chest heaving as I strained to listen. The lodge was silent, but I couldn't shake the feeling that I was being watched.

Another sound—a faint click—drifted through the air.

I crept toward the door, my pulse hammering in my ears, and peeked out into the hallway. The lodge seemed empty, the only movement the faint flicker of firelight from the lobby.

But I wasn't alone. Somewhere upstairs sat an old woman lost in the past, while somewhere outside was a person who would change the course of my entire future.

If it was the help I'd been calling for, they'd surely save us. If it was Rachel, I would have to save myself. I breathed through my panic and moved toward the door.

Chapter Fifty-Nine

Kate

W hen I opened the front door, the cold air rushed in, and a man in a brown sheriff's jacket stood in front of me. He was younger than I'd expected, clean cut, with sharp eyes that seemed to take in everything at once. His face was flushed from the cold, but his expression was calm and reassuring.

"Ma'am," he said, his voice carrying a quiet authority. "Sheriff Ronson. County plow just finished your road, so I came to check on you."

"I'm Kate, the winter caretaker." I said slowly, his words sinking in. Relief and apprehension warred within me. "I'm so glad you came."

"Yes, ma'am," he replied, glancing past me into the lodge. "Can I come in?"

I stepped aside, and he entered, bringing the crisp air with him. He stood just inside the door, looking around, his eyes lingering on the dark corners.

"You here alone?"

"No," I blurted, my voice trembling. "There's an old woman... Norma, the owner. She's upstairs. But she's confused. She thinks I'm her daughter. And Rachel, the manager—she's supposed to be here, but I can't find her. She's been gone for days."

The sheriff's brows knitted together. "Norma Whitaker? You're saying she's staying here?"

"She's been living at the lodge, but I'm not sure it's by choice," I said, trying to keep my voice steady. "She's in a hidden room upstairs. And there's... there's more." I hesitated, unsure how to explain the tunnel and what I'd found inside.

"Go on," he prompted.

I took a deep breath and told him everything—about finding Norma's hidden room, the tunnel, and the bodies I'd discovered there. The words spilled out in a frantic jumble, but I forced myself to finish, watching his expression shift from concern to something colder. Skepticism.

"You're saying you found human remains?" he asked, his tone careful, measured.

"Yes," I said, gripping the back of a chair to steady myself. "Eight of them. Lined up on benches, like they were on display. Someone decorated them, dressed them up. And I think Rachel —" My voice cracked, and I swallowed hard. "I think my boss Rachel is responsible."

The sheriff frowned slightly, then motioned toward the hallway. "Alright. Let's take a look."

Hope flared in my chest as I led him down the hall to the east wing. My hands trembled as I fumbled with the doorknob, but when I turned it, the door wouldn't budge. Locked.

"No," I whispered, shaking the knob. "It was open a few minutes ago. I swear it was open."

The sheriff stepped forward, testing the door himself before turning to me. "You don't have a key?"

I shook my head in confusion. "It wasn't locked before. I know it wasn't."

His lips pressed into a thin line. "What about this hidden room upstairs?"

I led him up the grand stairway to the maintenance closet where the hidden staircase to Norma's room was. But this door, too, was locked.

"She's up there," I said, desperation creeping into my voice. "She must have locked it from the inside." I knocked on the door, but there was no sound from inside.

The sheriff's expression remained neutral, but I could see the doubt in his eyes. "Without a warrant, I can't force these doors open. I'm sorry."

My chest tightened. "But I'm telling you the truth. You have to believe me—there are bodies down there."

He studied me for a moment, his gaze sharp but careful. "Ma'am, how long has it been since you've slept?"

The question hit me like a slap, and I faltered. "A few days, maybe," I admitted, my voice barely audible. "But I'm fine. I've just been keeping the fires going... and everything else."

His jaw tightened as he scanned the interior of the lodge before sighing heavily. He thought I was losing it.

"Look," he said gently, his tone patient. "I can't act on what you've told me without evidence to show a judge. If you're feeling unsafe, I'd be happy to give you a ride into town. We can figure it out from there."

"I—I'm not packed," I said, my thoughts scrambling. "And I don't want to leave Norma alone."

He checked his watch. "I've got a welfare check to do up near Condon. I can come back in a few hours. Or, if you're ready now, you can ride with me."

I hesitated, torn. The thought of leaving felt wrong, but

staying here—after everything I'd seen—felt like an impossible choice. And yet...

A few more hours would give me the time I needed. Time to pack. Time to check on Norma. Time to go back to the tunnel and take photos of the bodies. Even if I had to break the damn doors down.

The sheriff mistook my hesitation for indecision. "Think it over," he said. "I'll be back. And if you see Rachel, tell her to call me."

Right. The sheriff wants to talk to you about the bodies your delirious caretaker found in the basement...

I nodded numbly as he made his way to his truck. The door closed behind him with a hollow thud, and I was alone again.

My chest felt tight as I leaned against the wall, staring out the window at his truck pulling away. I'd been so close to escaping, to finding some kind of help. But now I was back in the same suffocating silence. And I did this to myself. I made this reckless, foolhardy choice because I needed answers. And I needed proof.

Grabbing my phone, I headed for the storage room, my heart pounding with every step.

Chapter Sixty

Rachel

The steady rattle of the big diesel engine beneath me was reassuring as I sped along the snow-packed highway. The truck Dale had loaned me—a favor he didn't realize he was granting—handled the conditions perfectly. The warmth from the heater poured over my hands, and I couldn't help the smile tugging at my lips.

It was done.

The papers were signed; the bankers were satisfied, and in less than a week, the money would be transferred to my account. *My account.*

I tapped my fingers on the steering wheel, the rhythm of the tires on the road matching my giddy thoughts. Dale's talk of Mexico had been circling around in my head, and now I could see it clearly: a little casita of my very own near the beach, the waves lapping at the shore, and a warm sun on my skin. I deserved that. After everything I'd given to the lodge—three and a half decades of my life, the best years of my life—it was time I reaped the rewards.

Norma would be fine. I'd find her a nice facility in

Missoula, somewhere warm and clean, where she'd have company and care. I'd prepay a few years, maybe even visit now and then to make sure she was happy. She deserved that much. A warm bed, regular meals, and people to dote on her.

The lodge, though?

I glanced at the rearview mirror, as if I could see it in the distance. The thought of it standing there, towering over the frozen lake, made my blood run cold. The investors didn't deserve it. They might have bought it, but they didn't understand what it meant, the years of sweat and sacrifice it demanded.

I'd thought about it for weeks now, the idea simmering in the back of my mind: burning it down. Once the deal was completed and the money was safe in my account, what harm would it do? The land was the real value, not the building. The lodge was just a shell, filled with memories no one cared about anymore. A little gasoline, a match, and it could all go up in flames.

Gone forever, its legacy would stay forever in the family circle, untouched by outsiders.

The thought sent a thrill through me, a sharp contrast to the warming satisfaction that warmed my chest. I'd outsmarted them all. Everyone. Norma would be gone, the lawyers duped, the bankers none the wiser.

And Kate.

My grip on the wheel tightened as I thought of her. My enemy. She'd appealed to me at first with her soft voice, her quiet nature and eager-to-please work ethic, but she'd become a stranger of late, defiant and stronger-willed than I'd ever expected. In short, she'd become a thorn in my side, poking and prying where she didn't belong, threatening everything I'd built.

More shocking than that, she'd somehow taken my place in

Norma's—my mother's—mind, stolen her affection, and now she thought she could control the lodge.

Not for long.

The thought of her lying there, perfect and still, all the newfound defiance drained out of her, brought a strange comfort. I knew how to do it. I'd done it before. The others had taught me that much. A few drops of morphine in her drink— enough to quiet her struggles. Then the silk pillow over her face, soft and final.

I'd dress her up in one of the old party dresses—the ones still tucked away in the closets from when the lodge had catered to families, letting girls play dress-up while their parents drank cocktails by the fire. The dress-up parties that I, the hired help, could never join. Kate had the perfect figure for those dresses. Her hair was beautiful, too, long and glossy. I'd style it myself, adding ribbons and lace, arranging her as though she were about to attend a grand ball.

She would join the others in the tunnel, the eternal dress-up party, a celebration no one else would ever see.

But then my stomach tightened.

What would happen when the lodge sold? When the bankers took possession? They'd find the tunnel. *They'd find the girls.*

I bit my lip, gripping the wheel harder as the snow-covered landscape blurred past. I hadn't thought of that. I'd been so focused on the money, on the escape, that I'd forgotten the details. But it was obvious now. I couldn't leave the tunnel as it was.

I'd have to seal it. Permanently.

Dynamite. The thought came quickly, fully formed. Dale had worked as an excavator for years, doing contracts for the Forest Service. He was always bragging about his skills with explosives, how precise he could be when grading a new road or leveling a rock face. How convenient that Dale was in Mexico, far away and unaware of what I'd need from him now.

The diesel truck beneath me was already proof of Dale's usefulness, even if he didn't know it. And now, he'd unwittingly provide the means to seal the tunnel forever. One more problem solved.

I smiled again; the elation bubbling back to the surface. Everything was falling into place.

Ahead, the highway stretched endlessly; the snow glowing faintly under the dull light of an overcast sky. The lodge was waiting for me, and so was Kate.

It wouldn't be long now.

Chapter Sixty One

Kate

The storage room door loomed in front of me. I had left the flashlight behind and locked it from the inside, and now the door refused to budge. I knelt in front of it, tools scattered at my feet—a flathead screwdriver, a small hammer, and a pair of pliers I'd grabbed from the maintenance closet.

My hands shook as I tried to wedge the screwdriver into the seam between the door and the frame, but the lock held firm. Each attempt sent the metal scraping against the wood with a grating sound that echoed down the hallway.

"Come on," I muttered, gritting my teeth.

I worked at the lock for what felt like hours, sweat prickling at the back of my neck despite the cold. Frustration mounted with every failed attempt. I tossed the tools aside and stood, wiping my hands on my jeans.

If I couldn't finesse my way in, I'd have to force it.

I scanned the hallway and spotted a small, heavy end table near the wall. Its legs were thick and sturdy, designed to survive a lifetime of abuse. I hefted it, the weight reassuring in my hands, and swung it toward the door. The crack of impact reverberated through the hall, but when I pulled back, the door remained stubbornly intact.

"Damn it," I cursed under my breath, swinging again.

The door groaned but held, the old wood defying my every effort. After a few more attempts, I leaned against the table, panting, my arms aching from the effort. This wasn't going to work.

Then it hit me. The tunnel started here. It led to Rachel's cabin.

I hadn't seen Rachel in days, but the idea of stepping into her space, of being surrounded by her presence, made my skin crawl. Still, it was my only option. I grabbed my snowshoes from the back entryway, strapped them on, and stepped out into the freezing morning.

The snow was deep and powdery. I felt myself sink down with every slow step, but the snowshoes kept me moving. Rachel's cabin came into view, its roof piled high with snow. The sight of it sent a shiver through me that had nothing to do with the cold.

The front door was old, its brass knob tarnished by time. The ancient lock was simple. I slipped the screwdriver into the narrow gap between the frame and the door, prying carefully. The wood splintered, and with a firm push, the door creaked open.

Inside, the air was still, carrying a faint scent of mothballs and something earthier. I stepped inside, closing the door softly behind me. The cabin was cold, colder than the lodge, and every creak of the floorboards under my boots made me wince. It felt like Rachel could step around the corner at any moment, her sharp eyes catching me in the act.

The cabin was a mess of clutter—old magazines, piles of papers, mismatched furniture. I searched each room carefully, opening closets and peering under rugs, looking for any sign of the tunnel's entrance. But there was nothing.

My pulse quickened as I moved toward the back of the cabin. A covered porch stretched out behind it, the wooden decking faded and worn. The porch was screened in, an old-fashioned sleeping porch that would have been charming in another era.

I stepped out onto the porch, my breath clouding the frigid air, and that's when I saw it.

A trap door.

The wood blended with the decking, almost invisible if you didn't know to look for it. I crouched, my fingers finding the edge, and heaved it open. A narrow staircase descended into the ground, stale air wafting up, damp and cold.

My hands shook as I gripped the flashlight and stepped down, the creak of each step echoing in the confined space. The walls narrowed as the stairs ended, and I found myself back in the tunnel.

I forced myself to walk forward, each step heavier than the last, until I reached the horrifying tableau I'd discovered earlier. The bodies lay as I'd left them, the fake flowers and bright ribbons clashing grotesquely with the mummified faces and hollow eyes.

My stomach turned, but I forced myself to steady my breathing. I pulled out my phone and snapped photo after photo, the flash casting harsh, sterile light over the grim scene. My hands trembled, and I clenched the phone tighter, telling myself I had to finish.

After capturing every angle, I turned and hurried toward the lodge. My heart pounded as I climbed the stairs back into the storage room, unlocking the door from the inside and slipping out into the hallway.

The lodge was silent, the halls echoing as I made my way to

my room. I dumped the flashlight and tools on the bed, then threw everything I could into my duffel bag—clothes, toiletries, anything I could grab quickly.

The Starlink terminal powered up as I plugged it in. My fingers flew across my phone's screen as I attached the photos and typed out a quick message to Dominic.

You need to see this. Rachel did this. I'm in danger.

I hit send, my chest tightening as I watched the message go through.

"Rachel?"

The sound of Norma's voice made me jump, the mug I'd been holding slipping from my hands and shattering on the floor.

"Rachel, dear," Norma called again, her voice carrying through the hallway.

I froze, the sound of her footsteps growing closer.

Chapter Sixty-Two

Kate

"Rachel, dear, I need you."

I opened the door to find her standing there, clutching a satellite phone with both hands. Her long white hair hung loose around her shoulders, and her eyes were wide with a mix of urgency and fear. Being called Rachel made my stomach ache.

"Rachel," she said again, looking straight at me. "They're trying to steal the lodge. The caretaker—she's trying to sell it to some New York bankers. Our lawyer just called me."

My mind raced, trying to keep up. "What?" I asked, stepping aside to let her in. "What do you mean, steal the lodge? Who called you?"

"Mr. Talbot," she said, holding up the phone as if it were evidence. "He's been our lawyer for decades. He told me the caretaker was trying to sell our family's legacy. We can't let her do this. You're the only one who can help me, Rachel. You're the only one who will rightfully inherit the lodge."

"Norma, let's go upstairs," I said gently. "We can talk about this in your room. I'll call Mr. Talbot, and we'll figure it out."

She nodded, clutching the phone tightly. "Thank you, my sweet girl. I knew I could count on you."

I guided her carefully up the stairs. The lodge was quiet, the shadows stretching long in the dim light. Norma's hidden suite was exactly as I'd left it—warm, with the fire crackling in the hearth and the scent of lavender lingering in the air.

Norma settled onto the bed, her movements slow but calm, and I took the phone from her trembling hands. "Let me speak to Mr. Talbot," I said softly, punching in the number she'd shown me on the screen.

The line rang twice before a deep voice answered. "Greg Talbot here."

"My name is Kate," I said, my voice shaking. "I'm with Norma Whitaker at the Holland Lake Lodge. She said you called her about someone trying to sell the property?"

There was a long pause before he responded. "Ah, yes. You are Norma's nurse, I presume?"

"No, I'm not—" I hesitated. "I'm not a nurse. But, I'm... helping her."

Another pause, then a sigh. "I see. Well, I'm glad someone is there with her. Yes, I received a call this morning from an investment firm in New York. They were trying to verify the transfer of ownership paperwork for the lodge. The documents list Rachel, the caretaker, as the new owner."

My breath caught. "That can't be right. Rachel's not part of the family."

"You're correct," Talbot said, his tone growing heavier. "Rachel isn't a member of the Whitaker family. And, for what it's worth, her name isn't even Rachel. Her real name is Carole Jean Palmer."

My mouth went dry. "What?"

"Carole Jean Palmer," Talbot repeated. "She came to the lodge in the early 1980s as an employee of the lodge, shortly after Norma's husband and children were killed in an accident on the lake. Over time, Carole Jean adopted the name Rachel. That was the name of Norma's youngest daughter."

"You're saying she's been pretending to be Rachel?"

"Not pretending, exactly," Talbot said. "Norma wanted to believe her daughter was alive. It seemed harmless at the time. She began to treat Carole Jean as though she were her daughter, and eventually, Carole Jean leaned into that role. It's a complicated dynamic, but it's clear she manipulated the situation to her advantage."

"She's not just manipulating," I said firmly. "She's dangerous. There are no caregivers here. No nurses. Norma's been alone except for me."

Talbot's tone hardened. "Then it's worse than I feared. If Rachel—Carole Jean—has forged documents or coerced your Norma into signing anything, she's committing fraud. You need to involve the police immediately. And protect Norma from Rachel, or Carole Jean, whatever you want to call her."

I swallowed hard. "She could be back any time. What can I do in the meantime?"

"I'll leave Bozeman right now," he said. "It's a five-hour drive, give or take. Until I arrive, stay with Norma. Don't let her out of your sight. And, Kate—if the caretaker arrives before I do, don't confront her alone. Call the police."

My pulse quickened. "Alright. I'll be waiting."

We hung up, and I turned to Norma. She was smiling at me, her face glowing with gratitude. "You handled that beautifully, my dear," she said, her voice full of warmth. "Your father would be so proud. He always deals with the lawyers."

My chest tightened, the weight of her delusion pressing down on me. "Norma," I said carefully, "I need to move you to another room, just for now. It's for your own good."

She tilted her head, her smile unwavering. "If you think it's best, Rachel, I trust you."

I helped her gather a few things and guided her to a beautiful suite on the far end of the lodge. The room had pale blue walls and heavy mahogany furniture, the kind you couldn't buy outside of antique shops. The bed was covered with a pristine white quilt edged in lace, and a gilded mirror hung above the dresser.

Norma's face lit up as she looked around. "Oh, this was my favorite room growing up," she said, running her fingers along the edge of the bedframe. "I helped your grandmother pick out this furniture. She let me choose the mirror—I thought it looked so elegant."

"It's beautiful," I said, helping her settle onto the bed.

She nodded, a wistful smile playing on her lips. "She would be so proud of you, Rachel. Taking care of the lodge, keeping our family together. It's what she always wanted."

I swallowed the lump in my throat, brushing her hair back. "Get some rest, Norma. I'll be close by."

She closed her eyes, her breathing evening out, and I stepped out into the hallway. My hands were trembling as I closed the door behind me.

Rachel—Carole Jean—was on her way back. Talbot was hours away. And I was running out of time.

Chapter Sixty-Three

Kate

With the satellite phone in my hands, I dialed the sheriff's office. The line rang twice before a calm, detached voice answered.

"Missoula County Sheriff's Office, this is Dispatcher Smith. How can I assist you?"

"This is Kate," I said, my voice raised. "I'm at the Holland Lake Lodge. I need the sheriff back here immediately."

"Ma'am, the sheriff is currently handling a medical emergency from a welfare check near Condon," the dispatcher replied. "He'll be tied up until paramedics arrive. It may be a few hours."

My pulse spiked. "No, you don't understand. I can't wait that long. There's a life-or-death situation here. There are multiple homicides, and there's an elderly woman in need of medical care. And someone—someone dangerous—is on their way here right now. We need help!"

There was a pause, the silence on the other end unbearable.

"I'll pass the message along to our other deputy in your area," the dispatcher said. "But my advice is to lock yourselves in a room and wait for us to arrive. Don't engage with anyone who comes to the lodge."

"That's terrible advice!" I snapped, my voice rising. "She'll come through the tunnel, and if she finds us, it's over. Send someone—anyone! A deputy, a park ranger, Forest Service—just send someone armed!"

"I'll radio the sheriff as soon as possible," he said firmly, though his tone remained calm.

"Radio him now," I said, my voice trembling with rage and fear. Before he could respond, I hung up.

My hands were shaking as I tried calling Dominic. The line went straight to voicemail.

"Damn it, Dominic!" I yelled into the empty room. I tried again, only to hear the same automated response.

I was alone against Rachel. Completely and utterly on my own.

Adrenaline surged through me as I grabbed the flashlight and sprinted toward the storage room. My boots pounded against the floor, each step echoing in the hollow silence of the lodge. I flung open the door and stared down the steep staircase leading to the tunnel.

If Rachel was coming, this would be her way in.

I grabbed the nearest pile of junk and started shoving it down the stairs. Boxes of old sports equipment, broken chairs, and rusted tools clattered and tumbled into the narrow passage. My arms burned as I heaved a long wooden beam, wedging it against the walls to create a crude blockade. I worked furiously, pushing and piling until the staircase was impassable.

It wouldn't stop her, but it would slow her down.

Sweat dripped down my forehead as I raced back into the lodge. I moved to the front door, dragging the heavy sofa and a heavy armchair and shoving them against the frame. I stacked a small side table on top of it, wedging it tightly into place.

The kitchen was next. I scanned the room, my eyes landing on the industrial-style refrigerator. It was old and bulky, and I knew moving it would take every ounce of strength I had left.

"Come on," I muttered, gripping the sides and bracing my feet against the floor.

The fridge groaned as it slid inch by inch, the sound of metal scraping against tile grating in my ears. I clenched my teeth and pushed harder, finally wedging it in front of the kitchen door.

Every muscle in my body screamed in protest, but I didn't stop. I couldn't.

I stepped back, surveying my makeshift barricades. They weren't perfect—far from it—but they were all I had.

I leaned against the counter, my eyes darting to the dark windows. The snow outside glowed faintly under the moonlight, an eerie, silvery landscape that seemed to stretch endlessly.

She was coming.

I grabbed the satellite phone again, debating whether to call the dispatcher back, but my fingers froze over the keypad. What more could I say? They didn't understand how urgent this was.

Instead, I turned and bolted upstairs, heading straight for Norma's new room. I opened the door to find her sitting on the edge of the bed, her hands folded in her lap. She looked up at me and smiled.

"Rachel, dear," she called. "What's all the noise? Is everything alright?"

I forced a smile, trying to steady my voice. "Everything's fine, Norma. I'm just making sure we're safe for the night."

She tilted her head, her expression serene. "You always take such good care of us. Your father would be so proud."

The mention of her father sent another pang through my chest, but I didn't have time to dwell on it.

"Stay here," I said. "I'll be back to check on you soon."

Norma nodded, humming a soft tune to herself as I closed the door.

I leaned against the wall, my pulse racing. The lodge was as secure as I could make it, but the sinking feeling in my gut told me it wouldn't be enough.

Chapter Sixty-Four

Kate

The thought hit me like a bolt of lightning: Rachel's rifle.

The same one she'd used to shoot at the grizzly bear. The same one she'd aimed—if I was being honest with myself—at Decker and me. I couldn't believe I hadn't thought of it sooner. Rachel was dangerous, and if she came back armed, I'd have no way to defend myself or Norma.

I had to find it.

I tore through Rachel's office. The desk drawers were empty except for a few scattered papers and an old stapler. Her filing cabinet yielded even less—just dusty folders filled with maintenance records and receipts.

I moved to the kitchen next, pulling open cabinets and peering behind stacks of dishes and jars. Nothing. The closets were just as fruitless, filled with old coats and boots, but no sign of a weapon. My frustration mounted with each failed search, my pulse quickening as the sense of urgency grew.

Then it dawned on me: Rachel's cabin.

My snowshoes were still there from my last trip, but there

were more in the sporting goods closet. I bolted for it, wrenching the door open and grabbing the pair Decker had worn when he was here. The leather bindings were still adjusted to his size, but they'd do.

I pulled them on, fastening the straps with shaking hands, and headed to the broken window I'd used a few nights ago. The plywood I'd nailed in place was still there, but I pried it off, tossing it aside. Cold air rushed in as I slipped through.

The trek to Rachel's cabin was quicker this time, my body fueled by a mix of fear and determination. I yanked off the snowshoes, propping them against the porch, and stepped inside.

I started in the living room, scanning the walls and corners, checking behind furniture. No luck. The kitchen and bathroom yielded nothing but more dust and clutter.

Finally, I stepped into the bedroom. My eyes darted to the bed, and my breath caught. There, beneath the bed, under a faded quilt, was a long, slender shape.

I dropped to my knees and lifted the quilt. Underneath was the hunting rifle, its dark wood stock polished smooth with age. Beside it was a small box of ammunition, the brass shells.

I slid the rifle out carefully, noting the weight of it. It was heavier than the little .22 my dad had taught me to shoot during summer vacations when I was a teenager, but the bolt action was familiar.

The leather strap was worn but sturdy. I slung it over my shoulder and pocketed the box of .300 H&H Magnum shells. The rifle was mine now.

The trek back to the lodge felt longer, the weight of the rifle pressing against my back. My thoughts focused as I trudged through the snow. The memories of those summers with my dad—plinking tin cans off a fence post, his patient instructions in my ear—mixed with the grim reality of what I might have to do now.

At the lodge steps, I paused and removed my snowshoes, propping them by the door. The bitter wind nipped at my cheeks as I pulled the rifle from my back. The scope looked brand new, a sharp contrast to the antique appearance of the rifle itself.

I pulled back the bolt, exposing the breach, and slid one of the long brass shells into place. The clack of the bolt locking forward and down felt final, a sharp reminder of what I was holding. The safety latch was on the right side, just next to the bolt—a simple, old-fashioned mechanism.

I slung the rifle over my shoulder and stepped inside the lodge through the broken window, glass still scattered on the floor. The cold air followed me in, swirling around the empty hallway.

I worked quickly to hammer the plywood back over the window with nails I'd grabbed from the storage cabinet.

As I finished, I stepped back and eyed the patchwork repair. It wouldn't stop Rachel if she broke another window, but it was better than nothing.

I leaned against the wall, resting for a moment. When this was over, and if I made it through, I would sleep for a solid week.

Chapter Sixty-Five

Rachel

The truck crawled over the icy road as the wipers scraped away the light flurries blowing across the windshield. I hadn't passed another vehicle for an hour. Everyone else had sense enough to be inside. I pulled onto Old Barn Road and into Dale's driveway.

The shed was where I remembered it—set back from the house, the roof sagging under the weight of snow. As I pulled up, the truck's headlights illuminated the rough wooden structure.

For a moment, I sat in the cab, letting the engine idle. My breath fogged the inside of the windshield, and my skin prickled with a mix of dread and exhilaration. I was so close now. So close to solving everything.

Pulling the crowbar from the truck bed, I made my way to the shed, where the padlock gleamed in the dim light. I wedged it under the shackle and gave a hard tug. The door snapped open with a satisfying clink.

Inside, my flashlight danced over shelves stacked with tools, boxes, and hunting gear. And there, on the far shelf, was what I'd come for: a small wooden crate marked EXPLOSIVES.

"Dale, you predictable bastard," I muttered, shaking my head.

He'd always bragged about his dynamite stash, joking about his work for the Forest Service and how he'd used a few sticks to blow up a stubborn beaver dam. He'd even invited me on one of his harebrained fishing trips, saying we could throw a stick in the lake and have trout for dinner without lifting a rod. The thought of a date with that fat idiot had turned my stomach.

I opened the crate slowly, my heart pounding as I peeled back the paper to reveal the dynamite sticks nestled inside. They looked old. The waxy red paper darkened in places where the nitroglycerin had begun to seep. Beside the dynamite were spools of fuse wire and a small box of blasting caps.

I swallowed hard, my fingers trembling as I lifted the crate and carried it to the truck. My steps were slow, deliberate, every jolt a potential disaster. Old dynamite was volatile.

I set the crate gently in the truck bed, packing it between a stack of old blankets to keep it from shifting. I closed the tailgate and climbed back into the cab.

The engine roared to life, and I eased the truck onto the road, driving slowly. The bumps and ruts in the snow-packed road felt amplified, each one jostling the truck and sending a fresh wave of anxiety through me. I gritted my teeth, my hands clamped around the wheel like a vise.

The lodge wasn't far now.

As I drove, my mind churned with thoughts of Kate. She'd ruined everything. She thought she was so clever, poking her nose where it didn't belong, stealing Norma's attention, her affection. She was trying to take what was mine, what I'd worked for.

The lodge was my life. My past and the means to my future. My entire life's purpose.

I had kept it standing, maintained its legacy, and protected it through the years when no one else cared. *I* was the one who stayed, the one who sacrificed everything to keep the lights on and the fires burning. It was mine.

And Kate thought she could take it all away.

My hands tightened on the wheel, anger bubbling under the surface. I'd fix this. Once and for all.

Norma would be fine. I had loved her with devotion once, sure, and still loved her to a degree. But she'd be comfortable and well cared-for in one of those memory care places with big windows and warm blankets. I'd pay for it upfront, make sure she had everything she needed. She didn't need the lodge—not anymore.

The bankers? They didn't deserve it. They wouldn't understand its history, its soul. The lodge was more than a building. It was part of me, part of who I was.

And if I couldn't have it...

The thought of flames rising against the snowy backdrop sent a dark thrill through me. The land would still be there, pristine and untouched, long after the lodge was gone. The bankers could deal with the ashes.

The truck jolted over a rut, and my breath caught as I glanced in the rearview mirror. The crate was still there, nestled in its makeshift cradle, but the sight of it sent another surge of adrenaline through me.

Be careful. One wrong move, and it could all end here.

The lodge appeared in the distance, its dark silhouette visible against the snow-covered trees. I slowed the truck to a crawl, my mind racing with the steps ahead.

First the dynamite. Then Kate.

It wouldn't take much. A few sticks at the front door, a quick light of the fuse, and the problem would solve itself.

As the lodge loomed closer, a bitter smile curled my lips.

Kate thought she could win.

But she'd underestimated me.

Chapter Sixty-Six

Kate

The sun was sinking lower, casting long shadows across the snow-covered grounds of the lodge. My fingers trembled as I punched the sheriff's number into the satellite phone yet again, the chill of the room doing nothing to steady my nerves.

The line clicked, and the same calm voice answered. "Missoula County Sheriff's Office, Dispatcher Smith speaking."

"It's Kate again," I said, my voice shaking. "I called earlier about the situation at Holland Lake Lodge. I need someone here now."

The dispatcher hesitated before responding. "Ma'am, I understand you're upset, but the sheriff is still tied up with a medical emergency near Condon. He's coordinating with EMS, and it may be a while before he's available."

My chest tightened. "What do you mean, a while? I've told you this is a life-or-death situation! There's a murderer on the way. There are bodies in the tunnel beneath the lodge, and an elderly woman here needs medical attention!"

The line went quiet for a moment, then the dispatcher sighed. "Ma'am, I'm just relaying what I've been told. The sheriff is aware of the situation."

"Then why isn't anyone here?" I demanded, my voice rising.

There was another pause before the dispatcher said, almost reluctantly, "Ma'am, I think you should know that we've also received a call from the lodge's caretaker, Rachel. She's expressed concerns about your behavior. She claimed you've stolen money—around $3,000—and that you might be a danger to yourself or others."

The words hit me like a slap, and for a moment, I couldn't breathe. "What?"

"Rachel said you've been acting erratically and might need mental health support. The sheriff is taking the steps to ensure everyone's safety."

My stomach boiled in rage and disbelief. "You think I'm the crazy one? Rachel is the one who's dangerous! She's murdered young women and hidden their bodies in the tunnel beneath this lodge! I have pictures on my phone—I'll send them to you right now!"

The dispatcher's tone softened, but it was patronizing. "Ma'am, I understand this is upsetting. The sheriff is gathering resources to properly handle the situation and ensure everyone is treated fairly."

"Fairly?" I snapped. "You think this is about fairness? Rachel is trying to kill me! She's been stealing this lodge out from under Norma, who's too sick to even realize what's happening!"

"Ma'am—"

"I've spoken to the family's lawyer," I pressed, cutting him off. "He's on his way from Bozeman right now. If you don't believe me, call him. His name is Mr. Talbot. He'll confirm everything I've said."

The dispatcher hesitated again, his calm demeanor faltering. "Alright. I'll pass along the information to the sheriff. But in the meantime, my advice remains the same: stay inside, lock the doors, and wait for help."

I slammed the phone down, anger and frustration boiling over.

Dominic. He'd believe me.

I dialed his number, but it went straight to voicemail, just like before.

"Dominic, please call me back," I said, my voice cracking. "I need you. It's urgent."

I hung up and stared at the phone, my breath coming in shallow gasps. The silence of the lodge pressed in around me, suffocating.

Decker.

My fingers fumbled as I dialed his number. The phone rang once, then twice, before his familiar voice answered.

"Kate?" he said, sounding genuinely happy. "I'm glad you called. I was just thinking about you."

Tears pricked my eyes at the sound of his voice. "Decker, thank God. Where are you?"

"Just outside Missoula," he said. "I'll be at the lodge in about two hours. Why? What's going on?"

"It's Rachel," I said, the words tumbling out. "She's been lying to everyone, manipulating Norma, and there are bodies— Decker, there are bodies in the tunnel beneath the lodge. She's killed people. She's trying to kill me!"

There was a long pause on the other end of the line. "Kate... are you sure? I mean, this sounds..."

"It's real!" I shouted, anger flaring at the doubt in his voice. "I have photos. I've seen them with my own eyes!"

"I'm on my way," Decker said firmly. "Just hang tight, okay? Two hours. I'll be there."

"Ok." I hung up, the tears still streaming down my face. The phone felt heavy in my hand as I set it down on the counter.

Chapter Sixty-Seven

Kate

The sound of tires on snow jolted me from my thoughts. My breath hitched as I peered through the window, the rifle resting across my lap. The truck I'd seen Rachel drive before rolled slowly into the lot, its headlights cutting through the fading light of the day.

She was back.

The truck stopped a few yards from the lodge, and Rachel stepped out. Her heavy boots crunched on the snow as she surveyed the building. She was bundled in her usual coat, her face shadowed by the brim of her hat. Her movements were deliberate, her head turning toward the front door, then toward the kitchen entrance.

I tightened my grip on the rifle, my heart pounding in my chest.

Rachel approached the front door first, her steps heavy and purposeful. I stood and moved to the door, positioning myself behind it, rifle ready. When the handle rattled, I flinched but held my ground.

"Kate," Rachel's voice called out, calm and even. "Let me in. It's freezing out here."

I swallowed hard, steadying my voice. "The door's locked, Rachel. You're not coming in."

There was a pause, then a dry laugh. "Kate, this is ridiculous. Open the door. We need to talk."

I raised my voice, forcing confidence I didn't feel. "I know what you've done, Rachel. I know about the bodies in the tunnel. I know about Norma and the fraud. It's over."

The silence that followed was deafening. Then, her tone changed—sharp and savage. "You don't know anything, Kate. You've been locked in here with that lunatic, and she's filled your head with lies."

"She didn't tell me anything," I shot back. "I found the bodies myself. I have pictures. You're the one who's been lying —to everyone. You've been lying for years."

Her boots squeaked on the snow again as she shifted, her voice dropping into something softer, almost pleading. "Kate, listen to me. You don't understand what's really going on here. Norma is dangerous. She's always been dangerous. Those girls... she did that. Not me."

I hesitated, her words hitting like a gut punch.

"She's kept me here all these years," Rachel continued, her tone turning desperate. "I came here to start over, just like you. I was young, lost, looking for a second chance. But Norma wouldn't let me leave. She's controlling, obsessive. Everything had to be perfect—perfect dinners, perfect guests, perfect caretakers. When those girls didn't measure up, she took care of them."

"That's not true," I said, though my voice wavered slightly.

"It is," Rachel insisted. "You've seen her, haven't you? How she talks about her dead husband and her kids, like they're just going to walk through the door any minute. She's delusional, Kate. Dangerous."

I tightened my grip on the rifle, willing my voice to stay steady. "You're lying. Norma might be sick, but she's not a killer. You are. You've been using her for decades, keeping her isolated, stealing the lodge right out from under her."

Rachel let out a bitter laugh. "And you believe her? You've been here for what—three months? You think you know everything? You're nothing but an outsider, just like all the others. You have no idea what this place does to people."

I braced myself, refusing to let her words sink in.

"I'm the victim here, Kate," Rachel continued, her voice softening again. "Norma has controlled me for thirty years. I've been trapped, just like you. Don't you see? We're the same. We've both had hard lives. We've both had to fight to survive. All I wanted was a second chance, and she took that from me."

Her words struck a chord, a flicker of doubt creeping in. But then I thought of the tunnel, the preserved bodies, their hair braided and adorned with ribbons. I thought of the fake flowers and the silk fabric, the grotesque parody of a princess dress-up party, or whatever it was supposed to be.

"No," I said firmly. "We're not the same. I'm not a murderer."

Rachel's voice hardened. "You don't know what she's capable of. If you're locked in there with her, you're the one in danger, Kate. You locked yourself in with the killer."

I swallowed, her words twisting in my mind.

Rachel took a step closer, her shadow darkening the window. "Let me in, Kate. I can help you. We can end this together."

"No," I said, my voice cold and steady. "Stay away from the lodge. I'm armed, Rachel. If you try to come inside, I'll stop you."

There was a long pause, and then Rachel sighed, the sound heavy with frustration.

"Fine," she said, her voice icy. "Stay with her, then. See how that works out for you."

I watched as she turned and stomped back to her truck. She paused for a moment, her head tilted as though she were thinking, then climbed into the cab and slammed the door.

The engine roared to life, and the truck backed away, its headlights swinging across the snow.

My heart pounded as I lowered the rifle, my hands trembling. I didn't trust for a second that she was leaving for good.

Rachel wasn't done yet.

Chapter Sixty-Eight

Rachel

The truck's engine coughed and rattled to silence as I pulled up to my cabin, the headlights casting long shadows over the snow-draped structure. My hands were trembling, not from the cold, but from the seething rage boiling inside me. *She knew.*

That conniving little brat knew everything.

I slammed the truck door shut, the sound sharp and jarring in the still night. The snow crunched beneath my boots as I marched toward the cabin, each step fueled by fury. She had dared to stand there with *my* rifle in hand, accusing me of things she couldn't possibly understand.

Inside the cabin, the air was heavy with the familiar smell of wood smoke and aged fabric. I yanked open a drawer in the small dresser near the bed, my fingers closing around the cold metal of the .22 pistol I kept there.

I slid the revolver open. Six rounds. It would be enough.

I only needed one.

I tucked the pistol into the waistband of my jeans, the weight of it pressing against my hip as I turned to grab the flashlight. My thoughts raced, tumbling over themselves in a chaotic loop.

Kate.

She had ruined everything. She thought she was clever, digging where she didn't belong, but she didn't realize what she was dealing with. She was just like the others, too full of herself to see what this place demanded.

And Mother?

My jaw tightened. She had always been my anchor, my reason for staying, for enduring everything. But now, even she was slipping away, poisoned by Kate's lies. If I was going to save myself, I had to act quickly.

I headed to the trapdoor on the back porch, the one leading to the tunnel. The old boards creaked as I pulled it open, revealing the dark staircase descending into the earth. The cold air rising from the tunnel was damp and musty, wrapping around me like a shroud as I climbed down.

The flashlight beam cut through the darkness, illuminating the familiar walls of the tunnel. The rough granite glistened faintly, the same way it had for decades. I moved quickly; the pistol bumping against my side with each step.

The beautiful decorations came into view, and I slowed, the tension in my chest easing just slightly. The silk flowers, ribbons, and lace draped lovingly over the benches. And there they were, my girls, my sisters.

I stopped in the center of the room, my heart aching as I gazed at them. "Oh, my darlings," I whispered, my voice thick with emotion.

I stepped closer to the nearest bench, running my fingers gently over the delicate ribbons in her hair. "You've always been so beautiful, so perfect," I murmured. "They never understood us, did they? But we knew. We knew how to make this place special."

My gaze swept over them, their still, silent forms a comfort in the chaos. "I'm going to miss you," I said softly. "Our dress-up parties, our stories... everything. But things are changing now. I have to fix this. I have to protect us."

The words hung in the air as I turned away, the sharp edge of determination hardening my resolve.

I moved deeper into the tunnel, the flashlight beam bouncing off the walls. When I reached the staircase leading up to the lodge, I stopped cold.

The way up was completely blocked.

Boxes, crates, pieces of wood, even beams and bricks were piled haphazardly against the stairs, creating an impenetrable barrier. My hands tightened into fists as frustration boiled over.

"That little witch," I hissed.

I shoved at the nearest crate, grunting as it barely shifted. The adrenaline coursing through me made me reckless, and I began pulling and flinging objects out of the way. A box of old sporting goods tumbled into the tunnel, scattering tennis rackets and ski poles across the floor.

I grabbed a heavy beam and heaved it aside, my muscles straining with the effort. Sweat dripped down my back, my breath coming in harsh gasps as I worked.

The piles seemed endless. Every time I moved one object, another was there to take its place.

"She thinks she can stop me," I muttered through clenched teeth. "She thinks she's won. But she doesn't know who she's dealing with."

The flashlight beam wavered as my hands began to shake. My strength was fading, the adrenaline that had carried me this far beginning to wane. I leaned against the wall, panting, my vision swimming.

"No," I growled, forcing myself to stand. "I won't let her win."

I returned to the pile, yanking and pulling with renewed ferocity. Pieces of wood splintered under my grip, and boxes crashed to the floor with dull thuds.

But it wasn't enough. The barricade was too much, and my body was failing me.

I stepped back, breathing hard, and stared at the mess in front of me.

I needed another plan.

Turning on my heel, I marched back down the tunnel, my mind spinning. I'd start a fire in the wood stove, rest for a few minutes, and then figure out my next move.

I returned to my cabin. I knelt and lit the kindling, watching as the flames caught and began to grow. The warmth seeped into my fingers, soothing my raw, aching hands.

I stared at the iron resting on top of the stove, its surface already beginning to heat. My eyes drifted to the pistol at my side, and my thoughts turned dark.

Kate thought she was safe. But she didn't realize how far I was willing to go to finish what I'd started.

The fire crackled softly, the only sound in the quiet tunnel.

The game wasn't over yet.

Chapter Sixty-Nine

Kate

Norma's temporary room was warm, the fire casting flickering shadows across the walls. She was sitting on the edge of her bed, her long white hair cascading over her shoulders, a faraway look in her eyes. Her serene expression faltered the moment I stepped inside with the rifle slung over my back.

She gasped, clutching at her chest. "Rachel! What are you doing with that gun?"

"It's not what you think, Norma," I said quickly, trying to keep my voice calm. "It's just for protection."

Her gaze hardened, a mix of worry and disappointment clouding her features. "That's your father's hunting rifle. We have plenty of deer and elk in the freezer. You don't need to hunt, my dear. Put that awful thing away."

I hesitated, feeling a pang of guilt despite the dire situation. "Norma, I need to ask you something."

She tilted her head, her expression softening. "What is it, sweetheart?"

"Do you know about the girls in the tunnel?" I asked, my voice quiet but firm. "The dead girls?"

Norma's face fell, and she looked away, her hands wringing in her lap. For a long moment, she didn't answer, the silence stretching between us.

"Yes," she said, her voice barely above a whisper.

I took a step closer, my pulse quickening. "How did they get there, Norma?"

She looked up at me, her eyes glistening with unshed tears. "The caretaker..." she began, her voice trembling. "She has very high standards. I'm afraid I... I ingrained those in her. And none of the girls could ever live up to them."

I stared at her, my breath catching in my throat. "You mean Rachel?"

Norma shook her head once before pausing in confusion. "The caretaker, yes. She's always been so... particular. Everything had to be perfect—the cleaning, the cooking, the way they behaved. When the girls didn't meet her standards..." Her voice broke, and she looked down at her hands.

"She threatened me," Norma continued after a moment. "She said she'd burn the lodge down if I ever told anyone. That she'd make sure I lost everything."

My mind reeled as I processed her words. "When the sheriff was here," I said, "you locked the door to the storage room. Why?"

Norma's voice was barely audible. "I was afraid. Afraid of what would happen if they found out. Afraid of what she'd do to me if she thought I'd betrayed her."

She looked up at me, her eyes pleading. "I didn't know what else to do, Rachel. I thought your father would handle it when he got back from his business trip. But he never... he never came back."

Her words hit me like a punch to the gut. This woman, so frail and lost in her own mind, wasn't the killer. She was just another victim, trapped by Rachel's manipulation and threats.

I forced myself to take a deep breath, steadying the whirlwind of emotions threatening to overwhelm me. "Norma, listen to me," I said gently. "Just rest here, okay? I'll take care of everything."

She nodded, her face weary but trusting. "You've always been such a good girl," she murmured. "Just like your father."

I turned and left the room, closing the door behind me. My heart pounded as I walked back toward the lobby. The sound of muffled crashes echoed from below—the tunnel. Rachel was down there, throwing things, trying to claw her way through the barricade I'd built.

I reached the storage room at the end of the hallway and positioned myself just outside the door. The rifle felt heavy in my hands as I lined up the scope with the entrance, my pulse racing.

Rachel would have to come through here, eventually. There was no other way up.

I dug into my pocket and pulled out three more brass shells, slipping them into the small pocket on the stock of the rifle. My hands trembled as I worked, the adrenaline coursing through me making every movement feel jagged and unsteady.

I lowered myself into a chair, angling another one in front of me as a makeshift rest for the rifle. My hands were still shaking as I looked through the scope, the crosshairs swimming in my vision.

"Steady," I whispered to myself, adjusting the rifle against the chair. The scope was bright and clear, the hallway sharp in its view.

I took a deep breath and exhaled, trying to steady my

nerves. The sound of Rachel's furious efforts in the tunnel continued, punctuated by the occasional thud of something heavy being flung aside.

I tightened my grip on the rifle, bracing myself for what was coming.

Rachel would emerge. And I would be ready.

Chapter Seventy

Rachel

The tunnel air was thick, damp, and suffocating as I stood again at the base of the staircase, staring at the mess blocking my way. My breath came in gasps, my arms and back screaming in protest with every movement. The pile of crates, wooden beams, and broken furniture that Kate had hurled down into the tunnel still seemed insurmountable.

I leaned against the cold granite wall, my legs trembling beneath me. I'd been at it for hours—or so it felt—yanking at the debris, throwing what I could down the passageway, and trying to claw my way to the top. But for every piece I moved, it felt like ten more were waiting behind it.

"Damn you, Kate," I hissed, my voice echoing back at me from the stone walls.

The flashlight beam flickered as I slumped to the floor, its weak light making the shadows in the tunnel dance and twist. My chest heaved as I tried to catch my breath, the anger bubbling inside me warring with the exhaustion that had taken over my body.

I still couldn't get through. Not this way.

I leaned back against the wall, letting my head rest on the cold stone. My throat was dry, and my limbs ached in ways I hadn't felt in years.

I was tired. Not just physically, but deep in my soul.

I reached for the canteen I'd stashed nearby, unscrewing the lid with shaking hands and taking a long drink. The water was lukewarm, but it soothed the burning in my throat.

How many nights had I spent her, dreaming of a future where everything was finally mine? How many years had I given to this place, to Norma, to the lodge?

It was supposed to have been my sanctuary. My reward.

Instead, it had become my prison.

I closed my eyes, the weight of my years at the lodge pressing down on me. This was supposed to be my legacy, the thing that proved I'd mattered. And now, it was all slipping away.

I would not let it end like this.

I pushed myself to my feet and made my way back through the tunnel to the trapdoor. The cold hit me like a slap as I climbed out, the night air biting at my skin.

The truck's dark shape was barely visible against the snowy backdrop. I opened the tailgate and reached for the crate of dynamite, my fingers brushing against the waxy paper. I selected a stick and grabbed a length of fuse wire. I worked methodically, attaching the fuse with hands steadier than I expected. My mind was calm now, focused on the task ahead.

The lodge loomed in the distance, its dark silhouette a stark reminder of everything I'd lost—and everything I still had to protect.

I trudged through the snow, the dynamite cradled in my hands like a sacred offering. Reaching the front porch, I set the stick down carefully, positioning it just in front of the main door. The fuse dangled in the faint moonlight, its frayed end almost mocking in its simplicity.

I struck a match, holding it to the fuse until it caught. The flame sizzled and danced, racing along the wire with a hiss.

I stepped back, my breath visible in the frigid air, and watched as the fuse burned closer and closer to the stick.

This was it.

I turned and made my way back to the truck, my boots crunching on the snow. As I climbed into the cab, I glanced at the lodge one last time, the glow of the burning fuse casting faint shadows across the porch.

The game was almost over.

Chapter Seventy One

Kate

The lobby was quiet. I sat on the chair, the rifle resting on the back of another in front of me, my eyes locked on the storage room door. My pulse was steady, but my chest felt tight, every second of silence stretching the tension further.

The sound from the tunnel had stopped. Rachel wasn't trying to clear the barricade anymore.

The fire in the hearth crackled, the sound doing little to calm my nerves. I shifted in the chair, my fingers gripping the rifle stock as I glanced at the window. Snow swirled outside, the dim light of the setting sun casting long shadows across the grounds.

Movement caught my eye.

Rachel emerged from the darkness, her figure outlined by the faint glow of moonlight reflecting off the snow. My breath hitched as I watched her approach the lodge. She was carrying something—a cylindrical object cradled in her hands—but I couldn't make out what it was.

My heart pounded as I watched her step onto the front

porch. She knelt near the door, setting the object down with deliberate care. My stomach twisted, unease prickling at the back of my neck. What was she doing?

I leaned forward, squinting to get a better look, but the shadows obscured her actions. She stood, brushing snow from her hands, and glanced toward the parking lot. Then, without warning, she turned and ran, her boots crunching through the snow as she darted behind the diesel truck.

"What the hell is she doing?" I whispered under my breath.

I tightened my grip on the rifle, my instincts screaming that something was wrong. My mind raced, trying to piece together what I'd just seen.

And then it happened.

The explosion ripped through the air, absolutely deafening. The shockwave hit me like a battering ram, throwing me backward out of the chair. I crashed to the floor, the rifle skidding across the room and out of reach.

The sound was everywhere, drowning out my thoughts, my heartbeat, even the wind outside. Splintered wood and shattered glass flew through the air, the acrid smell of smoke filling my nostrils.

For a moment, everything went dark.

When I opened my eyes, the world spun. The cold hit me first, the icy wind slicing through the room. I blinked, trying to focus, and realized the front of the lodge was gone.

The entire front wall of the entrance to the lodge had been blown apart, leaving jagged logs jutting out at awkward angles. Snow swirled inside, mingling with the thick haze of smoke and dust.

I pushed myself onto my elbows, my ears ringing as I tried to make sense of the chaos. My gaze darted around the room, searching for the rifle, but before I could move, a shadow loomed over me.

Rachel.

She stood over me, her face streaked with soot, her eyes wild with triumph. In her hand was a small pistol, the barrel pointed directly at me.

"Get up," she said sharply, her voice cutting through the ringing in my ears. She picked up the rifle from the floor and slung it over her shoulder.

My limbs felt heavy, my head spinning, but I forced myself to comply. She grabbed my arm, hauling me to my feet. The cold barrel of the pistol pressed into my side as she pushed me down the hallway.

"You just couldn't leave it alone, could you?" she hissed, her voice low and venomous. "Had to go digging where you didn't belong. Now take me to my Mother. I know you've hidden her from me."

I didn't answer, my mind scrambling for a way out. My thoughts were muddled, the shock of the explosion still clouding my senses. Like I was sleepwalking, I led Rachel to the suite where I had put Norma.

When we reached the room, Rachel shoved the door open and pushed me inside.

Norma was sitting on her bed, her hands folded in her lap. Her wide eyes darted between me and Rachel, confusion and fear etched into her face.

"There was a frightening sound. Are they working on the tunnel again?" Norma asked.

"Mother," Rachel said, her voice softening as she turned to Norma. "It's me. I'm here to take care of everything."

Norma's expression shifted, her fear giving way to something colder. "You are not my daughter," she said firmly.

Rachel froze, the words hitting her like a slap.

Norma straightened, her frail frame radiating unexpected strength. She pointed at me. "This young woman is my daughter. She will inherit this lodge. You are nothing but a liar and a thief."

Rachel's hand trembled, the pistol wavering as her face contorted with disbelief. "No... no, that's not true," she stammered. "You've always loved me. I've always taken care of you."

"The lawyer called," Norma said, her voice cutting like a knife. "He knows what you've done. You've tried to steal this lodge, but it will never belong to you."

Rachel's face paled, her composure slipping. "The lawyer..." she whispered, her voice trailing off as the weight of Norma's words sank in.

I seized the moment.

With all the strength I could muster, I lunged at Rachel, tackling her to the ground. The pistol clattered across the floor, sliding out of reach as we hit the hardwood with a heavy thud.

Rachel screamed, her nails digging into my arms as she thrashed beneath me, but I held on, my desperation overpowering her rage.

"Norma, run!" I shouted, my voice hoarse.

But Norma didn't move. She sat frozen on the bed, her wide eyes fixed on us as the struggle continued.

Chapter Seventy-Two

Kate

Rachel's face twisted with rage. "She's lying! You're not her daughter, Kate! You don't belong here!"

Norma's voice rose, trembling but defiant. "You are not my daughter, Rachel! You never were!"

Rachel's focus wavered as her eyes flicked to Norma. It was all the opening I needed.

I bolted.

Throwing open the door, I darted into the hallway, the sound of Rachel's furious scream echoing behind me.

"Get back here!" she shrieked, her footsteps pounding after me.

The dimly lit hallways of the lodge stretched before me like a labyrinth, the shadows twisting and dancing as I ran. My boots skidded on the polished floor as I rounded a corner, the adrenaline surging through me, making every sense sharper.

Behind me, Rachel's voice carried through the halls, sharp and venomous. "You can't outrun me, Kate! This lodge is mine!"

A deafening crack split the air as she fired, the bullet

striking the wooden paneling just inches from my head. Splinters flew, and I ducked, my breath coming in ragged gasps.

I burst into the stairwell, my hands gripping the railing as I stumbled down the steps two at a time. Rachel's footsteps followed, each one louder than the last, her fury propelling her forward.

"Stop running!" she shouted, her voice reverberating off the walls.

Another shot rang out, the sound deafening in the enclosed space. The bullet ricocheted off the metal railing, and I felt the sting of a sharp fragment grazing my arm.

Pain flared, but I didn't stop. I hit the ground floor and sprinted toward the front of the lodge, the gaping hole left by the explosion looming ahead. The frosty night air rushed in, carrying with it the faint scent of smoke and splintered wood.

"Kate!" Rachel's voice was closer now, each syllable dripping with venom.

I leapt over a fallen beam, my boots crunching on shards of glass as I bolted out into the snow. The icy wind hit me like a slap, but I barely felt it. My only thought was to keep moving.

My frantic pace was slowed by the deep snow, but then again, so was Rachel's.

The forest loomed ahead, dark and dense, and I plunged into it without hesitation. The branches clawed at my arms and face, but I pressed on.

Behind me, Rachel's voice carried through the trees, sharp and taunting. "You can't hide, Kate! I know these woods better than you do!"

Her footsteps crunched in the snow, faster and more determined than I'd expected. My lungs burned as I pushed myself harder, weaving through the trees in a desperate attempt to lose her.

The forest was alive with sound—the snap of branches, the thud of boots on snow, the frantic rhythm of my own heartbeat.

A sharp *crack* split the air, and a tree just ahead of me splintered as the bullet struck. I ducked, my hands brushing the snow as I scrambled behind a thick pine trunk.

"You can't run forever!" Rachel shouted, her voice closer than I'd thought.

I didn't respond. My breath was loud in my ears, my chest heaving as I tried to catch it. I peeked around the tree, my heart lurching as I saw Rachel emerging from the shadows.

Her face was a mask of fury, her hair wild, her pistol held steady. Her gaze swept the trees, searching for movement.

"I've worked too hard for this," she called, her voice almost conversational despite the menace beneath it. "I'm not letting you ruin everything!"

She fired again, the sharp crack echoing through the forest. Snow exploded from the ground near my feet, and I darted to another tree, my movements frantic and uneven.

I had no plan, no direction. The woods seemed endless, the darkness pressing in on all sides. My legs ached, my breath coming in shallow gasps as I stumbled forward.

Rachel's voice followed me, a chilling reminder that she was still there, still hunting me.

And then I saw it—the faint shimmer of the lake through the trees. The open expanse of ice stretched out like a silver mirror, reflecting the pale light of the moon.

I skidded to a stop at the edge, my boots crunching on the icy crust of snow. My breath fogged in the freezing air as I turned, searching the shadows for any sign of her.

The sound of her boots crunching on snow came first, deliberate and unhurried. Rachel stepped into view, her pistol raised, her eyes gleaming with triumph.

"No more running, Kate," she said, her voice low and steady.

The lake groaned faintly beneath the weight of the snow, the sound low and ominous. My heart pounded as I stared at her, the cold seeping into my bones.

Chapter Seventy-Three

Rachel

My pulse thundered in my ears, my hands trembling as I tightened my grip on the deer rifle. Kate had ruined everything—my plans, my life, my legacy. She'd fought back, she'd exposed the truth, and now she thought she could escape.

Kate had to die.

I slowed, the forest opening into a faint clearing. Kate had stopped and was staring at me. *This was too easy.* I and raised the rifle. My breath came in short bursts, the adrenaline coursing through me making it hard to steady myself. Kate turned and ran into the clearing. I pressed the stock into my shoulder, lining up the scope with her retreating form.

She was faster than a wild hare, darting left and right with a kind of desperate energy I both admired and despised. But desperation couldn't save her.

I took a deep breath, letting it out slowly to calm my shaking hands. The crosshairs in the scope hovered over her, bouncing as I tried to match her erratic movements. Another breath, slow and deliberate.

"Steady," I whispered to myself.

I squeezed the trigger.

The rifle roared, the recoil slamming into my shoulder. Snow exploded near Kate's feet, but she didn't stop. She bolted back toward the lodge, her form weaving unpredictably through the trees.

I cursed under my breath, shifting my aim and firing again. The second shot splintered a tree trunk just behind her.

"Stop running!" I shouted, my voice tearing through the stillness.

Kate didn't look back.

I started after her, my boots crunching on the snow. The rifle felt heavier with every step, the strain of the chase beginning to sap my strength.

A sound caught my ear, and I entered the clearing—faint and distant. I froze, tilting my head to listen.

"Rachel..."

It was Norma's voice, soft and haunting, carrying through the trees like a ghostly echo.

I scanned the forest, my eyes narrowing as I searched for her. Then I saw her—standing on a balcony off one of the lodge's upper rooms, her white hair catching the moonlight. She was leaning over the railing, her voice thin and wavering as she shouted into the night.

"Rachel... don't go on the ice... my sweet girl, please..."

Her words were swallowed by the snow and the distance, but the sadness in her tone pierced through the noise in my head.

"Shut up, Norma," I muttered, shaking her voice away.

I refocused on Kate, who had reached another clearing. The trees fell away, and the moonlight illuminated her silhouette as she ran, heading back toward the lodge.

I lifted the rifle again, my breathing ragged as I lined up the shot. She was exposed now, no trees to shield her.

The crosshairs steadied. I pulled the trigger.

The shot missed, the bullet kicking up a spray of snow just to her left. I fired again, the blast reverberating through the clearing. Another miss.

"Damn it!" I hissed, lowering the rifle as I started running again.

The ground beneath my boots changed subtly, the snow thinner, the air sharper and colder. A faint groan reached my ears, and I slowed, glancing down.

My breath caught.

The ice beneath me shimmered in the moonlight, the surface glossy and uneven. A hollow groan echoed beneath my feet, the sound sending a chill through me far colder than the wind.

This wasn't a clearing. *I was on the lake.*

The realization struck like a blow, freezing me in place. My head snapped up, searching for Kate. She was ahead of me, her movements sloppy as she slipped and darted across the frozen expanse.

Norma's voice drifted to me again, stronger now, the words sharp and pleading.

"Don't go on the ice, Rachel! Please, don't go through!"

I turned back toward the forest, gauging the distance. It was too far. Kate was closer.

The ice groaned louder beneath me as I moved forward, each step sending faint cracks rippling outward. The sound made my stomach twist, but I forced myself on.

I couldn't let her get away.

Ahead, Kate stumbled, her foot punching through the ice and plunging into the freezing water. She cried out, scrambling to pull herself up, the ice splintering further beneath her weight.

I slowed, the rifle heavy in my hands as I watched her crawl toward the shore.

And then I felt it—the ice shifting beneath me. The sound was different now, sharper and more urgent, the cracks beneath my boots spreading faster than I could react.

Panic surged through me as I glanced down. The moonlight reflected off the surface, illuminating the jagged fractures snaking outward.

"No," I whispered, my voice trembling.

The ice exploded beneath me.

For a split second, as the ice gave way beneath my feet, I saw her—Norma. She was leaning out over the balcony, her face pale and sorrowful.

Her image blurred as the icy water closed over me, the lake's frigid embrace dragging me deeper.

Cold water engulfed me, the shock stealing the breath from my lungs as I plunged into the lake. My arms flailed, clawing at the icy edges of the hole, but the surface crumbled beneath my fingers, each movement dragging me deeper.

The weight of the rifle on my back pulled me down, the leather strap digging into my shoulder. I reached for it, fumbling desperately as the freezing water numbed my hands.

Above me, the round hole glowed above, the moonlight a cruel beacon of what I couldn't reach.

My fingers scrabbled at the strap, pulling it loose as I fought to swim upward.

But my limbs were heavy, the cold sapping my strength. The rifle slipped away, sinking into the dark below as I reached for the shimmering light above.

It was too far.

The last thing I saw was the moonlight refracting through the crystalline water, its glow fading as I descended into the icy depths.

Chapter Seventy-Four

Kate

I dragged myself onto the snow-covered shore, the icy water biting at my legs and freezing me to the bone. I was hyperventilating. Each intake of breath felt knives in the frigid air. Behind me, the ice on the lake cracked and shifted, the sound low and mournful, as if it understood the weight of what had just happened.

Rachel was gone.

I was dizzy and almost blacked out as I pulled myself further up the bank, my knees sinking into the snow. My hands were raw and dumb, trembling uncontrollably, but I couldn't stop staring at the dark hole in the ice. She'd vanished, swallowed by the lake, and there was nothing I could do.

A pair of headlights cut through the trees, their beams reflecting off the icy expanse. Moments later, a white truck skidded to a stop near the lodge, and the sheriff's truck door flew open.

"Kate!"

Sheriff Ronson ran toward me. Another vehicle pulled in behind him, a sleek, black sedan that I didn't recognize.

The sheriff reached me just as my legs gave out, catching me before I hit the ground. "Easy now," he said, his voice calm. "What happened?"

"Rachel fell through the ice," I managed, my teeth chattering so hard it was difficult to speak.

Ronson's eyes darted to the lake, his face tightening. "We need to get you inside."

Another man approached. He was tall and distinguished, with neatly combed gray hair and a heavy wool coat.

"You must be Kate," he said.

I nodded, too exhausted to respond.

"I'm Greg Talbot," he said, crouching down to meet my gaze. "Norma's attorney. I came as soon as I could."

The sheriff registered Talbot would help me and he walked to the lakeshore, pulling his flashlight from his belt.

"Let's get you inside before you catch your death," Talbot said. "You're soaked through and absolutely freezing."

I smirked at his mention of death, but let him help me, my body leaning against his for support. Together, we made our way toward the lodge, the gaping hole in the front wall illuminated by the truck's headlights.

"My God," Talbot muttered, his voice low with disbelief as he took in the destruction before us.

I barely registered his reaction. My focus was on putting one foot in front of the other, each step a monumental effort.

As we reached the broken threshold, another vehicle came tearing into the parking lot. The sound of its engine roared through the night, and I turned just in time to see Decker's Jeep skid to a halt.

He leapt out, his eyes wild with panic. "Kate!"

"Decker," I whispered, relief surging through me.

He ran to me, his arms wrapping around me in a tight embrace. I buried my face in his chest.

"I thought..." His voice cracked, and he held me even tighter. "I thought I lost you."

"I'm okay," I said, though the words felt like a lie.

He pulled back just enough to look at me, his hands cupping my face. "Let's get you warmed up."

Together, we navigated the wreckage of the lobby. Talbot followed, his eyes scanning the room with a mixture of amazement and dismay.

I pointed toward the far guest wing. "Norma's in a suite down there, at the end of the hall. Please check on her."

Whitaker nodded. "Of course." He strode off, his coat billowing as he disappeared into the hallway.

Decker guided me to my room, his arm steadying me as I stumbled, my body too drained to protest. I dripped water all down the long hallway. Once inside, he turned the shower on, the sound of rushing water filling the space.

"Get in," he said softly, his hands brushing a strand of wet hair from my face. "I'll be right outside when you're done."

I nodded, tears prickling at my eyes as I stepped into the bathroom. I pulled off the frozen clothes, the cloth coated in a layer of ice, and stepped into the shower. The lukewarm water was a balm, washing away the cold, the dirt, the fear. I warmed the water temperature until it was piping hot and I stood under the stream for what felt like an eternity.

Once my core temperature returned to normal and my teeth had stopped chattering, my thoughts drifted to the events that had led up to this evening's tragic events.

Rachel. The bodies in the tunnel. Norma in the attic.

What had started as a way to get back on my feet had turned into a nightmare. But somehow, I'd made it through. I'd stood on my own, faced horrors I never could have imagined, and I'd survived.

Steam filled the bathroom, fogging up the mirror. My

muscles relaxed under the soothing heat, the tension ebbing away. I finally turned off the water, stepped out, and wrapped myself in a towel.

I wiped the steam from the mirror, staring at my reflection. My face was pale, my eyes hollow, but I already looked less haggard than I had in days. I took a deep breath and let it out slowly.

It was over.

I pulled on clean, soft clothes, the fabric warm against my skin. My body felt lighter, freer, as I opened the bathroom door and stepped back into the room.

Decker was waiting for me, sitting on the edge of the bed. He stood as soon as he saw me, his expression softened with relief.

I crossed the room and wrapped my arms around him, holding on tightly.

"I'm so glad you're here," I whispered.

He kissed the top of my head, his hands rubbing soothing circles on my back. "I'm not going anywhere."

Chapter Seventy-Five

Kate

The fire crackled in the hearth, sending flickers of light across the walls of my room. I sat in one of the worn armchairs, a blanket wrapped around my shoulders. The heat from the flames felt good against my skin, but my body still held a deep chill that no hot shower or fireplace toastiness could reach. Decker sat beside me, his hand resting on my knee, a steady presence that anchored me to reality.

Sheriff Ronson leaned forward in his chair, his elbows on his knees, his expression grave. Beside him stood a newly arrived deputy, young and wide-eyed, as if the events of the day were beyond anything he'd ever imagined.

"There's no sign of Rachel," the sheriff said, his voice low but steady. "We searched the shoreline but couldn't get out the ice where she went through. It's deep there—sixty feet, at least. If she's in the lake, we won't know for sure until spring, when the ice melts and we can send divers out."

I nodded, staring into the fire. Rachel's face haunted me, her wild eyes, her desperate fury as she chased me. And then the way she'd disappeared beneath the ice, her silhouette fading into the inky depths below.

"That doesn't surprise me," I said softly.

The sheriff shifted in his chair, glancing at the deputy before turning his attention back to me. "We've confirmed the tunnel and the bodies," he said, his tone heavy. "We'll start the process of identifying them—DNA testing, comparing missing persons reports, employment records at the lodge. It's going to take time, but we'll get answers."

I nodded again, my throat tightening as I thought of the women I'd seen in the tunnel, their mummified faces frozen in time. "There's one person you can identify without DNA," I said, my voice firmer now.

Ronson raised an eyebrow. "Who?"

I reached for Lydia's journal, sitting on the nightstand beside me, and handed it to him. "This belonged to Lydia Forsythe, the winter caretaker before me," I said. "She wrote about everything that happened to her. I think she's one of the women in the tunnel. She went through what I did—and worse."

The sheriff flipped through the pages, his brow furrowing as he scanned the words. He closed the journal and placed it on his lap. "This is helpful," he said. "Thanks for sharing this."

He leaned back in his chair, his gaze shifting to me. "What about the damage to the front of the lodge?" he asked.

"Rachel," I said. "She planted some kind of explosive at the front door and lit the fuse. I had locked and barricaded the doors and was in here with her rifle, trying to protect Norma and myself."

Ronson's face tightened, his jaw clenching as he processed the information. "We found a bunch of dynamite in the truck out front. She was ready for war."

Talbot entered the doorway, a grim look on his face. He wiped his glasses on his sweater.

"How is she?" I asked.

Talbot gave me a reassuring smile. "She's asleep," he said. "Resting comfortably." He paused and put his glasses on. "The sale of the lodge has been stopped. I've reviewed the documents. The signatures were fraudulent. Rachel must have forged them. I've already contacted the bankers to let them know the deal is void."

Ronson nodded, his face impassive. "What else can you tell us?"

Talbot and I took turns answering his questions, recounting the tangled web of lies, manipulation, and murder that Rachel had spun over the years. Decker sat beside me, his brow furrowed in disbelief as he listened.

When we finished, the sheriff let out a long breath, leaning back in his chair. "Jesus, this is a hell of a mess," he said. "Kate, do you want to go into town? We can find you a hotel. You shouldn't have to spend another night here."

I shook my head, exhaustion weighing down my every word. "I'd like to stay here in my room with Decker," I said. "But the pipes are going to freeze with all the cold air coming in. The generator is out."

I hesitated, my voice faltering. "Dominic said he'd come fix it, but he never showed up."

The deputy shifted uncomfortably, glancing at the sheriff. "Dominic's truck was found at the highway," he said, his voice hesitant. "It had a snowmobile trailer, but no snowmobile. I think he tried to get to you. We're searching the road and the woods alongside."

Ronson's expression darkened, and he rubbed a hand over his face. "We'll figure that out," he said. "In the meantime, we'll drain the water system to minimize damage. My team and I will be here all night, preserving the crime scene. We'll try to keep the noise down."

"Don't worry about that," I said. "I'll sleep through anything."

The sheriff stood, nodding to Talbot and the deputy. "Let's get to work," he said.

As they left, Decker stoked the fire. He came to me and pulled me into a hug, his arms steady and strong around me.

"It's over," he murmured.

I leaned against him, feeling the weight of everything lift. "Yeah, it's over," I whispered.

We climbed into bed, the fire casting a soft glow across the room. Decker pulled me close, his hand brushing my hair as we settled into the quiet.

For the first time in months, I felt truly comfortable in this space.

Chapter Seventy-Six

Kate

The morning air was crisp as Decker and I pulled away from the lodge. The snow-covered peaks of the Swan Range loomed in the rearview mirror, fading into the distance as we wound down the narrow road. I leaned my head against the cool glass of the window, watching the scenery blur into a patchwork of frost-covered trees and endless white fields.

The day stretched ahead of us—an entire day of driving through Montana, Idaho, and Washington to get home. Home. The word had never felt so sweet, so full of promise.

The morning had been hard.

The sheriff's face had been grave as he told me. They'd found Dominic. He'd been shot along the road from the highway, near his snowmobile, a large-caliber rifle bullet shattering his shoulder. Rachel had tried to kill him, but Dominic had survived. They airlifted him to Seattle early that morning for emergency surgery. He was stable, but would face a long recovery.

I'd stood there numb, the news landing like a stone in the hollow of my chest. Dominic—my friend, the one person who had consistently tried to be there for me through all this madness—was alive, but Rachel had still nearly succeeded in killing him.

Decker had wrapped his arms around me as I stood frozen in the kitchen, the weight of it all pressing down. But I couldn't break down, not now. There were things to do, loose ends to tie up.

Norma had been taken by ambulance early that morning, first to a hospital for a full examination, and then to a retirement community with a respected memory care unit, which she would have access to if her memory issues weren't resolved with proper nutrition and healthcare. I'd visited her before she left, holding her hand and promising her that everything would be okay. She smiled, her eyes filled with a distant warmth, and called me "Rachel"—the name of her long-lost young daughter —one last time.

The lodge was another story. Its future was uncertain, a gaping hole still yawning in the front wall where the dynamite had torn it apart. Local workmen had been hired to build a temporary wall to keep the winter storms at bay, but the repairs would require specialists come springtime.

And then there was me. I was leaving it all behind and, in a sense, I was leaving parts of myself behind as well. When I had arrived, still shaky after my stay in rehab, I had felt unsure of myself, disappointed in my own past actions and choices, weakened by my own insecurities, but I had emerged from the literal and figurative wreckage of the lodge stronger. I'd been tempered like steel in a forge. I had proved to myself that I was tough, resilient, and resourceful.

Decker squeezed my hand as the miles slipped past. The snow thinned as we left the Swan Valley, left Montana, crossed the Idaho panhandle, giving way to the rolling hills of sagebrush and brown fields in eastern Washington. By the time we reached the small cafe in the town of George for lunch, I felt a little lighter. A hot sandwich, a steaming mug of coffee, and Decker's easy smile were grounding me.

Crossing the Columbia River felt like a turning point. The verdant greens of the Cascade foothills rose ahead of us, a world apart from the stark winter landscape we'd left behind. Snoqualmie Pass was clear, and as we descended into the Puget Sound area, the rain-soaked evergreens felt like a soft embrace, welcoming me back to a world I was familiar with, a place I understood.

I pulled out my phone and called my parents as soon as we hit cell service. Their joy was palpable, their voices filled with love and relief. "We'll see you in a few hours," I told them, smiling despite myself.

"Drive safe," my mom said, her voice cracking just a little.

"We will," I promised.

It felt good to know they'd be there, waiting for me.

As we drove through the emerald green of the coastal lowlands, my phone rang again. A Montana number flashed on the screen, and Decker glanced over, curious.

"It's Talbot," I said, answering.

"Kate, good afternoon," he said, his voice smooth and professional. "I hope your drive has been pleasant."

"It has," I replied. "What's on your mind?"

There was a pause, as if he were gathering his thoughts. "I wanted to let you know that Norma expressed her gratitude for everything you've done. She asked me to handle something on her behalf, and I thought it was only fair to inform you right away."

"Okay..." I said slowly, sitting up straighter.

"Norma has transferred ownership of the lodge to you," he said.

I blinked, certain I'd misheard him. "What?"

"The Holland Lake Lodge and the surrounding 360 acres," Talbot continued, his tone matter-of-fact. "She wanted you to have it. Effective immediately, you're the legal owner."

The air seemed to leave my lungs. "You're joking."

"I assure you, I'm not," he said with a chuckle. "We'll go over all the details when you're ready, but I thought you should know."

"I... I don't know what to say," I stammered. "That doesn't even make any sense. She isn't in possession of all of her mental faculties. I mean, she doesn't even know who I am, not really. Surely her decision can't be considered legal."

"Kate, she knows enough. She recognized you as a hard-worker and a person who reflects the Whitaker values of diligence and personal responsibility. She wants this. She needs to know her family legacy will be in good hands, and since I have power of attorney, I was able to fulfill this desire."

I sat there stunned, speechless, my mind unable to process the enormity of his words.

"Just think about it," Talbot said kindly. "You've earned this, Kate. Take care."

He hung up, and I stared at the phone, my mind reeling.

"What was that?" Decker asked, his eyes narrowing in concern.

I looked at him, my voice trembling as I spoke. "Norma gave me the lodge."

He blinked, leaning back in his seat. "The lodge? As in... the whole thing?"

"Yeah." I let out a shaky laugh. The absurdity of it hitting me all at once. "The lodge. Three hundred and sixty acres of land. A murder tunnel. And probably the most haunted attic in Montana."

Decker grinned, his hand sliding over mine. "Congratulations?"

I laughed again, this time louder, feeling a strange, giddy relief. "I don't know if I should feel flattered or cursed."

Decker's laughter joined mine, and for the first time in what felt like forever, the weight on my chest lifted, if only a little.

"We'll visit Dominic when we get home," I said. "I want to see him. Make sure he's okay."

Decker squeezed my hand again. "We will."

The landscape of home stretched ahead of us, green and rain-soaked, leading back to Seattle. Back to home. Back to something that, finally, felt like the beginning of a new chapter.

Afterword

I hope you've enjoyed The Silent Guest. I would be forever grateful if you would leave a rating or a review. Follow me as an author on Amazon and you'll be first to know when the sequel to The Silent Guest is available. Kate is headed back to the lodge...

Best Wishes, Ian

Printed in Dunstable, United Kingdom